SEEDS OF REVENGE

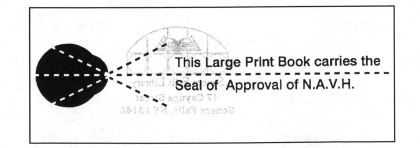

A GREENHOUSE MYSTERY

SEEDS OF REVENGE

WENDY TYSON

WHEELER PUBLISHING
A part of Gale, a Cengage Company

Farmington Hills, Mich • San Francisco • New York • Waterville, Maine
Meriden, Conn • Mason, Ohio • Chicago

Copyright © 2017 by Wendy Tyson.
Wheeler Publishing, a part of Gale, a Cengage Company.

ALL RIGHTS RESERVED
This is a work of fiction. Any references to historical events, to real people, or to real locales are used fictitiously. Other names, characters, places, and incidents are the product of the author's imagination and any resemblance to actual events or locales or persons, living or dead, is entirely coincidental.
Wheeler Publishing Large Print Cozy Mystery.
The text of this Large Print edition is unabridged.
Other aspects of the book may vary from the original edition.
Set in 16 pt. Plantin.

LIBRARY OF CONGRESS CIP DATA ON FILE.
CATALOGUING IN PUBLICATION FOR THIS BOOK
IS AVAILABLE FROM THE LIBRARY OF CONGRESS

ISBN-13: 978-1-4328-5695-3 (softcover)

Published in 2018 by arrangement with Henery Press, LLC

Printed in Mexico
1 2 3 4 5 6 7 22 21 20 19 18

For you, Aunt Carol.

ACKNOWLEDGMENTS

Special thanks to Frances Black, Rachel Jackson and all the folks at Henery Press, Rowe Carenen, Larissa Ackerman, Claire McKinney, and, of course, my family.

I'd also like to recognize Patricia Smith and the Friends of the Free Library of New Hope & Solebury, in particular Pamela Kerr and Kristin Reilly. Your support and encouragement have been a blessing.

ONE

Megan squinted through a sliver of windshield thick with ice and snow. The forecasters had been wrong again, and the storm predicted for the wee hours of the morning slammed the region early — with a vengeance. The untreated roads were slick with rapidly falling snow, and it was nearly impossible to see more than a few meters ahead. Megan slowed to a crawl, hoping the truck wouldn't slide along this stretch of deserted street.

It'd been a long evening. She'd visited with the chefs from four restaurants in Philly, trying to sell them on Washington Acres' winter hot house greens. She glanced back at the coolers of arugula, spinach, and pak choi, likely frozen in the cold truck bed. Only one restaurant, City Roots, had been interested. The chef, a sweet, passionate woman named Patricia Smith, had sampled the greens with enthusiasm. Chefs from the other three restaurants had promised to try the samples she'd left and would "call her soon." She knew that meant she'd be calling them. Selling greens was one way to extend her market and make some cash during the winter months. But as a new farm awaiting its organic certification, getting restaurants to take a chance was proving to be a challenge.

The truck's wipers were crusted with ice. After pulling over, Megan rolled down the window, stuck her arm out, and banged the left wiper hard against the windshield in an effort to break some ice loose. She increased the temperature of the defroster and pulled back out on the road. She was only about twelve miles from Winsome, but in this arctic landscape, it felt like a million.

The snow was coming down harder now, hitting the truck at an angle. Practically a white out. Her cell phone rang and she ignored it. A few more miles and she'd be on a busier, and hopefully plowed, stretch of road. The truck climbed, passing an abandoned Honda. Megan felt grateful for the truck's snow tires and four-wheel drive. With almost a foot of snow on this back country road, she wouldn't have made it up the hill either.

Megan was just approaching her turn

when she saw a shadowy figure walking along the road. As her car got closer, Megan could make out a shape encased in a snow-covered blanket. Long golden curls hung beneath a hat, past a broad set of shoulders. A halo of white snow lay atop the blonde strands.

Megan pulled over. "Do you need a ride?"

The figure moved closer. Megan saw a young woman, maybe mid-twenties, with a wide mouth and beguiling, fern-green eyes. She smiled warmly. "Car died on me, and so close, too." She frowned. "At least I think I'm close."

"Where are you headed?"

"Winsome. Is it near here? I'm afraid with all this snow, I may have gotten off track."

Megan smiled. "Heading that way myself. Climb in."

"Oh! Would you mind? I have some stuff in my car I need." She glanced at the back of Megan's truck, took in the coolers, and said, "They should be okay in the open for a while if I can stick them back there."

"Sure."

The woman smiled her gratitude. She stuck a gloved hand through the window. "Becca Fox." Her shake was firm, her expression affable. "You sure you don't mind giving me a lift?"

While the snow was starting to slow, it'd left a mess in its wake. "I don't mind at all. I'm not leaving you here in the dark and cold."

Megan unlocked the passenger door and made room for Becca. Then she turned the truck around and drove back to the stranded vehicle. She helped Becca lift three large plastic cases and a suitcase into the back of the truck. Becca pulled what looked like an oversized jewelry case out of the backseat of her car.

She held it up. "This is my bread and butter. Mind if it rides with us?"

Megan didn't mind, and she said so. Becca placed the case on the floor between her feet and snapped her seatbelt into place. Once they were back on the road, she pulled off her hat and gloves. Megan snuck a sideways peek at her passenger. Becca had an open, handsome face. There was a child-like allure to her that Megan found appealing.

"What do you have going on in Winsome?" Megan asked, navigating around a pile of snow that had blown across an intersection. She glanced at Becca. "Heading there for the holidays?"

"Sort of. My aunt is letting me set up shop in her store. I started a business and she thought the foot traffic would be help-ful."

"Who is your aunt?"

"Meredith Chance. People call her Merry. Do you know her?"

"I sure do. Merry is letting you set up a display in the nursery?" Every Christmas, Merry transformed her nursery into a holiday shop, complete with ornaments, Poinsettias, outdoor decorations, Christmas trees, wreaths, and even carolers and visits from Santa.

"She said she has the room." Becca shrugged. "I need to start somewhere."

The storm was waning, but the wind had picked up and Megan wound her way past three-foot drifts of snow. She saw headlights behind her and pulled over to let a plow pass, waiting until it had cleared the path ahead before moving forward.

"So what brings you out on a night like this?" Becca asked. "I see the coolers in the back. Not dead bodies, I hope?" Becca smiled. Deep dimples popped out on either side of her mouth.

"Nah, not this time." Megan explained that she was a farmer and café owner on a mission to sell greens to city restaurants. "We're still trying to figure out what works, what will bring in the most money during the down months."

"A woman farmer. Pretty cool." Another grin. "I've never met a female farmer before."

Megan found Becca's upbeat attitude infectious, and the disappointment trailing her time in the city lifted. It *was* pretty cool, and she and Bibi, her grandmother, had pulled the farm firmly into the black — finally. They just needed to keep it there.

"What kind of display will you be setting up?"

Becca sat back against the seat. She ran a large hand through her hair, tugging it into a loose ponytail, which she held behind her head. Everything about Becca seemed large, from physical frame to her personality.

Becca said, "I'm a love chemist."

"A love chemist?"

Becca nodded. "That's the name of my business — The Love Chemist. I make modern day love potions."

Megan let that sink in. A love chemist in Winsome. Seemed maybe her companion could have chosen a better time of the year. Valentine's Day? Then again, who knew? Perhaps Hanukkah and Christmas would prove to be ripe for romance.

Becca freed her hair and shook it loose. Damp strands clung to the collar of her coat. She dug a card out of a pocket on one of the boxes and held it out to Megan. Megan couldn't read it because she was driving, but she thanked her and tucked the card into her coat pocket.

"I'm actually a chemist. I have my Masters in Chemistry. But most of the jobs I found were in industry, and I was bored. My last stint was at a fragrance company, and that's where I learned about perfumes."

"So you make perfumes?"

"I make naturally scented love potions." She smiled mischievously. "My magic ingredient? Pheromones."

Before Megan could ask more questions, Becca pointed toward Canal Street, Winsome's main drag. She gasped. Covered in a marshmallow fluff of snow, with holiday lights and Christmas trees glowing against the backdrop of the cloudy night sky, Winsome must have seemed like a destination from yesteryear to a newcomer. The historic buildings, with their brick and stone fascia, were done up in holiday finery, and the tall streetlights wore caps of white over streams of plaid ribbon. The street was deserted at this time of night, and the snow remained untouched except for a semi-cleared path carved by the plow.

"It's like Christmas has come alive."

Becca's eyes widened. "That's where Aunt Merry lives?" She glanced at Megan. "It's been a while since I've been here."

"She's up the hill a bit. Want me to take you to her house?"

"Sure. She's not expecting me until to-morrow, but I imagine she's home. I think I'll just surprise her."

Merry Chance's statuesque four square was alit with white Christmas lights — Colonial candles in the windows, braids of lights outlining the window sills and doorways, blinking lights woven into wreaths, and miniscule bulbs incorporated into a doe and two fawns that adorned the front lawn. As Megan pulled up alongside the road in front of the home, she saw with relief that Merry was home. In fact, she was standing on her porch talking with a man.

Becca gave Megan a quick hug. "Thank you," she sang. "You saved me quite a trek."

Megan climbed out of the truck and pulled Becca's suitcase from the bed while Becca unloaded her boxes of love potions. Merry had noticed them, and she turned her attention toward her niece.

"Aunt Merry!" Becca called. "Hello!"

She hurried toward her aunt and stopped short just feet from the landing, Megan trailing behind. The man had turned to look at them so that his face was visible. He was older, mid- to late-sixties, but his resemblance to Becca was unmistakable. Strong features: a square chin, a broad nose, unnaturally black hair receding ever-so-slightly into his scalp line. He wore a tailored coat and carried an expensive bag. His bearing screamed money and privilege.

The man regarded Becca with an evenness that seemed unnerving, while Becca's whole body shook with emotion.

No one acknowledged Megan. She watched the scene unfold the way a bystander witnesses a car crash. Helpless and transfixed.

"No! Why is he here? Aunt Merry, why the hell is he here?" To him, "I told you I never want to see you again. Never. Do you know what that means? You brought him here on purpose."

"Rebecca, calm down," Merry snapped. "You're jumping to conclusions."

"He's here, I'm here. What conclusions am I jumping to?"

The man said, "Actually, I was just leaving."

"That might be best, Paul." Merry glanced at her niece, lips pursed into a frown. "Let's give Becca some time to calm down."

Paul nodded curtly. "Very well. Thank you, Merry. You know where I'll be in town." He walked down the steps, past Becca, without as much as another glance in her direction. Becca placed her bags on the ground. With a sudden rush, she darted toward the man in the slippery snow, hands outstretched. She would have pushed him had he not reacted with laser speed. He grabbed her wrists and held them out in front of her. Merry took a step forward. Megan dropped the suitcase, ready to intervene.

But Paul and Becca just stood there, staring at one another. Finally, Becca said, "You're hurting me."

He looked down at his hands, wrapped like bindings around her wrists, and let go. "I'm sorry." He backed away, his eyes unwavering in their focus on Becca's face.

He climbed into the car — a silver Mercedes — and Becca spat at the ground near his tire. She rubbed her wrists, shoulders hunched.

Becca watched as he pulled away, his rear tires slipping in the deep snow. "Why would you invite him here, Aunt Merry?"

"I wasn't expecting you until tomorrow."

"He's staying here. He made that pretty clear."

"He wanted to see you. He wants to make amends."

"I will never forgive him. You of all people should understand that."

Merry regarded her niece with a long, sad stare. Finally she said, "Megan, I assume Becca's car had some difficulty in this snow?" When Megan nodded, she said, "Thank you for bringing her."

It was a dismissal, at odds with Merry's normally saccharine insistence on hospitality. Megan placed Becca's suitcase on the porch and returned to her truck. She watched as Becca followed her aunt obediently inside. With the front door shut, the visage of the house returned to its festive façade.

A façade, indeed, Megan thought as she pulled away. That was all it seemed to be. She wondered what conversation was going on inside.

TWO

Megan left Merry's house feeling shaken and ill-tempered. It wasn't the weather or the unfruitful trip into the city exactly. Something else was bothering her. She was channeling Merry's unease. Merry had a reputation as the town busybody, but tonight she'd looked like she'd rather Megan stay out of her business. Megan was happy to oblige. She wondered, though, who Paul was and why Becca Fox had such a visceral reaction to him.

It had stopped snowing, but cold wind blew through the streets, creating swirls of snow and chilling Megan to her core. Megan was anxious to get back to Bibi and the farm, but she needed to swing by Denver's house first. Dr. Daniel "Denver" Finn was the town veterinarian and Megan's boyfriend. Megan knew animals didn't care about things like inclement weather and bad roads, and she'd promised him she'd swing by and check on his dogs while he was attending to the various barnyard emergencies.

Denver's driveway was empty. She parked on one side of the unshoveled pavement and unlocked the front door of his bungalow with her key. All five dogs — a motley crew of rescued pure breeds and mixed breeds, tiny and giant — met her with fawning and kisses. They were a well-trained lot, but like any dogs, they knew who would spoil them.

Megan laughed, petting them in turn, and slowly made her way to the kitchen and their dog food, her mood lightening. She found their bowls already lined up on the counter, Denver's square handwriting denoting which dish was for which dog and how much food they should receive. His Great Dane, a gentle giant if ever there was one, sat calmly watching her, while the blind Beagle ran in circles around her feet, whining with anticipatory joy.

They all ate in a matter of seconds. Megan was just leading them into the snow-covered backyard when she heard the front door open and Denver walking in. He met her by the back door. Without a word, he wrapped his arms around her, burying his face in her hair.

"Mm, Megs, ye smell fine." He tilted

Megan's face back, and looked into her eyes. Then he kissed her, his lips soft and insistent against her own. Pulling back, he said, "Long day?"

Megan was reluctant to let go. "You could say that. I have to get home to Bibi, but how about a nightcap first? I was just going to take the pups out —"

"Let me pour two brandies and I'll meet ye out back." Denver was Scottish, and his brogue became especially noticeable when he was tired or upset. Tonight he looked tired.

Like the rest of southeastern Pennsylvania, "out back" was buried in more than a foot of snow with more expected over the next day or two. But Denver's deck was partially cleared, and Megan found a spot on a dry bench under an awning, against the house. From that vantage point, she watched the dogs go about their business with reactions that ranged from total disdain for the white stuff to outright glee. Of all his rescues, his Golden Retriever seemed happiest to be in the snow, and the dog threw a ball into the drifts and dug around tenaciously until she found it again — her own solo game of fetch.

"Aye, that dog's a single-minded lassie." Denver handed Megan a small sifter of brandy. "Not unlike someone else I know."

Megan smiled. She wondered for a moment what it would be like to be that carefree and focused only on the moment. Somedays it felt like worrying was what she did best.

"Tell me about your trip to Philadelphia. Any takers for those winter greens Clay has growing in the greenhouses?"

"One chef seemed interested. Otherwise I gave away some samples, heard a few excuses. 'We'll wait until you have your organic certification,' 'we already have a provider,' or 'we don't know anything about Washington Acres.' " Megan sighed. She took a sip of brandy, her lips curling at the jarring flavor. She'd never gotten used to the taste of liquor. "Hopefully a few will pan out."

Denver eyed her with his biting blue gaze. "You're worried?"

"Yes and no. A steady source of income during the winter months would be nice. I'm hoping selling greens and microgreens to local restaurants will fill that void."

"Patience and tenacity."

Megan smiled. She had the latter; she struggled with the former.

Denver said, "You're back later than you anticipated. Roads that bad?"

"Once I got off the main thoroughfares,

they were awful." Megan told Denver about finding Becca Fox along the road, about what she'd witnessed at Merry's house. "In all the time I've known Merry Chance, I've never seen family there. I didn't even know she had a niece. As for the man, obviously Becca knew him, but I'm not sure who he is."

The Golden Retriever dropped a tennis ball in front of Denver, tail wagging expectantly. He tossed it out into the yard and the ball landed in front of the thick line of trees at the back of his property and sank into the snow. They watched the dog dig furiously for the lost treasure.

"If I had to guess, I'd say that was probably Paul Fox, Merry's brother-in-law. Becca is Paul's daughter. She had a big fallout with him years ago."

"Paul Fox? Blanche's husband? I'd forgotten Merry has a sister."

"*Had* a sister. She died about five years ago."

Megan wondered what had Becca and her father in town at the same time. Merry's attempt at reconciliation — or Paul's desire to see his daughter? Based on what she'd overheard, it was a do-good effort on Merry's part.

"How do you know so much about

Merry's family?" As the town vet, Denver often heard his share of gossip, but Merry was no animal lover. As far as Megan knew, she had no pets. "Your normal rounds wouldn't take you to Merry's house or business."

"Aye, you're right about that. I know about Paul from my Aunt Eloise. She had hired him for a spell to work with some of her patients."

"Becca's father is a doctor?"

"Psychologist. Specializes in trauma. I'm not sure what happened, but I do know Aunt Eloise asked him to leave her practice."

Interesting, Megan thought. "Eloise seems like a shrewd business woman on top of being a pediatrician. I wonder why she let him go."

Denver shrugged. "You'd have to ask her, Megs. She never much talks about that period in her life." Denver scratched the Beagle behind the ears. The dog leaned into his touch. "Why is Becca here? Just for the holidays?"

"Actually, Merry is helping Becca with her new venture. She's a chemist who calls herself a *love* chemist."

Denver laughed. "Now that's a new one. What exactly is a love chemist?"

"She says she mixes love potions and creams using pheromones — to increase attraction and affection from others. That's what she'll be selling at Merry's nursery: love potions."

Denver's eyes widened. He stood and let all the dogs back in the house except for the Golden Retriever, who showed no inclination to go inside. "So she's here at Merry's invitation. And her father shows up too? I don't know. Sounds suspiciously like Merry's playing family counselor."

Megan nodded. "And Becca was having none of it." The Golden dropped a ball at Megan's feet and she threw it with fingers stiff from the cold. Thinking of Becca's physical reaction to her father's presence, Megan asked, "Do you have any idea what Becca's fight with her father could have been about?"

Denver sat back down next to Megan. He took his hand in hers and rubbed her fingers with warm, gentle strokes. "Becca Fox claims her father murdered her mother."

It was Megan's turn for widened eyes. "Seriously?"

He nodded. "Based on what I've heard — and it's not much, mind you, and may be totally false — there was no evidence of foul play. Blanche's death was ruled an accident.

Becca is a bit mental, and she took her anger at her mother's death out on her father."

"Mental as in —"

"Based on what Aunt Eloise says, Becca is flighty and dramatic and always has been."

Megan remembered Becca's kind smile and warm eyes. Her easy demeanor and obvious intelligence. Definitely a contrast to the she-devil she'd become in her father's presence. "I don't know. The Becca I met seemed pretty together."

Denver shrugged. "There's a Scottish proverb that says, 'Bees that hae honey in their mouths, hae stings in their tails.' "

"Don't be fooled by appearances?"

Denver grinned. "You're learning." He looked out at his dog frolicking in the snow, a golden angel now dressed in white. His eyes darkened. "That about sums it up, Megs. Things — and people — are not always as they seem. But then, I think ye know that as well as anyone."

THREE

It was several days before Megan found herself in contact with Becca Fox again. This time she met Becca at her café, Washington Acres Café and Larder, where the young woman was deep in conversation with the café's ornery chef, Alvaro Hernandez. Becca looked up and smiled when she saw Megan. A moment later, she ended her conversation with Alvaro and met Megan by the storefront counter where Megan was stocking shelves.

"I was hoping to run into you," Becca said. "I'd like to introduce you to my products. As a thank you for helping me out the other night."

"It was no problem at all," Megan said. "Did you get your car squared away?"

"I did. It's in the shop. I'm borrowing my brother's until it's ready."

"You have a brother in town too?"

"Luke. Another one of Aunt Merry's

28

surprises. We hadn't seen each other in almost two years." Becca bounced up and down on boot-clad heels. She was dressed in striped Nordic tights, a wool miniskirt, and a black turtleneck. Her hair hung loose around her shoulders. "It's okay, though. I was happy to see him."

Megan put the box of ginger snaps she was stocking down on the counter. "The other night —"

Becca shook her head vehemently back and forth. "About that. I'm so sorry you had to witness that fiasco. I had no idea Aunt Merry had set me up that way. She knows how I feel about my father." She shrugged. "She wants peace in the family. It's just not in the cards."

Megan gave her a reassuring smile. "Well, I'm glad you seem more at ease with it. Would you like some coffee? Maybe a bite of Alvaro's pecan pie?"

"I already sampled the blueberry pound cake and the gingerbread. Divine." She rubbed her stomach. "Your chef's a sweet man. I wouldn't have guessed it based on his demeanor, but that's what I get for stereotyping people, right?" Becca dug around in her oversized shoulder bag. "But that's not why I came. Here, these are for you." Becca handed Megan a box gift wrapped in brown craft paper decorated with tiny Christmas trees and red ribbons. "Don't open it now. I hope you like it." She bent forward, winked. "Use it around someone you're attracted to."

"Thank you, Becca. You didn't have to do this."

"Nonsense. If you like it, spread the word. And come visit me at the nursery. I'm setting up today." She glanced around the café, her gaze falling on the one decoration Megan had put up, an elaborate holiday harvest wreath that sat on the far wall. "And while you're at it, why don't you pick up some decorations. This is the cutest little store and café I've ever seen, but it definitely needs more holiday cheer."

Megan arrived back at the farm after three. She found Bibi in the kitchen with Emily, a younger woman from Winsome who they'd befriended earlier that year. Emily had lived with them for a spell. Although she was back in her own home now, she visited regularly, and Megan often found her chatting with Bibi or Clay, the farm manager, her infant daughter in her arms.

Today Bibi was teaching Emily how to make German Christmas cookies — small spicy delicacies that Bibi formed using holiday molds passed down to her by her own mother — while Emily's daughter slept in a Pack-n-Play. Megan's two dogs, Gunther and Sadie, slept soundly next to the baby. They both looked up when Megan entered, their tails thumping against the stone floor. The kitchen was warm and smelled of cinnamon and vanilla — a wonderful contrast to the bitter cold and icy roads outside. Megan was happy to be home.

"There's some fresh coffee," Bibi said. "And the first batch of cookies are cooling. Help yourself." She nodded at her granddaughter, her eyes silently appraising.

"Thanks, Bibi." Megan gave each woman a hug, patted the dogs, and poured a cup of coffee.

"How did things go at the café?"

"Fine. A little slow still, but picking up."

Things had been slow since a pair of deaths a few months ago had rocked the small historical town of Winsome during Oktoberfest. The café had become a hub of activity, but folks seemed less likely to socialize — and that hit the café's bottom line. Megan was more worried than she'd let on to her grandmother, but Bonnie Birch was no one's fool. She saw what was happening and wanted success for the farm and café as much as Megan did.

"What ya got there?" Emily asked. She pointed to the gift-wrapped box Becca had given Megan.

"Ah, that. It was a present." Megan glanced at Bibi. "Remember the woman I told you about? The one I drove to Merry's."

"Her niece, Rebecca."

"Yes, Becca. She brought this by the café. As a token of thanks for the ride."

"Well open it." Bibi was pulling another tray of cookies from the oven. She transferred the cookies to a cooling rack, placed another tray in the oven, and then wiped her hands on her "Everybody Loves Winsome" apron — a leftover from Megan's father's souvenir shop. "Let's see."

Megan unwound the ribbon and carefully removed the wrapping, revealing a pink box with a single white orchid on the outside. She opened the box. Inside, two old-fashioned apothecary bottles were nestled side by side. One was pink — the same color as the box — and contained a clear liquid. The other was clear with a rubber-stopped dropper lid. It, too, was full. A parchment card labeled "The Love Chemist" lay inside atop the bottles. It held instructions for use.

Emily stood near. "So pretty! What is it? Perfume?"

Megan explained Becca's line of business. Perusing the directions, Megan said, "It looks like you place a few droppers of the pheromones into the perfume bottle and dab the perfume on your upper lip and other spots on your body. This perfume is called Promises."

"And voila, you have a boyfriend?" Emily looked skeptical.

"Something like that."

Bibi crossed the kitchen and picked up the box. "Well, if it's a scheme, it's a nicely packaged one. I wonder how much these sets sell for."

"No idea." Megan opened the cap on the clear bottle. The perfume was light and floral and quite lovely. "Who wants to try it?"

Emily glanced at Bibi. "Any older gents at Bridge club these days, Bonnie?"

"I want another husband like I want another colonoscopy. Megan already has Denver. Why don't you give it a go, Emily? Who knows?"

Emily shrugged. "Why not."

Megan followed the directions. Emily placed drops of the liquid on her upper lip, behind her ears, and on her neck. "There, do I smell sexy?"

Megan and Bibi both said "Definitely!" at

the same time.

While Megan put the bottles away, Emily read the card that contained the directions. "The Love Chemist." She looked at Bibi. "Do you remember Rebecca or her mother, Bonnie?"

Bibi stopped what she was doing long enough to consider the question. "I remember Blanche, Merry's sister. She was Merry's opposite. Quiet, deferential, soft-spoken. Pretty in a plain sort of way. Merry was thrilled when she married that psychologist. I think she wanted him for herself, to be honest. But to have a professional in the family? And a handsome one at that? It was all Merry could talk about for months."

"And Becca?" Megan asked.

"I saw Becca and her brother, Luke, a few times, especially during the holidays. They lived in Winsome for a spell while you were in college, Megan. I remember Becca as a shy child, afraid of her own shadow. Shy and awkward. The boy was very outspoken. Smart, definitely more precocious than his younger sister." She paused before returning to her task. "Despite what Merry said, they never seemed like a happy family."

"Denver said his Aunt Eloise and Becca's father had a falling out."

"I wouldn't know anything about that.

One day, the family was just up and gone." Bibi waved her hand in the air. "Merry said Paul found a better opportunity, but maybe there was more to it. Wouldn't surprise me one bit. Merry says a lot of things."

Bibi was not Merry's biggest fan, so Megan took her opinion with a healthy dash of salt.

"Where's Becca staying?" Emily asked.

Megan said, "With Merry, I presume. That's where I left her."

"How about Paul Fox?" Bibi asked.

Megan shrugged. "I figured he left town."

"Oh, no," Emily said. "He's still here. Merry arranged for him to rent my grandmother's old house. They have it until early January. Until now, I didn't put two and two together. I didn't recognize the name."

The oven alarm went off and Bibi pulled out another tray of cookies. Megan could see crispy brown squares and rectangles molded with festive designs — Christmas stockings, wreaths, even larger cookies with tiny Bavarian villages. Once this round of cookies was cooling, Bibi pulled out a plate from the cabinet and placed a few of the cooled cookies on it. She held the plate out to Emily.

"Oh, Bonnie, I've eaten my fill."

"They're not for you. They're for Clay.

He's up at the main greenhouse tending to the spinach." Megan saw the spirited glint in her eye.

"I can take them, Bibi," Megan said. She wanted to protect Emily from her grandmother's ninja-style matchmaking. "I still have my boots on."

"Nonsense." Bibi stacked a few more cookies on the plate and poured a thermos of coffee. "Let's see if that love concoction works. Take it, Emily, and report back."

Emily's light complexion flushed rose. "Bonnie."

"He won't bite. And anyway, with cookies this good, you'll be hard pressed to know if it was the cookies or the perfume."

Emily laughed. "Well, if you put it that way." She glanced at Lily, still asleep by the door.

Bibi waved a dishtowel in the direction of the door. "We'll tend to her. Go."

Megan and Bibi watched the younger woman head out into the cold. "You're bad," Megan said. "Always trying to set people up."

"That girl's shy and Clay is clueless when it comes to women. If sparks fly, we'll know that love chemist stuff works. 'Cause only a miracle could bring those two together."

Megan wasn't so sure. But before she

could comment, Bibi surprised her with a request.

"Winter is long for us older folks, Megan. The snow, the ice . . . it can start to feel tiresome, if you know what I mean. How about I finish up these cookies, and when Emily's back, you and I take a ride over to Merry's nursery? She has the lights going, and tonight is one of her caroling evenings. Hot chocolate, cookies, apple cider." She held up another plate. "We can bring some of these to share."

Megan agreed. She wasn't sure if Bibi really wanted to get out of the house for the evening or if she was just being nosy. Either way, Megan was curious too. And while she was there, she could pick up some decorations for the café. Becca was right — 'twas the season to celebrate, and the café needed a little festive bling.

Upstairs, Megan changed into black pants and a red print peasant blouse, one of her vintage finds. She glanced in the mirror, and unhappy with the pallor of her skin, dabbed on some blush and tinted lip balm. She left her dark, shoulder length hair down. "And that's as good as it's going to get," she told the image in the mirror.

Debating, she reached for her cell and left

a message for Denver to meet them at the nursery if he was available. She headed out the door to fetch Bibi but thought better of it. She returned to her bureau and opened The Love Chemist box. She dabbed the concoction behind her ears, on her throat, and above her upper lip. She expected a tingle, a sting — something. But the potion felt just like any perfume on her skin.

Probably rubbish, she thought — no more than a nice idea. But at least it smells nice.

FOUR

Merry Chance's nursery, aptly named Merry's Flowers & Shrubs, offered a tribute to the traditional English Christmas. Ropes of gold and green garland had been strewn across the rafters and along the tops of windows, tiny gold stars hanging from their centers. Advent candles sat atop counters near rows of blood-red Poinsettias. The nursery's centerpiece, a twelve-foot spruce awash in Victorian finery, was encircled by a toy train carrying a bounty of tiny wrapped gift boxes. Puffs of smoke rose from the train's engine while a whistle punctuated the silence at regular intervals. Row upon row of decorations — from tree ornaments to yard Santas — were on display, their prices handwritten on small parchment tags. In the far corner, a table was set for English tea, with miniature mince pies, tiny scones, and butter cookies shaped like crowns presented on tiered dishes.

"Leave it to Merry to flaunt her British heritage," Bibi whispered. "Crown cookies? Seriously?" Still, she took one, nibbled, and finding it worthy, stuffed three of them in her sweater pocket.

A small crowd had gathered at the other side of the cavernous enclosure. Megan could make out a group of carolers organizing under an elaborate canopy of garlands. She recognized Roger and Anita Becker, Merry, and a few of the café regulars. She didn't see Becca.

"Don't look now," Bibi said, reaching for a scone. "Here comes the Ice Princess herself."

Merry had left the carolers to talk with Megan and Bibi. She was wearing ivory from head to toe: ivory pants, an ivory tunic belted with an ivory leather belt, an ivory tasseled shawl, and even ivory and gold ballet flats. She looked at Megan over ivory readers, smiled broadly, and said, "Megan, I'm so happy to see you."

It was a far cry from the reception Megan had received a few days prior. "Well, thank you, Merry. Your nursery looks very festive."

Merry grinned at the compliment. "Thank you, thank you. I tried to lighten everyone's spirits this season." A shadow crossed over her features. "You know."

40

Megan did know. The town of Winsome was still grieving the loss of two of its own. Healing would come slowly.

Merry forced another smile, took Megan's hand, and said, "Don't you look pretty tonight. That doctor of yours coming?"

"I hope so."

Bibi cleared her throat and Merry turned her attention to the other woman. Merry's mouth turned down. "I don't see you wearing your caroling clothes, Bonnie."

"I'm not here to sing. I just thought it would be nice to get out, be part of the party."

"Well good, I'm glad you came. We're waiting on Sarah, Eloise, and a few others, and then we'll get started." She waved the papers in her hand, which appeared to be sheet music. "Roger keeps insisting we sing Leonard Cohen's 'Hallelujah' as a tribute. I told him there's no 'Hallelujah' at a proper British caroling. What do you think, Megan?"

Only Megan had spied Becca's display by the handmade wreaths and she left Bonnie to opine on tonight's music selection. Becca seemed engrossed in conversation with a short, slender man with a neatly trimmed beard and thick curly hair. They stopped speaking as Megan approached.

41

"Megan!" Becca turned to the man next to her. "This is my brother, Luke. Luke, this is the woman who rescued me the day I arrived. Megan Sawyer. She's a farmer!"

Luke eyed Megan up and down before holding his hand out. His shake was clammy, but his expression was warm and welcoming. "Appreciate you helping Becca."

"It was my pleasure. We've had more snow this year than in the last three combined. Becca had bad luck coming in during the worst of it."

Luke glanced at his sister. "Luck favors the prepared, Becca."

"I know, but what could I have done? My car is front-wheel drive. And how was I to know it would give out on me?"

"Snow tires."

Becca snorted. "Yeah, like I could afford snow tires. I'm not the rich entrepreneur you are."

Luke frowned, but he seemed pleased by Becca's remark. "You will be if you continue." He motioned toward the table behind them. "How are sales?"

"Starting to pick up." She leaned in and kissed him, grabbing his arm and squeezing. "Thank you for coming by. For supporting me."

Luke nodded. "Of course. Will you stop

over tomorrow? I'd like that."

"Not if he's there."

"He's busy with another one of his business deals. I don't think he'll bother you."

Becca made a face. "The only place I want to see him is jail."

"Becca —" Luke glanced at Megan and seemed to think better of whatever he was going to say. "Never mind. We can talk about it another time. I'll see you later?"

"Sure."

Megan watched Luke walk by the exit and pause near the large Advent candle on the cashier's counter. He took out his phone and glanced at the display. Whatever was written there seemed to upset him. He shook his head before stuffing the phone back in his coat pocket.

"Don't let the protective exterior fool you," Becca said, watching Luke leave. "He's a teddy bear. Too much so."

Megan picked up one of the boxes on The Love Chemist table. This one was chocolate brown and had the silhouette of a stag emblazoned on the front.

"That's the same stuff, but for men. With aftershave, of course."

Megan returned the box to its spot on the table. "Thank you for the gift, Becca. Unnecessary but appreciated."

"You're wearing it. I can tell."

"I am." And if Merry's pleasant reaction to seeing her earlier had been any indication, it was working. "I thought I'd take a look at the rest of your wares."

Wares was a loose term. The table held a bouquet of flowers, a poster with Becca's credentials, photo, and a few testimonials held up by a small easel, and boxes in four colors and designs: the pink and white orchid box, the brown stag, one lavender with a vanilla bean on it, and one white with a gold rose. Megan picked up the rose box.

"That's just a different scent for women. Some like florals, some prefer something less perfume-like, such as the vanilla bean. I'm working on two other scents — jasmine and seascape. They won't be ready for another few months."

"Nice." Megan picked up the vanilla package and flipped it over. She tried not to react at the price tag — $175.00.

"Remember, that includes the pheromones and the perfume. Many products that claim to offer pheromones only give you the product. No scent."

"But you could mix this with your favorite scent?"

Becca nodded. "Add drops to your favorite alcohol-based perfume and you can use that instead. I sell the pheromones separately too. Through my website."

Megan was busily taking this all in when the carolers walked by. They stopped briefly to peruse the table.

"Megan, how are you?" Roger said. He gave her a quick hug and a pat on the shoulder. "Looking good."

Megan was amused. It was unlike Roger to be so affectionate.

"Hey, Megan. We missed you at book club," Amber Daubney said. Amber was the town librarian. She'd been trying unsuccessfully to lure Megan back to the book club ever since the first disastrous meeting during which no one but Megan had read the assigned book. "Maybe in January?" Amber smiled. "We miss your insights."

Because they were the only insights offered, Megan thought. But she returned the smile anyway. "Maybe."

The carolers slowly drifted off until only Merry, Becca, and Megan were standing by The Love Chemist table. Megan busied herself reading Becca's literature, a treatise on the science behind her products. It was fascinating — although the conversation between Becca and her aunt made it hard to concentrate.

"Are you coming home tonight?" Merry

asked Becca.

"Probably."

"I promise you don't have to see him again."

"You said that last time, and then you invited him to Winsome." Becca lowered her voice. "He killed your sister, for God's sake, Aunt Merry. You of all people should be able to see through my father's pretenses."

"That's not a conversation for here," Merry hissed. "And you really need to stop saying that. Your father did a lot for Blanche, and he's done — or is trying to do — a lot for you."

"I don't need his help."

"He wants to make up for missed time."

"He wants to buy my silence."

Megan could feel the weight of a stare upon her. She looked up to see Merry watching her over those ivory readers. Megan nodded and went back to the report. She wanted to walk away from this private conversation, but she wasn't sure which would be more awkward — leaving and letting on that she'd heard, or staying and pretending not to hear.

She was saved from making a decision when Roger popped over. "Merry, we're ready. Everyone's here except Sarah. Amber says she's outside in her car."

To Roger, Merry said, "Great, everyone in position." She turned to Megan. "Be a dear and fetch your aunt? She's probably answering fan mail and will be out there all day if someone doesn't move her along."

In addition to being Megan's great aunt, Sarah Birch was also a famous mystery author who wrote her bestselling novels under the penname Sarah Estelle. Megan hadn't seen much of her grandfather's sister over the past few months. Their last few conversations back in the fall had been laced with resentment and peppered by accusations. But she said "sure" to Merry now, happy for a chance to grab some fresh air and text Denver.

Megan spotted Sarah in the corner of the nursery parking lot talking with Becca's father, Paul Fox. A light but steady snow was falling and both stood with arms crossed against the cold. It wasn't until she got closer that she heard the raised voices and harsh tone of angry words. She was about to turn around when their conversation stopped. It was too late to retreat. Sarah had seen her.

"Megan? Are you looking for me?" Aunt Sarah flashed a half smile. She beckoned with her hand. "I feel like you've been avoiding me for months. It's so nice to see you."

"Merry said the carolers are ready to start. They're just waiting for you."

"Better go then." Sarah looked at Paul, frowned. "Take care of that cold."

"You should take care as well." He coughed, the violence of the spasm doubling him over. When he finally regained his breath, he stood and wiped his mouth. His eyes looked teary and slightly red. "And think about what I'm saying. You know it makes sense, Sarah."

"I don't need to think about it, Paul. Please don't ask me again." Sarah seemed to remember Megan's presence. She recovered quickly. "Forgive my manners. Paul, have you met my niece, Megan Sawyer? She owns Washington Acres Farm and the café on Canal Street."

Paul managed another smile. "I don't believe we've formally met." He held out his hand.

Megan returned his handshake, getting a better view of Paul Fox up close. He was a handsome man in an unsettling way. Medium height, broad shoulders, with sharply intelligent eyes, and what would be construed as a cruel mouth if it weren't for the amused half smile that played on his lips.

His gaze was intense, and right now he was aiming it at Megan with laser-like focus.

He said, "A farmer? At the risk of sounding old-fashioned, you don't look like any farmer I've ever met."

"No?"

"Not at all." His tone was teasing and self-deprecating at the same time. "Perhaps if more farmers looked like you, I would spend time at the local outdoor markets."

Megan tilted her head. "Perhaps if you spent more time at your local outdoor markets you wouldn't have such a wicked cold now."

Paul laughed. He contemplated Megan for a long moment, his stare both challenging and appreciative. He turned to Sarah, coughed again, and like that his demeanor changed. "You'd better start singing, Sarah."

"I'm only too happy to sing. For the right person."

Paul glanced back at Megan. He smiled again, but this time the smile didn't reach his eyes. "Your aunt's a smart lady. Smart people know when to open their mouths — and when to keep them closed."

As Megan and Sarah walked back inside Merry's nursery, Megan pondered those words. Was that a veiled threat directed at her aunt? And anyway, how did Aunt Sarah know Paul Fox? Not that it mattered. But her aunt certainly had an interesting life.

FIVE

Denver never showed on Wednesday night because of a lame horse and an injured cat, but he stopped by Thursday morning between farm rounds to sample Bibi's waffles and sausage and catch up with Megan.

The farmhouse kitchen was unusually crowded. Denver and Clay occupied one end of the long table, Megan and Emily the other. As usual, Bibi bustled around the kitchen, her eighty-four-year-old body wrapped in a red long-sleeved "Winsome Rules" t-shirt, complete with a list of Winsome's "rules" for vacation fun on the back.

"Bonnie, sit. I'll get the coffee." Clay, Megan's farm manager, stood halfway up before Bibi pushed him back down.

"The day I can't treat guests right in my own kitchen is the day you can bury me," Bibi said. She stopped by Megan to stroke Lily's cheek. "I won't say the baby suits you,

51

Megan, because I'll get an earful later." She looked pointedly at Denver. "Isn't that right, Daniel?"

Bibi had started calling Denver by his given name, a habit the veterinarian seemed not to mind.

"Oh, no you don't, Bonnie. That's a trap. If I agree with ye, I'll be getting an earful later too."

Everyone laughed, including Megan. Lily was eight months old and a darling package of rosy cheeks and inquisitive round eyes and roving fingers. Right now, those chubby fingers were wound around Megan's locket, the one her mother had given her before she left home more than twenty years ago.

Megan's cell phone rang. Emily held out her hands, and Megan reluctantly returned the baby. She frowned when she saw the name on her phone display: Bobby King. King was Winsome's youngest-ever police chief. It'd been a baptism by fire for the young cop, and Megan knew a call from Bobby typically portended problems.

"Bobby," Megan said. "How can I help you?"

"Morning, Megan. I'm looking for Emily Kuhl. Any chance she's with you?"

"She happens to be right here. Everything okay?"

"I'm afraid I need to speak with her. Can you pass the phone?"

"Of course." All eyes were on Megan, and all conversation had stopped. Even Lily's gentle gurgling had transitioned to a silent stare fixated on her mother. Megan knew after the trauma of the last few months, Emily would want nothing to do with Bobby King, but she had no choice but to pass the phone to her.

"I'm here, Chief," Emily said. She was silent after that, nodding along as though Bobby could see her. She ended with, "I see."

Emily handed the phone back to Megan. Her face was snow white, her fingers shaking. "He wants to talk to you."

"Bobby?"

"That damn house should just be burned to the ground. Nothing good seems to come of it, that's for sure."

"Bobby, you're not making any sense."

Lily, sensing her mother's distress, had begun to wail. Bibi took her gently from her mother's arms and walked her into the parlor, crooning all the while in her ear. Megan waited for King to say more.

"There's been a death at Emily's grandmother's house, Megan. The medical examiner is here now, but the circumstances are unusual, to say the least."

"Unusual in what way?"

"Let's just say someone had a very rough night."

Megan tensed. "Someone as in —"

"Paul Fox. Paul's son found him dead in his bedroom this morning."

Megan's breath quickened. Her thoughts shifted from the man on the phone to Emily to a memory of the night before. Paul Fox. A little bit charming, a little bit aloof. But alive. "He seemed okay yesterday. What happened?"

Bobby sighed, a novice quickly becoming a veteran. "We're not sure."

"Could it be . . ." Only she let her words trail off, unwilling to give voice to her fear with Emily and Lily sitting so close by.

"We don't know. I'll tell you more when you get here."

"Me?"

"I'm hoping you can bring Emily. We need her here to answer some questions, but I'm thinking that after what happened last fall, she could use some moral support."

"Yes, of course," Megan said. She clicked off her phone, tension rising like bile in her chest.

Winsome's town center was a cobblestoned

reminder of simpler times, but its surrounding area suffered from the very real problems associated with modern life — such as occasional gridlock. The storms from earlier in the week had knocked out power to parts of the town, and crews were on the scene, cutting down branches and repairing downed poles. As a result, the fifteen-minute drive to Emily's grandmother's Cape Cod took two detours and almost forty minutes.

Emily and Megan arrived to a frustrated Bobby King circling the house beside a man Megan recognized as Winsome's fire chief, Don Friar. When Bobby saw Emily, he waved noncommittedly, leaving them to loiter by Megan's truck. Megan recognized the scene before her. She had lived through a death on the farm property the year before when the local zoning commissioner was murdered in her barn. While Bobby hadn't made it sound like this was murder, the presence of so many police and firetrucks — plus two ambulances — gave her pause.

Megan looked around at the property before her. The broken down trailer had been removed, but the second trailer still sat abandoned on the side of the yard. Snow hid the vast lawn and gave the bordering trees a closed-in, ominous feel. Megan's gaze trailed to the Sauer farm across the road. Glen Sauer had reduced his stock, and what was once a bustling agro-business sat still and quiet on this winter day.

"You okay?" Megan asked Emily. Emily had been quiet since the call came in, not protesting when Megan said she'd drive her, and barely responding when Bibi offered to watch Lily.

"As okay as I can be." She gazed toward the recently renovated house. All of the windows on the house were open, as was the front door. "There goes my heat bill."

Megan saw a firefighter leave the building holding a gas mask and watched his progress. Had there been a fire? She saw no signs of smoke or damage. This property had belonged to Emily's grandmother, and after her grandmother died, it was to be Emily's father's. He'd planned to make it a rental property. When he died, Emily followed suit — at least for the short term, until she could sell it. In the meantime, she'd hired contractors to clean it up: new floors, fresh paint, matching kitchen appliances. Megan hoped those renovations hadn't been for nothing.

As though reading her thoughts, Emily said, "I almost moved in there. But I just couldn't, not after everything that happened. I've been hoping for a long-term renter, so when Merry's call came . . . well, it seemed like a perfect chance to pay some overdue contractor bills. Looks like it was another bad decision."

"You couldn't know something like this would happen. How long were Luke and his father supposed to stay?"

"Until the second week in January." Emily looked at Megan with a faraway glaze. Blonde hair stuck out from beneath a green cap, making her look younger than her twenty-eight years. "I wonder what happened. Bobby wouldn't say."

A car started up and Megan watched one of the police cruisers pull out of the driveway. The temperature was warmer today, but a biting wind blew through the property, kicking up snow and causing a shiver to run through her. Megan wrapped her arms around her chest, wishing Bobby would hurry up. A few minutes later, he ended his conversation with Friar and waved for Megan and Emily to join him by the front door.

"Don just gave us clearance to go inside." He looked from Emily to Megan and back again. "Ready?"

Both women nodded. Bobby led the way. Before entering, he turned around. "Emily, you had work done here recently?"

"Lots of it."

"Were the contractors finished?"

"For the most part. Why?"

But Bobby had turned back around and was now over the threshold. Emily looked at Megan before joining him, her eyes wide with alarm.

The first thing Megan noticed was the bitter, permeating cold. The windows in the entire downstairs had been opened, and a frigid breeze blew winter indoors.

Emily seemed affected by the cold too. She pulled her scarf tighter around her neck and tucked her gloved hands in her pockets. Her shoulders hunched, matching the despair on her face. King led them through the living room, pausing by the door to the back bedroom. The living room looked considerably different than it had in October. Amazing what new floors and a fresh coat of paint could do. But even the renovated interior couldn't mask the aura of death.

King said, "He died in the bedroom, Emily. His body has been removed and the place has been thoroughly gone over, but I wanted you to see the room. Get your thoughts on whether anything seemed out of place. Ready?"

Emily nodded. King walked into the bedroom and moved to the side to let Emily and Megan join him. Megan glanced around, taking in the scene before her.

Like the living room, the back bedroom had been remodeled. The walls were painted a trendy slate grey, the trim bright white. White curtains hung in the two small windows along the back wall, their sheer material billowing wildly in the wind. A full-size bed sat against one wall, its blankets askew; a three-drawered bureau had been placed against another wall.

A black suitcase sat propped on top of a small table, its strewn contents showing evidence of a search, and an open closet housed neatly hung pants and a row of button-down white shirts. The closet was otherwise empty. The room was tidy, clean, and wholly unremarkable.

King looked at Emily. "What do you think?"

Emily looked perplexed. "This room looks the way it did when I rented it to Merry. Why the open windows?"

"Gas leak?" Megan said.

King frowned. "Just a precaution. Nothing was found. We can close them now."

Megan walked to the open window and glanced outside. A uniformed man from the

59

local gas company was walking around the back of the property. She closed the window, latching it carefully. "How did Paul die? Do you know?"

"We'll have to wait for test results. Luke Fox found his father dead in his bed this morning. His efforts to resuscitate him were unsuccessful. He says his father hadn't been feeling well. Just a cold."

"I saw him yesterday," Megan said, remembering Paul's cough and watery eyes. "He did seem under the weather."

King glanced toward the bed. His shoulders sagged. "Poor guy was devastated. I'm not sure how reliable he was about his father's health. Could be he wasn't thinking too clearly."

"Cold medicine overdose?" Emily asked. She'd been quietly looking in the closet, and she closed the door and turned back toward Megan and King. "Prescription or otherwise?"

"Maybe," King said.

Megan thought about the violence of Paul's coughing spasms. She glanced at the bed, then met King's gaze. "But you don't think so."

"History has taught me to delay forming opinions until all the facts are in." He shook his head. "But no, I don't think so."

Emily asked, "Did Luke smell gas?"

"He thought there might have been a faint odor in the room."

Megan sniffed. She could smell *something,* but she couldn't quite identify the scent. It seemed sharp, sweet, and very faint.

King studied Emily. "Have you had an issue with gas before?"

"No. Never. The house does have gas heat, but we've never experienced a leak."

King said, "We didn't see any carbon monoxide detectors."

Emily frowned. "I should have installed them when I rented the place. I guess I forgot."

King nodded. "Well, the gas company didn't find evidence of a gas leak, but because there's no apparent cause of death, this is one for the medical examiner."

"Did she have preliminary thoughts?" Megan asked.

King hesitated. "She thought Paul's death was consistent with asphyxiation. Of course, that could have been brought about by a heart attack or some other natural cause. We won't know for sure until the autopsy is completed."

King asked Emily a few more questions about the contractors: what chemicals or supplies they may have used, and when the work was slated to be completed.

Megan, only half listening, paced around the room. She didn't know what she was looking for, or if she was looking for anything, but the conversation she'd witnessed between Paul and her Aunt Sarah at Merry's nursery bothered her. Other than that annoying cold, Paul had seemed fine. Yet he went to bed and never woke up.

Why? Simple as a heart attack? Overmedication?

"Did Paul have a history of heart disease?" Megan asked during a lull in King's questions.

"Both Luke and Merry said no."

Megan thought about that. She paused by one of the windows and again looked outside. The contractors had redone the windows, and each had fresh paint on the trim and the muntins.

Megan pulled off a glove and was running a finger across the base of one window, appreciating the meticulous workmanship, when something caught her eye. A tiny piece of blue in the sill, near where window meets frame.

"Look at this, Bobby," Megan said. She showed Bobby the blue tape.

"Just paint tape," he said. He turned back to Emily. "Your contractors probably left this here when they finished."

"Probably."

Megan touched the end of the tape with her index finger. She felt something sticky next to it.

"There seems to be some type of residue here."

King touched it, rubbing a thick finger back and forth across the surface. "Just leftover tape glue," he said. "From the contractors."

"Makes sense," Megan said. Only she wondered what contractor would be so careful with a paint job only to leave residue on the frame. And paint tape didn't leave a residue — that was the point of using it. But duct tape did.

"Who else had access to this house?" King asked Emily. "Besides you, that is."

Emily thought for a moment. "My contractors. I gave Merry two keys. She may have given one to Luke and one to Paul, or she could have kept one for herself."

"How about Becca?" King asked.

Emily shook her head. "I didn't give one to Becca. Merry may have, though."

Megan thought about Becca Fox. How would The Love Chemist react to her father's death?

Upset about the time wasted, time that

could have been spent reconnecting? Would she lament her unwillingness to forgive him now that he was dead? Or would she brush aside his death as justice done?

Something told Megan that Becca's feelings for her father had hardened over time, and it would take more than a love potion — or his untimely death — to soften her angry heart.

Six

Paul's death quickly became the topic de jour. Megan heard it discussed in the café like a morbid game of Whisper Down the Lane. Some said he'd had a heart attack, others alleged he was asphyxiated with a pillow, and some surmised that he'd been poisoned by arsenic. The fact remained that King had shared nothing new, and Merry insisted Paul's death must have been natural. A heart attack or an aneurysm, perhaps triggered by an undiagnosed condition in combination with the medication he was using to treat his cold.

Megan ran into Becca Fox Saturday morning, right before the town's Holiday Stroll was scheduled to begin. The concept behind the stroll was simple: each business along Canal Street adorned their shop with holiday lights and other decorations and offered a sale table or special offering at the front of the store. The town's Beautification

Board and Historical Society had decorated the main thoroughfare, and Historical Society volunteers were manning carts that offered hot chocolate, hot apple cider, and roasted chestnuts to visitors. The Winsome Historical Society wanted to recreate a Colonial Christmas experience. While Megan appreciated the concept, she thought Winsome's visitors simply looked like they were suffering from the cold. Including Becca.

"Such a pretty town," Becca said. She unwound a scarlet scarf from around her neck, giving Megan a wan smile. "I feel like it's two hundred years ago."

Megan and Clover, Clay Hand's sister and the Washington Acres Café and Larder manager, had placed a table of Pennsylvania-made goods at the front of the store. Clover was folding linens hand embroidered by a local woman while Megan arranged the organic soaps and creams produced by a neighboring farm. Clay, Clover, Bibi, and Megan had spent Friday night decorating the place, and now the café and store looked like the holiday edition of *Ladies Home Journal*. A modern version — not one from the 1800s.

Glancing at the electric icicle lights, Megan said, "That's the idea, Becca. Harken back to simpler times."

Alvaro was even baking butter cookies, gingersnaps, and gingerbread men for the occasion — so the store smelled like Christmas too.

Becca rubbed her hands together. "It was the scent of baked goods that drew me inside. Oh my god," she exclaimed, taking off her hat. "It smells *amazing* in here." She put her hat on the table next to an embroidered blue and white Menorah towel. "Alvaro's a genius."

"Go on back," Clover said. "Tell him to give you a ginger snap. They're delicious." She glanced at Megan. "I know because I've already eaten seven."

With a laugh, Megan said, "Why don't you go get Becca some cookies, Clover? And have an eighth and a ninth while you're at it. Just don't let Alvaro catch you."

Clover smiled. "You really want me to be on Alvaro's bad side."

Megan and Becca watched Clover walk back toward the café. In her early twenties, Clover had long brown hair, an easy smile, and a propensity for super short skirts. The skirt she wore today — with thick black lacy tights — was mini enough to get lost under her baggy sweater. Clover was also the live-in girlfriend of Chief Bobby King, and while Megan implicitly trusted Clover, she was mindful of not placing her employee in a compromising position. Like talking about Paul Fox with Paul's estranged daughter in front of her.

With Clover now safely out of earshot, Megan said, "I'm sorry about your father, Becca. It's never easy to lose someone."

Becca picked up a bottle of Mandy's Mango Foot Cream and stared at the label. "He's been dead to me for years." She looked up, seemed to notice the look of surprise on Megan's face, and said, "He killed my mother, Megan. No one believes me. Not even Aunt Merry. But it's true. My father was a man who could make you believe he was upright and just. A therapist, a business leader, a church goer. But it was all a lie." She replaced the mango foot cream and moved on to another product. "I didn't wish him dead, but I can't say I'm sorry to see a killer go."

"Did you ever go to the police about your mother?"

"Of course I did. They had no proof, so they ruled it an accident." Becca flipped her hair over her shoulder. "And it *looked* like an accident. I get that. But by then, I was on to him. No one could verify his where-abouts that day, and he had reason to want my mother out of the picture." She scowled. "I saw him for the monster he was."

Megan looked at Becca with sympathy. How awful to carry around such a burden, to lose one parent to death and another to hatred. She said, "Those are very strong words."

Becca turned her full attention on Megan. "My father had an unimaginable cruel streak. Oh, he could hide it from the public, but behind closed doors he reveled in it. He would do little things — rip up my favorite stuffed animal in front of me, tell me how fat I looked right before the prom, give away our beloved family dog — to show who was really in charge. It wasn't until I was in high school and saw how other parents were that I realized what a bastard my father was."

Gently, Megan said, "That's awful, Becca. But those things don't make him a murderer."

"My mother was a healthy woman. Depressed, yes. But not so out of it that she'd miss a gas leak in her house. My father set her up. He killed her."

"You need to stop saying that, Becca," a man's voice said. "You sound mad. And by mad, I mean crazy."

Megan and Becca looked up to see Luke standing there, his hands in his pockets.

He'd entered the café while they were engrossed in conversation. He stared at his sister, eyes rounded with concern. Becca turned away with a huff.

Luke grabbed Becca's arm. "You need to watch what you're saying." He glanced at Megan. Voice lowered, he said, "Dad is dead, Becca. *Dead.* Not the best time to be mouthing off about how much you hated him."

But Becca would not be deterred. "You weren't there, Luke. You didn't see the way he degraded her. The more she sank into depression, the more he berated her, blamed her for every bad thing that had ever happened in his life. It's not hard to believe he wanted her out of his life for good —" Becca seemed to catch herself. She looked at her brother, eyes watery.

"You should get some rest," Luke said slowly and deliberately. "We need to meet at Aunt Merry's later. To start dealing with Dad's cremation."

Becca nodded. Clover arrived with cookies and hot chocolate, but Becca refused the offerings. Clover shrugged and shoved a cookie into her own mouth. She held the hot chocolate out to Luke, who also declined.

"Megan, do you sell eggs?" Luke asked.

"Aunt Merry sent me to get some."

"Of course." Merry always wanted eggs. Megan wasn't sure what she did with so many eggs.

Megan walked to the cooler and fetched a dozen eggs from the cooler. She returned to the table and handed them to Luke. By that time, Becca was gone.

Luke started to reach for his wallet, and Megan shook her head. "No need."

Luke muttered his thanks.

"Where did Becca go?" Megan asked.

"She said she was heading back to Merry's to rest." Luke shifted the eggs from hand to hand absentmindedly. "Please don't pay her much mind. She . . . well, let's just say my father's authoritarian nature had a greater effect on my rebellious little sister."

Megan's eyes wandered to the storefront window and the small crowd gathering outside. She spotted her Aunt Sarah in the pack. The famous mystery author, who was living mostly incognito in Winsome, was eating chestnuts and talking with Amber, the town's librarian. Sarah turned, saw Megan looking at her, and waved.

Megan said to Luke, "Did your mother die of carbon monoxide poisoning?"

Luke nodded. "An unfortunate accident, despite what Becca says."

Megan was thinking about Paul Fox, about the potential similarity. Only the police had ruled out a gas leak. But there was that smell in the room . . . it reminded her of the crisp scent of the New Zealand Sauvignon Blanc Denver preferred. An odd association, and she wished she could place it. She said, "If I can help Becca in any way, let me know."

Luke bit his lower lip, a habit that was making his lip red and swollen beneath his beard. He stared at the lotions and creams on the sale table, his eyes settling into resignation. "Merry said to invite you and Bonnie to tea tomorrow. She's having some women over to introduce Becca's products."

"She still wants to have that, even with your dad . . . ?" Megan's voice trailed off. The pain in Luke's eyes softly echoed the pain she'd felt when her husband died, and the rest of the words wouldn't come.

Luke's smile was apologetic. "Remember, this is for Becca. My sister is already angry that Aunt Merry coordinated his homecoming. Aunt Merry can't very well cancel based on Dad's death. She'd be furious."

Megan watched Luke leave the store. His words about Becca rang true. Becca's anger seemed genuine — and while aimed at her father, she didn't seem too pleased with her aunt either. Warranted? Megan didn't know. But thinking of her own mother, and her newly discovered grandfather, Megan understood that some feelings defied explanation.

Megan was about to head back toward the café when something caught her eye. It was the bright pink of Aunt Sarah's scarf twirling behind her in the wind as she walked down Canal Street. Twenty yards behind her was Luke Fox, deep in conversation with a tall man whom Megan had never seen before.

SEVEN

Bibi had a bridge tournament on Sunday that conflicted with Merry's high tea, so Megan went alone. She pulled into Merry's driveway for the second time in a week. The snow that had blocked her steps and littered her drive was now piled in three- and four-foot heaps along Merry's property. But snow and ice couldn't stop Merry Chance from celebrating Christmas properly, and all of her yard ornaments and house decorations were clear and clean.

"Megan, I'm glad you came. Becca will be happy to see you."

Megan followed Merry through an expansive foyer and into an elaborately decorated living room. A thick white carpet covered the floor. Two damask loveseats faced one another across a coffee table, near a brass-ensconced gas fireplace. Queen Anne chairs in matching material flanked an antique round conversation table. Everything was decorated for Christmas. There were wreaths and candles and angels and Santa and sprays of white and red roses. The air was scented with pine and cinnamon. A catalog come to life.

Merry walked through the living room and into the dining room. A twelve-person table dominated the center of the vast square room. A Christmas tree done completely in white lights and Victorian ornaments stood in one corner. An ornate buffet stood against a far wall, and on it were tiered trays of crustless sandwiches, scones, cookies, and an assortment of china teacups.

Merry sure liked her English teatime.

"Lovely," Megan said, feeling suddenly underdressed in jeans and a sweater.

Merry thanked her. "The ladies should be arriving shortly, and Becca will be down any minute."

"Let me help you in the kitchen, then," Megan said.

Merry hesitated. "I'm just filling teapots." She sighed, evidently letting go of whatever unwritten rules caused her to push away the offer of help from invited guests. "I could use an extra hand or two."

Merry's kitchen was awash in teapots. Megan counted nine, and each had a label identifying a different type of tea. Merry had also created small thank you notes for the invitees, each with a different tea bag and information about Becca's business. "Tokens of thanks," Merry called them.

Megan was impressed.

"You really want to help her succeed, don't you?"

Merry was removing wet tea leaves from the inside of a ball strainer. Without pausing, she said, "Becca has no one else." Merry looked up. "What did you think of her perfume?"

What *did* she think? Megan had to admit that people had been nicer to her while she was wearing it, if nothing else. "I think I need to try it out a few more times. See what happens."

Merry nodded. She looked distracted, even slightly agitated. She wore a red sweater embroidered with tiny holly leaves and berries, black pants, and a lot of gold jewelry. Her reading glasses were red, white, and black and they hung from a red rope chain around her neck. She slipped the glasses on to read the label on a box of loose mint green tea leaves.

Megan said, "I'm so sorry to hear about Paul's passing."

"Thank you. I'm sorry too." She frowned. "To come to Winsome and then have that happen." She shook her head. "I feel responsible. If I hadn't been sticking my nose in their business, maybe he'd still be alive."

"How could this be your fault, Merry?"

She shrugged. "I know it could've happened anywhere, but it didn't. It happened here in Winsome. Under my watch."

"He was a grown man. Capable of making his own decisions. And if it was a heart attack or some other natural event, it would have happened regardless of where he was staying." Megan paused. "Any more information from Bobby?"

"Not yet. But frankly, Paul didn't care for doctors. It wouldn't surprise me if they found a latent heart issue." She looked at Megan over her readers, her guard back up. "That's what killed him. Denial." Merry put the box on the counter and tilted her head, as though listening for the presence of her niece in the other room. "I'd been hoping to give Becca some closure with this trip. She's angry that I invited Paul, but I thought maybe enough time had passed that she could see her father for who he is. Was. A good man, but not a perfect man. A man who tried to do what was best for his family." Merry shook her head. "I wasn't always there for Blanche the way I should have been."

"Were you and Blanche close?" Megan remembered Merry from her own childhood in Winsome, but she couldn't recall more than a ghostly image of Merry's sibling.

Merry nodded. "Blanche was my older sister. She had Luke when she was young, soon after she and Paul got married. She worked for a while to help put Paul through graduate school and to start his practice, and then she stayed at home with the kids. It wasn't an easy life. He was often short-tempered and a penny pincher, and my sister was . . . well, rather passive. She was kind at heart, but never liked making decisions. Paul suited her in the sense that he was happy to take the lead and she was happy to be led. I think he liked that about her — her warmth, her faith in him."

"Becca resented their relationship?"

Merry poured water from a tea kettle into two of the teapots. She sniffed the spout, and seemingly satisfied, wiped the bit of water that had pooled beneath the pot on the granite countertop.

"As much as she will never admit it, Becca is her father's daughter. While Luke was willing to take his father's rules and proclamations in stride, Becca fought everything. I mean everything." Merry's smile was tinged with sadness. "Paul could be funny and smart. He had what some might call charisma. People wanted to be around him."

Megan found that at odds with what others had said about the late psychologist. Instead of pointing this out, Megan said, "Becca insinuated things weren't good between Blanche and Paul in the end."

Merry leaned against the counter. "Have you ever witnessed what happens when two people have extreme parenting styles? When one is exceedingly permissive and one exceedingly authoritarian?"

Picturing her permissive father and her strict paternal grandfather, Megan said, "I've had some experience."

"Then you know that each pushes the other to further extremes. The authoritarian parent cracks down overly hard, causing the child to react. The permissive parent then attempts to sooth by loosening reins, perhaps spoiling the child. This angers the authoritarian parent, who perceives an undermining of his or her authority, a threat to his or her control. That parent acts in turn in an even more punishing manner, and so on." Merry paused, thinking. "This was the dynamic I saw with Blanche and Paul. First with the kids, and then later in their own relationship. She became more passive and depressed, and that made him more angry and controlling. I think each was blind to their role in the dance."

Megan thought it interesting that Merry seemed to unconsciously lay the blame at her sister's feet for starting that pattern. But Merry's characterization of Blanche as depressed matched Becca's description of her mother. "And Becca witnessed the dance, as you say, between them?"

"Becca lived at home for part of college. I'm afraid she saw more than she may have liked. She'd always been close to Blanche in a way Luke never really was. And where Blanche's passivity angered Paul, it made Becca fiercely protective. She never understood the complexities of her parents' relationship, or the ways in which they balanced one another." Merry frowned. "It was easier to blame poor Paul."

Megan thought that was unusually insightful for Merry. It made her wonder how closely Merry had witnessed her sister's downward spiral. "Did your sister get help for her depression?"

"Oh, I tried to get her to see someone. I'm sure Becca did as well."

"Not Paul?"

"We never talked about it. I'd like to believe he did."

Just then, the doorbell rang. Merry looked relieved. "I need to get that."

A teakettle whistled. Megan pulled it off the stove with an oversized Christmas mitt and began filling a china teapot, her mind on all the ways people could destroy the very things they loved in another person.

Megan was glad Bibi had chosen bridge over this. Her grandmother was frugal, and her brand of frugality meant not wasting money on what she viewed as unnecessary things. Bibi would have rolled her eyes at the way the ladies of Winsome were opening their wallets for a chance at love.

But Becca presented her love potions with aplomb, calmly explaining the purported science behind her products. As women passed around the scents and dabbed pheromone-laden perfume behind their ears and on their upper lips, Becca read testimonials written by happy customers and encouraged attendees to "live life a little more fully, love a little more deeply."

At one point, Becca caught Megan's eye and winked. Megan wasn't sure if Becca was simply pleased or if she was sharing a joke with Megan. The joke being the hundreds that were flowing into her small cash box.

Megan excused herself before it was over, while the attendees were drinking tea daintily from the mismatched china cups. She had chickens to attend to and goats to feed, and if she didn't spend adequate time with Heidi and Dimples, her Pygmy goats, the pair would find some mischievous way to show their displeasure. A swallowed cord. A stolen boot. A goat stranded on a barn roof. Megan had been there before.

Becca met her at the door and thanked her for coming. Megan hugged the box of rose-scented love potion she'd purchased as a gift for Emily and thanked Becca for inviting her.

"Did it work for you?" Becca asked. "The perfume, I mean."

Megan told her people seemed nicer, friendlier.

"Ah, yes, that's often the first thing you notice. Men and women pay you more attention. Keep wearing it and you'll find men hitting on you more frequently. You might even have a better and more active sex life."

Out of curiosity, Megan asked, "Do you use it, Becca?"

Becca laughed. "Me? Nah. I don't actually like attention all that much."

"That's ironic, don't you think?"

"I suppose. I've never felt the need for

male attention. Or friends, for that matter."

"Then how did you come up with this idea?"

Behind them, Merry called out for Becca to come back and answer questions for their guests. Becca smiled apologetically. "That's a story for another day." She brightened. "How about I meet you for coffee one day this week? You can tell me how things are going with the pheromones, and I'll share their origin."

"Better yet, why don't you come to the farm?" Megan said. "We can talk freely there, with only goats and chickens to disturb us."

"Goats and chickens?" Becca turned back toward her aunt and held up one finger in a "be right there" gesture. "Sure, that sounds fun." She said, "Coming!" to Merry, who was calling her again. With a last glance at Megan, Becca rolled her eyes. "And peaceful. I bet there's no one to bother you on a farm."

EIGHT

Becca arrived unannounced at the farm two days later, her tall frame ensconced head to toe in a puffy black coat. It was snowing lightly, and when Becca knocked on the door, a fine layer of white flakes covered her wild hair and the shoulders of her bulky coat. She apologized for showing up without calling first, but she seemed tense, and although Megan had been ready to help Clay pick greens for the café, she agreed to that coffee date — as long as Becca would help her collect eggs first.

"Are the chickens always in their coop?" Becca asked. She watched as Megan reached into the beds to gather the eggs, her body pressed against the frame of the chicken tractor. "And why are the eggs so many different colors?"

Megan glanced down into the basket she was holding. The farm raised a variety of laying hens, and the eggs reflected that diversity. Within the base of the basket were brown, light blue, green, and white eggs of varying sizes. She explained this to Becca — along with the fact that her chickens had access to the outdoors, but they often preferred the heated interior of the tractor to the below-freezing temperatures of winter. In fact, given the recent weather, Megan was surprised her girls were still laying at all.

Becca seemed to only be half-listening. She glanced around at the chickens and then over her shoulder, toward the barn. "Aunt Merry told me someone died there."

Megan stopped mid-bend and turned to her guest. "That's true, someone did."

"Aunt Merry also said the police suspected your grandmother — and you."

"Perhaps. But the killer was arrested and is in prison now." She gave Becca a hard look. "Didn't Merry tell you that?"

"She did. I was just wondering."

Returning to her chore, Megan said, "You seem preoccupied, Becca. Did something happen?"

"No, no. I just thought it was interesting. A murder in your barn. Doesn't seem like the kind of thing that would happen in Winsome. That's all."

Megan headed back toward the farmhouse, Becca trailing behind.

Becca said, "How about a tour?"

"Sure. And then some coffee?"

Becca nodded. Megan led her through the greenhouses and down to the goats' pen. Both girls were standing on their hay bales waiting for someone to feed them. Becca gave them only a cursory pat, even when Heidi nuzzled the newcomer and tried to pull a tissue from Becca's pocket.

"Cute," Becca mumbled. She patted the goat on the head as though she were a dog.

Odd, Megan thought. The goats loved people and most visitors found Dimples and Heidi irresistible. They left the goats' enclosure and Megan walked Becca through the old barn, stopping to show her the portion that marked the original barn from the 1700s.

Becca glanced around, taking in the dirt floor, the thick stone sills, and the murky light pouring through leaded glass. "Is that where the man was murdered?"

"No. Simon died in a newer portion of the barn."

Becca rubbed her hands up and down her arms. Condensation from the cold air blew from her mouth. "I can almost feel it, the presence of death." Becca bent down and touched the earthen floor. "It's weird to think about, isn't it?"

"Do you want to talk, Becca?"

Becca straightened, her eyes rounded in surprise. "No, why?"

Because you seem preoccupied with death, Megan thought. Instead she said, "How about that coffee?" She no more wanted to dwell on Simon's death than she wanted to think about nuclear disaster or a zombie apocalypse. "Bibi's at the café helping Álvaro make Christmas cookies, so we have the house to ourselves. Well, other than the dogs."

Becca nodded. She still had a faraway look in her eyes, but she made her way out of the barn ahead of Megan and didn't stop until she reached the house.

Megan placed two cups of steaming coffee down on the table. She opened a tin of Bibi's gingersnaps, gave one to each of her begging canines, and placed the tin on the table alongside a plate of banana nut bread. "So, you were going to tell me the story of how you got the idea for The Love Chemist. I'd love to hear about it."

Becca added cream to her coffee and stirred it in with languid circles. "I guess in an odd way, I can credit my dad with my business idea."

"Oh? How is that?"

Megan settled in across from the younger woman. Sadie and Gunther laid on the floor next to Becca, forever hopeful.

"He expected me to fail."

Megan waited while Becca placed two cookies and a slice of banana bread on a small plate.

Picking at the edge of her bread, Becca said, "During college I studied animal science, eventually focusing my research on pheromones. You know what they are, right?"

Megan nodded. She knew pheromones were chemicals animals released into their environment to affect the behavior of other animals, especially when it came to mating behavior. She also knew the existence of pheromones for humans was still a topic of debate.

"Well, after college I worked for a fragrance manufacturer, Tempest — I already told you that. Tempest creates the tastes and smells for food and fragrances. Quite literally. The flavored corn chips that are so popular? Tempest manufactures the exact spice blend that makes them irresistible." Becca gave Megan a wan smile. She took a sip of coffee and replaced her cup in the saucer before continuing. "The scientists there can make you want anything. Anyway, it was a fine job and I learned a lot, but I was bored. And kind of sickened by the ways companies manipulate, if you know what I mean. So I quit after two years."

"And started The Love Chemist?"

"No, actually. I lived with Luke abroad for a year and tried to help him with his business. He's an engineer who works with overseas start-ups. He helps companies looking to offshore their manufacturing facilities. I basically played glorified secretary for Luke." Becca eyed Megan over the rim of her cup. "Until my dad visited Luke while we were living in Mexico."

"By then you weren't speaking with your dad."

"Right." Becca pushed her seat back, away from the table, and stared at the uneaten baked goods on her plate. "Dad didn't know I was working for Luke — I'd forbidden Luke from telling him — and he showed up unexpectedly at Luke's office. I was using the photocopier, but the machine was broken, so I was bent over, my back to the door, struggling to fix it. Dad came in and let out a long, slow whistle." Becca's face flushed. "He said 'glad you finally got some attractive help' to my brother."

Horrified, Megan said, "What did you do?"

"I turned around slowly, letting him get a full look at the 'attractive help' Luke had hired. I thought I'd embarrass him." Becca shook her head, the scowl on her face indicating she was clearly reliving the unpleasant memory. "He wasn't embarrassed. In fact, he snorted and said 'I stand corrected. You continue with your old ways, Luke.' In other words, I was just another one of the ugly women Luke usually hired or dated."

Megan let that sink in. A father humiliating his daughter that way? A man humiliating his son's employee that way? Even if Paul had been joking, or if he hadn't known that the woman at the copier was Becca, his behavior was reprehensible. Megan said, "You must have been hurt."

Becca laughed. "He'd been telling me I was fat or ugly or unlovable since forever. That was nothing new. What bothered me — what really irked me — was having him see me like that, bent over a copier, as though my Master's Degree in Chemistry meant nothing. It was a defining moment."

Yet it still didn't quite explain the love potions. "So why The Love Chemist?"

Becca grinned. "I combined the two

things I knew — pheromones and scent manufacturing. Voila! A company is born."

"Very creative. And it seems like it worked for you."

"Perhaps, but it's been a huge financial struggle ever since. I've poured literally every cent back into the business. Makes it hard to have a life."

Megan stood to refill their coffee mugs. Becca's had barely been touched, but Megan filled hers to the brim. "Becca," she said while sitting back down. "The comment your dad made to Luke about continuing with his old ways. Did he usually talk to Luke like that?"

Becca's eyes darkened. "My dad acted like he and Luke were brothers, not father and son. When Luke was young, dad would comment on his girlfriends. You know, little things about the size of their busts or the length of their hair. Sometimes he'd rate them. When Luke got older, it became more of a friendly competition. They thought it was funny."

Megan put down the cookie she was about to eat. Just hearing about Paul's treatment of women was making her feel ill. "Compete in what way?"

"Who had the hottest girlfriend? And after Mom passed, who had the most sexual encounters. That kind of thing." Becca paused, thinking. "I know it's gross, but maybe I was a little jealous of their relationship. At least they had one."

Megan felt a wave of sympathy for Becca Fox. If even a few of her stories about her father were true, she could understand Becca's disdain for the man. Looking at her now, she'd managed to get through her father's demented view of the opposite sex — and parenthood — in one piece. Or were the scars just not immediately visible? Megan had to wonder.

Becca opened her mouth to say something else, but before she made a sound there was a strong knock at the door.

"Megan? It's Bobby King."

Megan stood and opened the door, a knot forming in her gut. "What can I help you with, Bobby? Clover's not here — she's at the store."

"I'm afraid it's not Clover I'm looking for." With the door into the kitchen open, Bobby looked over Megan's shoulder. "I tried calling you, but no one answered. I've been looking for Becca." He fixed his stare to Becca, who still stared right back at him. "Becca, you need to come with me," he said softly. "I have a few questions."

Megan turned toward her guest, unsure

what to think. A personal visit from Bobby King not long after your father's death was unlikely to be a social call. But if Megan was expecting fear or surprise, she was wrong. Becca grabbed her coat and nodded, the look on her face one of relief.

NINE

After King and Becca left, Megan felt ill at ease. She knew she should mind her own business. It was just two weeks before Christmas and she had plenty to keep her busy at the farm and the café. Customer and restaurant orders. Catering local parties. The daily upkeep of the greenhouses, barn, and animals. And then there were her own holiday preparations — gifts to buy, food to prepare, a tree to cut down and decorate. Nevertheless, the look on Becca's face stayed with her. It could have been the look of someone who just wanted answers. But it could also have been the look of someone flirting with the dodgy side of sanity.

Reluctantly, Megan returned to her chores, but her mind remained on Paul's death. As she made her way through the snowy courtyard toward the goats' enclosure, she considered King's visit. If King was looking for Becca, he likely had news from the medical examiner. Megan hoped it was relatively benign news that wouldn't mean more trouble for Winsome or Emily. A natural cause. But King's presence could portend something more ominous. And Megan had gotten to know Winsome's police chief well over the past year. If she was honest with herself, she recognized the stiff bearing, the formal demeanor, as King's way of dealing with bad news.

Foul play?

Megan set out hay for the goats. The smell of the fresh hay was particularly sweet today. Sweet and fresh, a distinct contrast to winter's earthy smells, reminding Megan of summer. And that's when it hit her: the aroma she'd noticed at Emily's rental house. Like fresh-cut hay. Or grass. Reminiscent of summer. And certain wines.

She knew that scent.

Inside she did a little more research, confirming her suspicions before she called King after dinner, once the animals were secure in their heated enclosures and while Bibi was playing Solitaire at the kitchen table. King didn't answer, but he called her back from his personal cell phone within the hour.

"I figured I'd hear from you," King said.

"I'm *that* predictable?"

"Back in Winsome for less than two years and already you're in the thick of things."

"I'm not in the thick of this one, I hope." Megan paused. "That is, if there is a 'this one.' So is there, Bobby?"

Bobby sighed. "You mean why did I come looking for Becca Fox today?"

"That's what I mean."

"You know I can't tell you that."

"Then tell me this. Was her father's death ruled suspicious?"

"Did she tell you that?"

"I haven't talked to Becca since she left." Megan stood up from her perch on the bed and walked to the window. She pulled the curtains aside and looked outside at the farm yard below. "But I think that's a question you should be able to answer. A matter of public record."

King took his time responding. Megan heard the sound of a car horn beeping, then the click of a door closing. Finally, the police chief said, "Yes. Based on the examination, Paul's death was ruled suspicious."

"I knew it," Megan said to herself. Then, "Did Paul's lungs show indications of noncardiogenic pulmonary edema?"

"Yes." Bobby sounded surprised. "How did you know?"

Fluid in the lungs not caused by heart failure. Megan knew if she kept naming symptoms, King would continue saying yes. She was that certain about the smell. "Are they testing him for poisons?"

"Further tests are needed to confirm, but they think they have their culprit." His voice went up an octave. "Why, Megan? What makes you ask this line of questions? Did Becca tell you something? Because if Becca told you something —"

"Are they testing for phosgene poisoning, Bobby?"

King's silence was answer enough. It was Megan who spoke first. "That's it, isn't it? The medical examiner found extensive damage to the trachea, bronchi, and lungs, including edema. Maybe red, irritated eyes too. I could probably spout all sorts of medical terms, but in the end, they're looking at phosgene. One of the chemicals used in World War I." Megan slowed her speech, let Bobby absorb what she was saying. "Which probably means Paul was murdered."

"How do you know all of this?"

Megan crossed her room and closed the door. From what she could tell, Bibi was still downstairs, but she didn't want to take any chances.

"Don't forget that I was an environmental lawyer. I once got called in to a case involving accidental phosgene poisoning at a pesticide factory. It wasn't pretty — nine people died, fourteen others were hospitalized. All of the survivors reported smelling a pleasant fresh-cut hay scent before they fell ill."

"And you noticed the smell while you were at Emily's house?" Bobby's tone was stern. "You could have told me."

Megan brushed aside the rebuke. "I noticed a smell. I couldn't place it at first, but then I was feeding the goats . . . anyway, I realized it was the lingering scent of phosgene."

"Yes, nothing that could have harmed us while we were there, but then it would have dissipated. We think the gummy substance you found was duct tape on the windows."

"Makes sense. Someone created an airtight space for quicker reaction." Megan closed her eyes, thinking. "You know, phosgene doesn't always work right away. Some of the people who got sick in the industrial accident took days to show severe symptoms."

"So you think he was poisoned earlier?"

"I saw Paul the night before he was killed. He was breathing heavily, coughing. His eyes looked irritated. He blamed it on a cold. I think he *thought* he had a cold."

"But it was exposure to phosgene?"

"It's a possibility. He could have thought he had some form of respiratory virus, if the symptoms were mild. Or allergies, given the eyes."

"If he was showing symptoms then, that could mean it was accidental. That there was a leak somehow in the house."

"Phosgene's not like natural gas. It doesn't just leak under normal residential circumstances."

"Emily had contractors there. We'd need to rule out an accident." King sighed. "But if the victim was showing symptoms before the night of his death, it could also mean —"

"That whoever poisoned him had been poisoning him for days. And had access to the house."

"The autopsy should show that. Why would someone target Paul?"

Megan considered what she'd heard about Paul Fox. A man who elicited such strong reactions — someone willing to bend reality to his own needs, someone who took sadistic pleasure in wounding others — would have enemies.

"I don't know, Bobby," Megan said. She

clutched a pillow to her chest, as much for protection as for comfort. "But whoever killed him wanted him to suffer. Phosgene poisoning is a horrible way to go."

The conversation with Bobby King haunted Megan long after lights were out. Tucked under the thick quilt Bibi had made her when she returned to Winsome, Sadie nestled against her legs, Megan thought about the man who'd died and the legacy of pain — at least in Becca's eyes — that he'd left behind. She thought about Becca, a young woman who'd made her own way in the world but who carried so much hate. She thought about the death of a mother, and the subsequent death of a husband.

She thought about another murder in Winsome.

She thought about Bobby King, a police chief whose heart was in the right place, but who'd had to deal with more in his young career than many cops endured over a lifetime. And she thought about the fact that he'd confided in her. He trusted her.

She'd earned his trust.

Phosgene. A nasty chemical. When she left the practice of law she thought she'd left nasty chemicals and environmental hazards behind. At least that had been her intent.

Megan turned over, punched her pillow. The air in her room felt heavy, matching the weight on her chest.

Another murder. She told herself this wasn't her problem.

Only she never had been very good at listening. Or at taking her own advice.

TEN

Denver was already in the farmhouse kitchen when Megan came down for breakfast the next morning. His reddish-brown hair was tousled, and several days' growth of auburn beard shadowed his face. He wore jeans and a thick navy blue sweater that perfectly highlighted broad shoulders and a tapered back. He gave her an appreciative smile when he saw her, his eyes full of warmth — and questions.

Megan kissed him. She knew he was wondering why she was up so late, and what was going on with Paul. She glanced in Bibi's direction, silently pleading with Denver that any discussion wait.

Denver nodded, stood, and said, "How can I help you with breakfast, Bonnie?"

Bibi was making pancakes at the stove. She turned toward Denver. Flipping a slightly burnt pancake to Gunther, she said, "Why don't you get yourself some more coffee if you want it. Otherwise, just sit and I'll have breakfast on the table in no time."

While Denver poured coffee for himself and Megan, Megan settled at the table. There were five place settings. It was only 5:47 a.m. Megan had overslept, but she knew that was early for anyone who didn't own a farm or make early-morning veterinary calls. "Who else is joining us?"

"Clay's already up at the barn, so I told him to come down." Bibi glanced warmly at Denver, looking, perhaps, for an ally. "And your Aunt Sarah is stopping over."

"Aunt Sarah? Why?"

Bibi wiped clean hands on a red and green checked apron that had "Celebrate the holidays in Winsome!" scrawled across the front in fancy script — another leftover salvaged from Megan's father's failed souvenir shop. Bibi twisted the well-worn twill material in her hands. "She wants to see you."

"She wants to see *me*?" Megan hadn't had any meaningful conversation with her great aunt — her grandfather's sister — since the fall. Their short interaction in the parking lot of Merry's nursery hardly counted. As casually as she could, Megan said, "What about?"

Bibi placed a high stack of blueberry

pancakes on the table next to a glass pitcher of warmed Vermont maple syrup. She returned to the stove, pulled a baking dish out of the oven, and placed hot sausage on the table. Megan breathed in the fragrance of home, grateful for the respite.

She forked a pancake and a piece of sausage on her plate. If she didn't eat, Bibi would harass her. And she suddenly felt ravenous. "Well?" she said between mouthfuls. "What does Aunt Sarah want?"

"Sounds like ye can ask her yourself," Denver said. He smiled over his coffee mug. "She just pulled in."

Megan frowned. It wasn't unusual for Denver to stop by after morning rounds, or even earlier if he had to make early morning house calls — like today. Bibi loved cooking for him, and Megan loved seeing him in their kitchen. But today she wanted to pull him aside and speak to him alone. She'd been shaken by her conversation with Bobby King, and she wanted to bounce some ideas off someone. But that wasn't going to happen. The door opened and Clay came inside, followed closely by Sarah.

Sarah was always a sight. A towering woman with a solid frame, Sarah's style could be described as artsy-bohemian. She was fond of soft kaftans and native prints in saturated colors, her long gray hair typically braided in one long rope. Today she wore all black — black pants, black sweater, black coat. And her hair hung in loose waves around her head. But most noticeable were her hands. While her body slid into the kitchen chair with military bearing, her hands danced and flitted across the worn wooden surface, a traitor to their host.

"Coffee or tea," Bibi said, her voice firm. Sarah could choose which — but she would have one.

"Coffee, please, Bonnie. Thanks."

While Bibi poured her coffee, Sarah turned to Megan. She looked like she wanted to say something but couldn't. She let out a sigh, adjusted her silverware. Those hands continued to dance. Bibi finally handed her a cup, and with her hands occupied, she seemed to relax. A little.

Megan speared two more pancakes and passed the dish to Sarah, who declined. Clay took three pancakes and passed them to Denver.

"Have any more over there, Bonnie?" Clay asked. Her farm manager acted oblivious to the tension in the room. A lanky, handsome man in his twenties, Clay had morphed from employee to friend. He was highly attuned to people's emotions, and Megan knew he'd probably picked up on Sarah's case of nerves. He was politely ignoring the sense of unease, preferring to adhere to morning ritual to make other people more comfortable. That was Clay's way.

Bonnie returned to making pancakes. A few minutes of pregnant silence blanketed the room. Gunther broke the quiet with a deep bark in the direction of the driveway.

Megan glanced at her watch. It was 6:08. "Who could that be?" She stood, pulling her heavy gray cardigan sweater tighter around her chest. It was still dark outside. "I'll go see."

Denver stood. "I'll come with ye, Megs." He pulled a hat over his ears and tugged on his coat.

Outside, the air felt frigid against her skin. A fine snowy mist blew across the courtyard, and the exterior lights captured swirls of snow mid-dance. Megan looked up, toward the woods and Potter Hill, remembering a time when she was being watched, when every one of Gunther's barks shot sparks of adrenaline down her spine.

Megan had let Gunther out too, and the dog raced down the long driveway, barking madly, and disappeared into the misty dawn. He stopped barking, and the sudden quiet made Megan turn to Denver. He grabbed her hand and squeezed.

"Gunther," she called. "Gunther, come!"

To her relief, the dog barked again. Then he raced back up the drive, darting back and forth between Megan and a figure behind him. The man's face became clearer as he entered the light.

"Luke?" Megan said.

"Good morning, Megan."

Gunther growled, more of a warning than a threat. A firm word from Denver had the dog back by their side, but his unwavering canine gaze remained on the stranger.

"Luke, are you okay?" Megan took a step closer. Luke was standing there, his face ashen.

"I'm fine," he said. "I'm looking for Becca. Is she here?"

"No. I haven't seen her since yesterday."

Luke nodded. "Can I take a look around?"

Megan glanced down at Gunther. "What makes you think she's here?"

"She's not at Aunt Merry's, and she doesn't really know anyone else in Winsome."

"Well, I'm not hiding her," Megan said. "Maybe she got a hotel room somewhere. Decided not to stay with Merry."

"She left her stuff at my aunt's. Her perfumes." His neck strained to look beyond

Megan, toward the barn. "Maybe she's in your barn."

"She's not in the barn. My farm manager just came from there. Had anyone been in the barn, he would have known." She glanced back at the looming structure and frowned. "But you can take a look if it will make you feel better."

Luke thanked her. "My sister . . . you don't know her, the things that she does. She could have decided to hide from the world for a spell, and a warm barn may have been the spot she chose."

"I don't think the barn is too warm," Denver said. His eyes narrowed. "If you want to check, come on. I'll take you."

Megan kept Gunther by her side with a touch to the large dog's back. The two watched as Denver and the shorter man walked through the snowy courtyard and entered the barn. "Good boy," Megan muttered to her dog. He whined. "It's okay. Denver will be back."

The search seemed to take longer than Megan would have anticipated. Finally she watched as the two left the barn. Denver continued to wait while Luke walked around the perimeter of the property, peeking into greenhouses and checking behind the looming barn. When he returned to Denver, the two checked the goats' pen, and then they trod back down toward the house.

"Satisfied?" Megan asked.

Luke nodded. Snow had crusted his beard and eyebrows, and he wiped at his face absentmindedly with the back of a leather-gloved hand.

Megan said, "Would you like to come inside for some coffee and breakfast, Luke? My grandmother made pancakes."

"No, thanks. I should keep looking."

"If you're that worried, have you considered calling the police?"

"Nah, I don't want to call attention. Becca does stuff like this. She's sensitive. Always has been."

"Maybe the lassie is reacting to your father's death," Denver said gently. "Needs some time."

Luke gave a noncommittal "maybe." He turned to go. Megan reached out a hand to stop him and pulled it back. He looked tired and broken and like he needed some warmth and company. But he knew his sister better than she did, and so she let him go.

On the way back inside, Denver's eyes clouded with worry. "Have Gunther do rounds, Megan."

"Why? Did Luke say something while you

were at the barn?"

"No, but he didn't need to. His father's dead and now he can't find his sister. I'd be worried too." Denver's gaze strayed to the barn, and Megan knew he was thinking about another death, not that long ago. "The farm is vulnerable out here on the outskirts of town." To Gunther, he said, "Watch over the farm, boy."

Megan opened the screen door. "Think he understands you?"

"He understands love and protection. That's all he needs to understand."

Truer words . . . Hadn't the dog already proven his loyalty once?

"Wonder why Becca left."

"Whether she hated the man or not, her father's death was a blow. Some people can't deal with grief. She may just need to nurse her wounds — alone."

Megan nodded. "Given Becca's unannounced visit yesterday, and now Luke's visit so early this morning, I suspect you're right. Something's up in the Fox family, and surely it centers around Paul's death."

Denver opened the main door to go back inside, holding it open for Megan. Megan took a last glance at the driveway, taking comfort in the rising sun and Gunther, who was sitting by the barn, now stoically watching the property spread out below.

"What was that all about?" Clay asked when they were back in the kitchen.

"Luke Fox. He was looking for Becca." Megan hung her coat on the hook in the entrance and took her seat once again. Her appetite gone, she pushed her plate away. "Kept insisting she could be in the barn."

"No one's in the barn," Clay said. "I was up there this morning. Anyway, why would she be hiding in the barn?"

"We said the same thing, but he insisted, so Denver took him up."

Bibi looked at Sarah. "Maybe you know why he'd think Becca was hiding?"

Sarah frowned, deepening the lines around her mouth and eyes. She stood. "Megan, can we talk in the other room?"

Curious, Megan said, "Of course." She caught Denver's eye. With an apologetic smile, she said, "Will you be here when we're done?"

"I'm afraid I have to leave. Morning surgeries start soon, and I need a short nap and a shower beforehand." He glanced at his watch. "Plus, the dogs will be wanting some relief and some breakfast. I left at three this morning."

Megan nodded. After kissing Denver

good-bye, she placed her dishes in the dishwasher and gestured for Sarah to follow her. A look passed between Bibi and Sarah, one that made Megan suspect Bibi knew exactly why Sarah was there.

Sarah had information about Paul Fox. And whatever it was, Bibi didn't like it one bit.

ELEVEN

Megan closed the French doors while Aunt Sarah sat down on Bibi's recliner.

Megan regarded her aunt from a spot on the couch. Sarah's normally self-assured countenance seemed marred by worry. "What's going on?"

"I need to know what Becca told you about Paul. About her conversation with Bobby." Sarah couldn't hide her impatience. Her hands were acting independently again, picking at the strands of yarn hanging from Bibi's knitting basket, which sat alongside the chair. Her gaze darted between Megan's face and the window. A soft sleet pelted the windows, its *ping, ping* a rhythmic white noise in the stuffy room.

"Becca didn't tell me anything. I haven't seen her since Bobby came to collect her yesterday."

Sarah looked crestfallen. "Then what did Becca tell you before that? About Paul."

Megan wondered why Sarah wanted to know about the Fox family. Her mind reflected back on their encounter in Merry's parking lot, to the heated argument she'd witnessed between Aunt Sarah and Paul. Admittedly Megan didn't know her aunt that well. Years of conflict between Sarah Birch and Megan's grandfather had caused a rift in the family. Conflict that started when Sarah helped Megan's mother leave her young daughter and husband. It was only recently that Sarah had been welcomed back to Washington Acres. And not quite with open arms.

Nevertheless, Sarah was Megan's only real connection to her mother and to the maternal grandfather she just recently found out she had. As much as Megan resented Sarah, she also clung to the hope that someday there could be reconciliation with her mother, Charlotte Birch. A childish hope, she knew. But somehow she was always made to feel like a child around Sarah.

And so she didn't quite trust her instincts.

"It might be better if you told me what you're worried about," Megan said. "I spoke to Becca about a lot of things, her father just one of them."

Sarah rubbed long arthritic fingers down the length of a muscular thigh, kneading away some invisible tension. "Paul and I had a falling out many years ago." The corners of her mouth turned down as though whatever had happened had been painful then — and was painful to think about now. "He threatened me. I reported it. He left Winsome."

"Doesn't sound like he was a very nice guy."

Sarah smirked. "Understatement."

"Did he leave Winsome because of your falling out?"

"No. Well, maybe. I wasn't the only one he rubbed the wrong way. Paul Fox was a liar and a cheat, and few people around here were willing to tolerate a liar and a cheat." She seemed embarrassed about her outburst and lowered her voice. "We tolerated him for a while. Until we figured him out." She paused. "And for Merry's sake."

Megan did some quick math. Sarah hadn't lived in Winsome for years. She said as much.

"Oh, I've had the cottage for many years. It was my writing retreat before I moved in full-time. It wasn't until I heard you were coming back to town that I decided to make Winsome my permanent residence."

Megan let that sink in. "So what happened between you Paul?"

"It doesn't matter, Megan. What matters is that he's dead." Sarah looked down at her hands as though they belonged to someone else. She looked up, her gaze intense. "And someone killed him."

"I know."

Sarah's eyes registered her surprise. "So you did talk to Becca."

"No, I haven't seen Becca since yesterday, just as I told Luke. But I suspected Paul's death was intentional. Bobby confirmed."

Sarah pulled her long hair away from her face in an angry swipe. "He's causing trouble even in death."

Megan stood. She walked to the window and looked out toward the barn, which seemed out of focus in the hazy light and sleety drizzle. When she turned back around, Sarah was standing by the fireplace mantel, looking at the photos Bibi had placed along its surface.

"Did Becca mention anything about me?"

"Nothing. Why?"

"Bobby King had me in for a visit early yesterday evening. We had a . . . long talk."

Megan waited. Years of questioning witnesses at the law firm taught her that silence often elicited more information than questions.

"I wrote a book," Aunt Sarah said drily

116

after a moment. "It seems the plot line has certain things in common with the way Paul Fox died."

Megan twisted toward her aunt in surprise. Sarah Birch was well known within the crime writing community. She'd won awards, been a constant presence on the *New York Times* and *USA Today* bestseller lists, and had a solid fan base. There was even a movie based on one of her novels. Megan hadn't known about her aunt's occupation, and before she'd found out, she'd read many of her mysteries. But she couldn't think of a plot line that had the victim die by phosgene poisoning.

"It's an old novel, if that's what you're wondering," Sarah said. "One of my earliest mysteries, written under a different pen name — Lydia Kane." Aunt Sarah's smile took on a self-deprecating curl. "More of a literary mystery. Critics loved it, the public not so much."

"And the murderer used —"

"Phosgene." Sarah frowned, her eyes piercing Megan's. "Yes, I know. That's what killed Paul."

"Bobby told you?"

"I figured it out from his questioning. I may be old, Megan, but I'm not stupid."

"I never doubted your intelligence." Your

loyalty, perhaps, Megan thought — but not that. "And the windows?"

Sarah closed her eyes. "Duct tape. And my killer slowly poisoned his victim in the days before the big dénouement. Just like with Paul. I figured that out too." She opened her eyes, and the brightness of them was startling. "His cough."

"And his reddish eyes." Megan rubbed her temples, thinking. To have a killer use a novel as the basis for their crime? Well, that was either the world's most ardent fan — or a true nightmare reader. "Do the police suspect you? Surely they can't think you would be so dumb as to kill someone after having written a book about it."

"Who knows what the police think, but Bobby's questions were more about the book, who might have read it, that sort of thing."

Megan took this all in. "And your questions to me about Becca?"

"*Someone* tipped the police."

"You think it was Becca who told them about the novel?"

"Something tells me Bobby King does not read literary mysteries." She raised her eyebrows. "But who knows. I saw Becca at the police station when I arrived. I think they questioned her before me. Again, if

Bobby didn't put two and two together, then who told him? Becca's a reader — Merry told me that. Becca's also a little . . . unstable."

"Perhaps she has reason to be."

"Perhaps. Nonetheless, I don't need her shifting focus to me. For all we know, it was Becca Fox who killed her father. She had motive — she hated the man. And she had means. She's a chemist, after all. If anyone would understand the properties of a horrible chemical like phosgene, she would."

Megan had to admit that was true — and the same thought had occurred to her. "Aunt Sarah, what was the name of the novel?"

"*To Kill Again.*"

Megan sat back heavily on the couch. "It's doubtful this is a coincidence, which would mean —"

Aunt Sarah leaned forward, her posture conspiratorial. In the early morning light, she looked off-center, a little insane. Her lips twisted into the shadow of a smile. "Which would mean that someone used my book to plot a murder."

Megan's first stop after Aunt Sarah left was to her study. She powered up her laptop and looked for a copy of *To Kill Again.* It was out of print, but it didn't take Megan long to find a used edition sold by a third party on Amazon. She ordered it.

If the killer was using a playbook, she'd like to know what to expect.

TWELVE

It didn't take long for the news that Paul Fox's death was a murder to spread through Winsome. By that afternoon, Megan heard Paul's name whispered in the aisles of the store and speculation about his death seemed to be the prime topic of conversation at the café tables. Even Alvaro was in on the gossip. He cornered Megan in the café's kitchen while she helped him chop vegetables for that evening's winter stew.

"It's all I hear from back here," Alvaro said. "Buzz, buzz, buzz. They're like flies devouring a piece of rotting watermelon." He shook his head, his dark eyes crinkling in disgust. "The man is dead what, not even a week? The carcass is ripe for the picking, I guess."

Megan chopped a rutabaga into small pieces, all the while trying not to visualize carcasses and rotting fruit. Alvaro was right, of course. Paul's death had been one thing

— but a murder?

"I hear he was poisoned," Alvaro said. "Not a heart attack like we thought in the beginning."

Megan nodded. "That's my understanding."

Alvaro was sautéing onions and garlic in a large stock pot on the commercial cooktop. The smell reminded Megan of a thousand winter days at the farmhouse in Winsome, and she longed suddenly for a simpler time.

"I don't think he was such a nice man."

Surprised, Megan looked up. "Why do you say that, Alvaro?"

He shrugged, his thin shoulders sharp under an impeccably white chef's jacket. "I read."

"What did you read?"

"Newspaper articles. Old ones." Alvaro grabbed a bowl of chopped carrots and added the carrots to the contents in the pot. "Someone left them on a table. I saw them when I was cleaning up."

Megan stopped chopping. "When was that? Do you remember?"

"*Sí,* of course I remember. Last Tuesday. It was snowing. We had a rush at dinner — I served my tortilla soup, which everyone loves, especially on a cold day — and the café was a mess. The papers were there under a *New York Times.*"

"Were they actual news articles or print-outs?"

Alvaro pursed his lips. "Does it matter?"

"I don't know. Probably not. Just curious."

"They were cut from an old newspaper. Like if you were making . . . what you call it?"

"A scrapbook?"

Alvaro snapped his fingers. "Yes, that's it. Clipped for a scrapbook."

A scrapbook about Paul? Megan handed Alvaro a bowl of rutabagas, which he added to the pot, wondering who would go to that degree of trouble.

"Do you remember what the articles were about? What newspaper they were from?"

Alvaro waved his hand, clearly annoyed he had brought the topic up. "He was a cheat. Didn't pay money he owed. A bad guy. I have no idea what paper they were from."

"How about the date?"

Alvaro seemed to think about this. "They were a little yellow, a little crispy. Old, I think. But I don't recall the date."

"Did you tell the police?"

Alvaro stirred the pot with a long spoon. His arm churned with added vigor. "No one asked me. What am I going to say? That someone left newspapers? Someone always leaves newspapers. I threw them away."

"And the man was still alive then," Megan said. How was Alvaro to know he'd die just days later — and that those papers could be important. Megan would tell Bobby when she saw him, but she doubted he'd get much more from her chef.

Megan went back to chopping. It was snowing outside, and the café would have its usual evening visitors — Winsome residents who didn't mind braving the inclement weather to share some company and savor Alvaro's comfort food. But the articles bothered her. Someone had gone to the trouble of clipping them. And saving them.

And leaving them at the café.

Megan was still thinking about the articles and Paul Fox when she left the café after five o'clock. The café was crowded despite the snow, but Clover had arrived to help Alvaro, and Emily was giving them a few hours once her workday at the spa ended. Megan had promised to have dinner with Denver that evening, so she headed to his house directly from the café.

It wasn't until she reached his bungalow that she remembered Luke's visit early that morning. Had Becca ever shown up?

Once parked in Denver's driveway behind

his 4Runner, Megan dialed Merry's house phone. Merry didn't answer — but Becca did.

"You're okay," Megan said, relieved. "Your brother was worried about you."

"Worried?" She laughed. "I doubt it. He just wanted to keep tabs on me."

Megan turned off the truck ignition. "He seemed pretty worried to me."

Becca seemed to be doing something that involved running water. She said, "Hold on," and was back after a few seconds. "Sorry. Washing my equipment."

"Becca, is everything okay?"

"Of course. Why wouldn't it be?"

"Your father, Luke, you disappearing."

"I didn't disappear, I just had some stuff to attend to. How are you, Megan?" she asked in a transparent attempt to change the topic. "Have you used your pheromones recently?"

"I'm afraid not."

"The women of Winsome are *loving* my products. Soon there may be more competition for that handsome vet of yours."

Speaking of her handsome doctor, Megan glanced at Denver's house. She could have sworn the lights had been on just a few minutes ago. The snow was falling harder now, and the gray skies eclipsed the remnants of the setting sun. His house, his large yard, and the deep woods beyond loomed dark in the burgeoning night.

"Perhaps," Megan said. "I'll take that chance."

Becca's laugh sounded hollow — a little too perky, a little too positive.

"Are you sure you're okay? I know Bobby King spoke with you yesterday. That has to be hard. For anyone."

"I have nothing to hide." A note of defensiveness.

"I wasn't implying that you do."

"Well, Chief King did."

"He needs to turn over every rock. Ask questions — some of which are bound to be uncomfortable."

"He's looking under the wrong stones. I didn't kill my father. If I had, it would have been slow and painful. And it would have happened long ago."

A light went on toward the back of Denver's house. The truck was getting cold with the ignition off. She needed to get going.

Megan said, "I wouldn't make comments like that, Becca. Not now."

Becca make a "pfft" sound. Megan heard water running again.

"Seriously. If your father was murdered, the police will be looking for motive."

"I've made no attempt to hide my feelings, so that cat's long out of that shopping bag." Becca was quiet for a moment. Megan heard the clanking of glass, the hum of a dryer. Finally she said, "Look, I'm fine. Don't worry about me, okay? Big girl and all that."

Only Megan was worried about her. She seemed so alone, and despite the false bravado she wore when it came to her father's death, she sounded afraid. Nevertheless, Megan said, "Of course."

"Use the perfumes, Megan. They work. And spread the word."

"I will, Becca."

"Okay. Thanks for checking on me."

"Good night."

Becca didn't answer. Megan waited for Becca to hang up first, and in the meantime, Megan could still make out the sound of water — and the harsh whispers of someone else in the room.

There was a note taped to Denver's front door. Megan removed it carefully and turned it over. Plain white envelope, "Megan" written on the front in Denver's slanted scrawl. Snow drifted beyond the glow of the outdoor fixtures, a thousand points of glittering light. She opened it under the protection of the small vestibule, curious.

> The door's open. Come in, grab the container from the refrigerator, and meet me out back. WEAR GLOVES AND A HAT. There are extras in the front closet.
>
> — Denver

Intrigued, Megan entered the house. She could make out a light on in the kitchen, behind the sparsely furnished dining room. She found the kitchen empty. She opened the refrigerator. Inside was a large container with another envelope attached to the outside. *Bring me,* it said.

Megan pulled the container out of the refrigerator. It was heavy. She tucked it under her arm and headed for the front closet, where she grabbed a pair of ski gloves — warmer than her wool ones — and a fleece hat. She pulled an extra parka from the closet too. One never knew quite what Denver had in mind.

Making her way through the house to the back door and Denver's deep backyard, Megan stopped. She realized what had caught her attention: silence. Denver's five rescue dogs weren't here either.

Thoughts of Becca and Paul Fox and Aunt Sarah still lurking in the back of her mind, Megan went outside through the back door. On the back deck under a small awning sat a pair of snow shoes. A sign that read *Wear me* was taped to the front. Megan laughed. A pair of boots — her size — sat next to them, just in case. Another envelope was taped to the boots.

Megan didn't need the boots. She opened the letter, though. It was short and sweet:

You don't have nearly enough fun in your life, Megs, so I thought I would add some silliness to your evening. Plus, the daft dogs were feeling restless — and I have this thing I need to try out. You'll see — it's what happens when you're a country vet. So just strap on the snow-shoes and head straight back toward the wooded end of the property. I imagine you'll know what you had been looking for once you find it. Isn't that often the case? Don't get lost in the backcountry. If you do, call me.

— Denver

With another chuckle, Megan strapped the snowshoes on and headed out into the yard. She figured there was a good eighteen inches or more on the ground — unusual for the Philadelphia area — and the snow-shoes made trekking in the snow much easier. Once Megan was over the rise in Denver's fenced-in property, she saw smoke billowing from near the tree line. The pines were thick, and she strained to see where the smoke was coming from. As the back of the property became more visible, she eventually saw where she was headed: a large tipi. The pipe protruding from the top was the source of the smoke.

Denver's Great Dane and Golden Retriever emerged from the tipi and darted in her direction. They greeted her like a long-lost best friend and led her back to the shelter. When she arrived, she saw Denver standing in the doorway. He wore jeans, boots, and a flannel shirt. His tousled hair fell into his eyes, and he was smiling at her with a mixture of affection and amusement.

"I know I've found a special woman when she'll humor me this way," he said, taking the container and the extra coat from Megan. "Give me the coat you're wearing too. Ye won't need it in here."

Megan peeled off some layers. The inside of the tipi felt plenty warm thanks to a small red stove that sat in the dead center. The floor was covered with a thick tarp, and a stack of firewood sat on the floor next to the stove. The structure was big — large enough for the two of them and the five excited dogs. Megan said hello to each of the pups, and they eventually lost interest, preferring to bask by the fire entwined around one another.

"Lazy lot," Denver said, his eyes betraying his words. "Wouldn't let me be here alone. It's the fire. Give them a good fire, and they become worthless."

Megan laughed. The Golden was snoring, and Denver's Beagle, snuggled up against the Golden, was waving two paws in the air in the throes of some happy canine dream.

Megan sank down on a thick comforter that Denver had spread out next to the stove.

"I've had a few dates in my day," she said. "But none quite like this." She glanced around. "Where in the world did you get a tipi? And for the love of all that is good in this world, why did you put a tipi up in your backyard?"

Denver pulled the container in front of him. "Well, that's a long story. It begins with a wee lassie of a dog named Betsy."

"Betsy, huh?"

"Betsy. Now Betsy is not a fancy breed kind of dog. In fact, she's probably got more breeds in her than Max there." Denver pointed to one of his dogs — a true mutt who looked like a cross between a Jack Russel and an Afghan hound. "But Betsy is the beloved pet of little Ryan Simons. Know Ryan Simons?"

Megan did. Ryan was the grandchild of Delores Simons, Winsome's primary pharmacist. Ryan had Down Syndrome, and he lived with his grandmother and his father after losing his mother and grandfather in a horrible accident. Winsome had rallied around the Simons family, but the accident had shattered their lives, and Delores had a lot of challenges to contend with.

"I can see by your eyes that you know of the Simons family and their misfortunes. Well, Betsy is Ryan's dog and wee Betsy became very ill. She ate something she should not have, as dogs are apt to do, and it poisoned her. We spent a long time nursing Betsy back to health."

"I remember. You were gone for nearly forty-eight hours straight."

"Aye. I didn't think she would make it, quite honestly. But God was looking out for Betsy — and Ryan — that day." Denver seemed lost in the memory. "When she finally woke up, first thing she did was lick that boy's face. Could barely move, wee thing, but that tongue shot out." Denver looked away. "Well, as my people say, *Whit's fur ye'll no go past ye.*" He looked at Megan and she saw the gleam of moisture in his eyes. "What will be, will be. And so Betsy lived."

"And you inherited a tipi?"

"Mrs. Simons was so grateful that she sent her youngest son over here with this bloody tipi. Said it was her late husband's back-country hunting tent and she had no use for it." He laughed. "Guess she figured with a nickname like Denver I must like back-country trips." He stood and touched the walls. "Have to admit, it's nice. Quite warm."

Megan nodded. It felt oddly homey inside. "Are you going to keep it?"

"For now. I'll eventually donate it, if it's okay with Delores. But I thought we could try it out since it's here."

Denver knelt down in front of the container and opened it. He pulled two craft beers, two sandwiches, and a container of crudités from its depths. He smiled. "Dinner."

"You do spoil me." She peeked in the container. "You forgot dessert," she joked.

Denver's smile broadened. He leaned over and kissed her, hard. When he spoke, his voice was husky. "Oh, I didn't forget about dessert, Megs."

Understanding made her face flush. She returned his grin, all other thoughts gone.

THIRTEEN

Sarah's novel arrived the same day that Bibi fell. It had been colder than normal for December — in the teens — and snow had fallen every day for the past three. The parking lot at Merry's nursery shone with a mix of ice and hard-packed snow, but it was someone's discarded umbrella, half buried under a drift, that tripped Megan's grandmother and sent her to the local emergency room. Thankfully, the only thing badly bruised was Bibi's ego. But orders to stay off her feet for a few days coupled with tender shins and knees had Bonnie Birch on edge — and Megan knew from experience that dealing with Bibi in such circumstances was a job that required thick skin and even thicker patience.

It was hard to get things done while lying on a couch. And in Bibi's world, things needed to get done. Time didn't stop because of a few leg injuries. Ironically, Megan didn't get much done either, including finding the time to read Sarah's novel.

By Saturday, Bibi was feeling better. Her legs had mostly healed, and the aches and pains that went along with a sudden fall had subsided — or so she told Megan. In usual Bibi fashion, she refused anything stronger than ibuprofen, ice, and her evening tea with a shot or two of whiskey. But two days of rest had some benefits: an entire stack of quilted holiday placemats to sell at the store and a new scarf for Megan. As testy as Bibi seemed to feel, Merry Chance's daily visits were worse.

The morning Bibi was allowed back in the kitchen, Merry arrived at eight a.m. under the pretense of needing more eggs. Megan didn't believe her for a second.

"Merry, I was just about to have some toast. Will you join me?"

Merry eyed the thick harvest bread Bibi was slicing. With a glance at the giant slab of butter Bibi had set on the table, Merry shook her head.

"I'd better not, Bonnie. Right to the waist, you know." She glanced knowingly at Megan. "I look at bread and I gain weight."

"Then don't look at it. Just eat it," Bibi said. She limped her way to the table and sat down. "Well, don't just stand there,

Merry. Sit with me." Bibi glanced at Megan. "Do you want some more toast or are you heading out to the barn to get those eggs?"

Megan knew Bibi wanted Merry gone, and the sooner the eggs appeared, the sooner she'd leave. But Megan figured she should remain to play referee should things get out of hand. Besides, watching the two of them was rather amusing. She sliced a small piece of bread and sat down, waiting for the fun to begin.

"So how are things, Merry?" Megan asked.

Merry unwound her navy blue scarf, taking the time with the delicate wool weave. "Well, things have been better. For one, I'm worried about Bonnie here. And that fall."

Bibi took a sip of tea, her eyes glued to Merry. She put her cup in the saucer, wiped her mouth, and said, "You can stop worrying. And you can stop coming by to check on me. No one needs that many eggs, Meredith. No one."

"But —"

"No buts. I'm not going to sue you, if that's what's got your knickers in a bunch." Bibi looked at Megan for confirmation. "Right, Megan? I'm as likely to sue somebody over a stupid fall as I am to dance at that so-called gentleman's club two towns over."

"I didn't mean to insinuate that you were going to sue me."

"No?" Bibi pursed her lips. "Okay, then. I've saved you the trouble of worrying about it in the future. As to my health, I am just fine. Old bones take a little extra time to heal, but they do heal. And I've sat around long enough."

Bibi took the last bite of toast and picked up the plate and napkin. After placing both by the sink, she walked toward the hallway. Megan suspected she would have run had she been able.

At the doorway, she turned. In a softer voice, she said, "Thank you for visiting me, Merry. I understand in these litigious days that everyone worries about lawsuits. I fell. It was dumb of me not to pay attention to where I was placing my feet. I just feel . . . old . . . I guess."

Bibi disappeared around the corner. Merry, open-mouthed, watched her leave.

Megan smiled. "I think you just received the Bonnie Birch version of an apology. Savor it. Doesn't happen often."

Megan grabbed her coat off the hook. When she turned around, Merry was still sitting at the kitchen table. Fat tears were running down her face, and her shoulders were shaking with chunky, silent sobs.

Megan put the coat back and returned to the table. "Merry, she didn't mean anything. You know how Bibi is. She's just —"

Merry waved her hand. "It's not Bonnie."

Megan sat. "What is it?"

Megan waited while Merry composed herself. She'd never seen Merry this emotional. In fact righteous indignation was generally the extent of Merry's outbursts. Something tugged at Megan. Who did Merry really have to confide in? Her own fault or not, Megan figured Bibi was as close to a confidant as Merry had.

"It's Becca," Merry said. "She's not herself, Megan. The other day she disappeared for hours. And she's been surly. That's not like her." Merry sniffled. Megan handed her a tissue and she blew her nose daintily. "And then there's the man."

"The man?"

Merry nodded emphatically, skewing her glasses. "I don't know who he is, but I've seen him around a few times. I'm worried." She bit her lip.

"Worried about what?"

Merry sighed. "Worried it's another one of Becca's flings."

Megan recalled Becca's stance that the

pheromones weren't for her. That she didn't like people and wasn't looking for male attention. "I didn't think Becca was into dating."

"She's not, exactly." Merry rubbed her temples. She suddenly looked very tired. And old. "It started when Blanche died. Becca would hook up with these men who weren't nice to her. She'd stay with them for a few days, then dump them. But she flaunted her affairs. I think she did it to anger her father." Merry blew her nose again. "It worked."

"Becca made it sound like she was focused on work, not men."

"Oh, she's not into boyfriends, if that's what you mean. These could hardly be called relationships, and most of the men were well beneath her, if you ask me. She'd sleep with them a few times, and then the rest would be drama. Stalking, threats." Merry's skin turned a hot shade of pink. "Horrible."

Megan considered this. She had trouble reconciling the Becca she'd met with a woman who'd casually pick up the wrong kind of men — and then stalk them. Or put up with them stalking her.

"I'm sorry to hear this, Merry."

Merry nodded. "Thank you." She looked

up, the tears welling in her eyes again. "Maybe you could talk to her? She seems to like you."

"I don't think that's my place. I don't know her that well." Megan glanced toward the door. She could see Clay milling about, probably waiting to come in and talk to her about some issue on the farm. "Why don't you have Luke talk with her?"

Merry's thin lips pressed into a smirk. "Pot and kettle, those two. I don't think so."

"He has relationship issues too?"

"Luke prefers bimbos. Loose women who are only after his money."

Loose women? Megan didn't think anyone used that term anymore. Again, Megan flashed back to her conversation with Becca. She'd described her brother's girlfriends as intellectual types — not "hot" enough for his father's liking. Perhaps with such a messed up relationship with their own father, both Fox children had issues bonding. Or maybe they didn't share much with their aunt.

In any case, this wasn't a conversation she had any right to have with Becca. Megan stood. Merry took the hint and stood as well. "Let me get those eggs."

"Thank you," Merry said.

"I didn't do anything."

141

"You're a good listener." Merry sniffled again. "It's a rare quality in a person these days."

Megan forgot about her conversation with Merry until later that day. She left the farm at eleven to help Alvaro at the café. While Bibi was feeling well enough to fend for herself around the house, she wasn't quite up to cooking at the café and being on her feet all day, so Megan was bouncing back and forth. She was grateful for Clover and Emily — both of whom had been stalwarts all week.

When she arrived at the café, there was already a queue at the store register, which had Clover busy. And Megan could see that the back section of the store, where the café was, looked crowded as well.

Megan walked through the property toward the restaurant portion, taking notice of the store shelves and making mental notes about what needed replenishing. Almost everything.

The scent of stewing meat and cloves wafted from the back of the building. Megan's mouth watered. Today's lunch menu — which changed daily based on what was available at the farm and what Alvaro felt like cooking — was a rich Mexican stew served with pozole, homemade corn tortillas, and a simple salad. Based on the empty plates in front of her customers, it was a hit.

"Morning," she said to her chef.

He grunted. "Nearly nighttime now."

Megan smiled. It wouldn't be Alvaro if he didn't have a surly remark. "Emily show up?"

"She called. Said she would be here by noon. She was spending some time with the babe. She's teething." Alvaro's voice softened, as it normally did when talking about Emily — or babies.

He nodded toward the large pot simmering on the stove. "I am only serving two dishes today. The stew. And a cheese Panini for vegetarians."

He spit the word "vegetarians" out as though he'd eaten a piece of rotten meat. "Panini is just a fancy word for grilled cheese." He shrugged. "But if these hipsters want to pay $12 for a grilled cheese, who am I to complain?"

Megan wasn't sure hipsters were hanging about in Winsome, nor was she convinced Alvaro's hefty grilled sandwich was quite the same as a typical grilled cheese, but she let it go.

"Alvaro," she said. "Have you seen Becca

Fox in the café?"

"The girl with the crazy hair and the silly perfumes?"

"That's the one."

He frowned, thinking. "Yesterday or the day before. She was hawking those perfumes of hers to anyone who would listen. I told her to talk to you. That she could not solicit in the store."

He stood taller, puffing up his bulky chest. "She didn't like my answer."

"Did she leave?"

"She ordered a pastry and coffee and sulked at me. I remember that."

"Was she with anyone?"

"No. She was alone." Alvaro squinted. "Well, she was alone in here. But I saw a man outside the store. He seemed to be waiting for her. I remember because he was smoking and you don't like anyone smoking near the store."

"Do you remember what he looked like?"

Alvaro shrugged. "Like a man. Dark hair. Couldn't see much from here."

"A beard?"

"No beard. Why do you ask so many questions?"

"No reason."

Megan thanked him and walked to the back of the kitchen to place her bag in the office. No beard. That meant it wasn't Luke. So maybe Becca did have a lover in Winsome. That in and of itself meant nothing.

But a stranger in town might mean something when it came to a murder investigation.

FOURTEEN

Megan still had the package of pheromones she'd bought for Emily sitting on her dresser in her bedroom. She decided to run it over to Emily before dinner in the hopes of convincing her to join them. Time with the baby would lift Bibi's spirits and help her feel useful. And Lily adored Bibi. It was fun to see them together.

Only Emily wasn't home when Megan swung by her house. Alvaro said she'd left the restaurant at four to pick up Lily. Maybe they were running errands? Megan dialed Emily's cell. She answered right away.

Megan told her why she was calling.

"Oh, I'd love to join you tonight, but I'm kind of tied up right now." There was a pause, and when Emily came back on, her voice was lower. "I'm at my grandmother's Cape. With Chief King."

Megan's gut tightened. "Everything okay?"

"He has some questions about the house. Oh, hold on."

Megan heard the shuffling, and then the sound of Lily cooing. The next thing she knew, Bobby King was on the line.

"Megan, can you stop by here?"

"I guess. Why?"

"I thought you might be able to answer a few questions for me." King sounded tense, a little brusque. "I promise it won't take long."

Megan agreed. She didn't like the sound of Bobby's voice. He was clearly under pressure now that Paul's death had been ruled suspicious. But the fact that he had Emily at the house meant he was reexamining the scene. New information? Or had something else happened since Paul died?

The sun had already dipped below the horizon by the time Megan arrived at Emily's grandmother's property. She saw Bobby's car, and Emily's sedan parked next to it. One police car had been pulled haphazardly onto a snow mound, half off the road. All of the lights in the house appeared to be on.

Megan didn't need to knock. King opened the door as though he'd been waiting for her. No one wore masks, and the baby was

147

there, so Megan assumed the house had been declared free of phosgene or other chemicals. Still, Megan paused by the door, looking questioningly at the chief.

"It's fine. We had the house cleared. Again. Come in." He stepped back to make room. "We're headed outside in a moment anyway. But first, follow me."

Megan followed King into the kitchen, where Emily was already standing by the counter looking down at a set of photographs. She smiled gratefully when Megan entered, and then looked at King as though asking permission to speak. He nodded his consent.

"Paul's death is being considered a homicide," Emily said.

King put up a hand. "It's been deemed suspicious. I don't want to fuel the gossip fire even more. We still need to completely rule out an accidental poisoning. That's why you're here, Megan."

"Okay, suspicious." Emily's hand was shaking. She glanced down at it, frowned, and then tucked it by her side, out of sight. "The police wanted to know who had keys, who had been in the building, things like that." She pointed to a piece of lined paper. "All of the contractors and their numbers."

"Which brings me to the reason I asked

you to come down, Megan. We've requested an expert, a chemist who consults with the Philadelphia Police Department, to come up tomorrow afternoon. I know you did some work on a case involving the chemical in question. I was hoping — unofficially, of course — you could tell me more." King glanced at Emily. "I did my own research, but I'd love to hear your thoughts."

"I don't know that I can add much, Bobby, but I'm happy to help if I can." Megan's gaze strayed to the back of the kitchen where a rectangular table sat surrounded by four chairs. Beyond the table, and awkward to reach, was a door that led to the backyard. "How do you think the killer, if there was one, got in? Was the back door locked?"

"The son says it was." King walked back and turned the knob on the door. "We didn't pick up any prints, including Paul's or the son's." His attention turned toward Emily. "Only Emily's."

"Which makes sense," Emily said. "No one would have reason to enter through the kitchen door. The back patio isn't shoveled, and the door doesn't really lead to anywhere."

"How about the front door? Signs of a break in?"

Bobby shook his head. "None."

Emily said, "And like I told you before, Chief, only Merry, Paul, and Luke had keys."

"Along with you and your contractors."

Emily's eyes darkened. "Correct."

King seemed to mull something. "Megan, can you come with me? Emily, why don't you stay here with Officer Brown and Lily?"

Emily hesitated, then agreed.

Megan touched Emily's arm lightly. "When we're done, we can head to the farm for dinner. Sound good?"

"I think some time at the farm would be great. How about if I go home and get Lily's things and meet you at your house?" Emily glanced at Bobby King hopefully. "Would that be okay? I've given you everything I have."

Bobby looked about to say no, but Lily whimpered and he nodded. "Keep your phone on in case we have more questions. And if you think of anyone else who had access to the house, please call me right away."

While Emily packed up the baby's things, Megan followed King out the front door. He paused on the outside stoop. Glancing down at Megan's feet, he said, "You're wearing boots. Good. Where we're headed, you'll need them."

King led Megan on a trampled path of snow around to the back of the house, where a set of Bilco doors marked the entrance to the basement. The doors and the surrounding area had been cleared of snow. Faint footprints marred the adjacent backyard, but even as they spoke the prints were being swept away by wind and a gentle falling snow.

"This is how I think someone may have gained entrance," King said. "There's a set of steps that leads from the basement into the hall on the first floor. We found these Bilco doors unlocked and mostly free of snow. Emily says she never thought to lock them, so they were probably open from day one."

"How about the door at the top of the steps?"

King shook his head. "Handle is broken and the lock doesn't work. Emily said she never bothered to have it fixed because the contractors were in and out of the basement. It was on her to-do list."

It wasn't that unusual for folks in Winsome to leave their doors unlocked. Many had dogs or alarms, but even those who didn't trusted their fellow townspeople. Megan stared at the Bilco doors. Like the house, they were a little aged, frayed around the edges. One handle was gone, the other mottled with rust.

"The lack of a second handle was probably why she didn't bother locking it. What would she have attached a lock to?"

King waved his hand toward the yard and the trailer beyond. "And as you can see, the backyard doesn't get much use."

Megan hopped up and down on her toes. It was cold out, and standing here made her feel even chillier. Eyeing the trampled lawn, she said, "So there could have been footprints. Were there?"

"There were definitely marks, but it snowed the night he died, if you recall. So any footprints had been filled in."

"And Luke didn't notice anything? A sound inside the house, noise in the basement?"

"Luke says he didn't go back to the house that night. He ran some errands, went to scope out a piece of property up north, and then had a beer at the brewery. Stayed at Merry's house, which she and Becca corroborated. As for the time he was scoping out property?" King shrugged. "No one can confirm that."

"And the others in that household? Alibis?"

"Together by the end of the evening, but everyone — even Merry — had gaps. Periods when they hadn't actually seen one another."

King finally seemed to notice that Megan was cold. With some effort, he opened one of the Bilco doors. He shined a flashlight into the basement's depths. "Come on."

"I don't know that my civic duty includes creepy basements, Bobby."

King's laugh sounded forced. His face looked ghostly in the glow of the artificial light. "I know this is above and beyond, but I want you to take a look at something. I'd appreciate hearing your thoughts."

King was looking at her with something akin to warmth. After the traumas of last fall they'd developed a bond. She'd come to respect his abilities and toughness as a new police chief, and he seemed to appreciate her insights. It was a relationship that worked, and so Megan descended the dark steps that led into the house. A house in which someone had been poisoned.

The basement felt damp and chilly. The first thing that hit her were the smells: a lingering scent of gasoline, moth balls, dust, and a healthy dose of mildew. As her eyes adjusted to the glow from the flashlight, she could make out a hoarder's haven of stuff.

Broken chairs. An old workbench, now covered with moving boxes and what looked like a bowling ball. Broken lamps, crates full of decorations, even what appeared to be a pile of rocks. It was a basement that had not seen serious use or a cleaning crew for some time, probably since Emily's grandmother had died

"Can you turn on the overhead light?" Megan asked.

"Bulb is shattered." King shined the light on a fixture hanging by a bunch of wires from the low ceiling. Jagged shards of glass hung down. He shined the beam toward the back of the basement. "What I want to show you is over here."

King stepped over a dissembled picnic table. "Watch your step." At the far end of the room, he paused next to a freezer. Like most things in the basement, the appliance had seen better days. But it wasn't the freezer King was after — it was the shelf of solvents and paints that stood next to it. This area had been recently disturbed. Fresh cans of paint — clearly marked with color and date — sat next to rusty cans and milky bottles containing older chemicals.

A standing fire hazard.

"We went through this basement thoroughly. Dusted for prints — nothing's turned up so far. Everything checks out in terms of the work Emily's had done to the house." He swept the beam back and forth across the chemicals. "Still. I need to rule out that this wasn't an accident. And this shelf has been bothering me."

Megan got closer so she could take a better look. She had to wipe cobwebs away from a coffee can of nails — it had obviously been there a while. In addition to the paint, she saw two plastic containers of pesticides, mouse traps, paint thinner, some weed killer, and what looked like another solvent, but the label had long since faded.

"You're concerned that someone accidentally made phosgene with these chemicals?"

"Or ones like them." Bobby picked up the pesticide. "It could happen."

"You're right, it could." Based on the research she had done, Megan recalled that certain chemicals, when mixed, produced phosgene.

"When you were working on that case, you said phosgene was released at a pesticide plant. That's what got me thinking. What if one of the contractors did something to create the poison. He could have had no idea." King ran the light over the chemicals on the shelf. "It could have been one of these, or maybe something he brought with him."

Megan leaned in for a closer look. "The plant where the accident occurred was using phosgene as part of their chemical process. It was industrial strength, and a large amount was released." She took the pesticide container from King. "This doesn't look like it's been used in years. And while phosgene can be a byproduct of certain solvents, why would it be used accidentally in Paul's bedroom? And why would the windows be taped shut?"

King couldn't hide his disappointment — or his sense of resignation. "That's what I was afraid you would say." The ceiling above them creaked, and his eyes followed the bits of plaster that flurried from the ceiling. "I guess I was just hoping." He shrugged. "So this stuff could cause phosgene as a byproduct, but not in sufficient quantity to kill someone? Does that mean we're looking for someone with an industrial connection?"

Megan thought about his question. She had wondered the same thing: had the killer pilfered phosgene from a chemical or pharmaceutical plant? "Not necessarily. It's possible to die from phosgene produced as part of a chemical reaction, and the killer could have purposefully mixed certain chemicals to create that reaction. Of course releasing an industrial supply would be the surest way to cause death. Although I would think most companies would report missing phosgene given its toxicity."

"Not if the person who owned the company killed Paul. Or if Paul's killer otherwise had control of the company's supply."

"An expert," Megan said. "Or someone with resources."

They looked at each other across the flashlight beam. The Love Chemist came to Megan's mind. King's somber expression suggested he was thinking about the young entrepreneur as well.

FIFTEEN

It was after ten that evening when everyone finally left the farm. Bibi, still a little off from her fall, seemed tired, so Megan suggested she head to bed early while Megan cleaned up the kitchen. Bibi refused, of course, but by ten thirty, she was dozing by the television, her head lolling to the side. Megan placed a pillow behind her and spread a coverlet over her knees. She turned down the television volume but left it on; Bibi liked the background noise.

Tired but restless, Megan headed to her study where she turned on her laptop. Sadie and Gunther curled at her feet in perfect mirror images of one another. Megan was thankful for the alone time — and the quiet. Until Gunther started snoring.

Megan glanced at Aunt Sarah's novel, *To Kill Again,* still sitting on her desk. She was apprehensive to start it for some reason, feeling, she supposed, like it would open a

Pandora's Box of fear — about her aunt, about the type of person who kills another person based on a fictional work. Thinking of the evening spent with Bobby, and the puzzle he had on his hands, she couldn't very well ignore the book. Perhaps it would offer some clues.

Megan opened a search engine and input Paul Fox's name. She was curious about his history. Why did people seem to have such a visceral reaction to him? What about those old articles Alvaro had found? There seemed to be so many layers. A man who would threaten Aunt Sarah, belittle his daughter, dominate his wife. Yet his son seemed quite attached, Merry respected him enough to invite him here, and Megan had to admit — Paul had seemed charming. Was he as cruel as Becca made him out to be? Or was Becca a poor judge of character? She was interested in knowing more — but beyond that, she wanted to reassure herself that Paul's death was targeted at him — and no one else.

Isn't that always the way, she thought. We tell each other stories to avoid the reality that these things could happen to us — or worse, to the ones we love. Life was so uncertain. She thought about her late husband, Mick, too young to die in the service of his country. You live, you love, you hope, Megan thought. There are no promises.

A general Google search came up with all of the hits Megan would have expected. Paul's professional LinkedIn page, updated to reflect his multiple graduate degrees and years of experience treating trauma victims. Mentions on professional pages. A few hits for sites that related to voter registration, real estate, addresses. All-in-all, nothing unusual.

Megan found Paul's professional website. The only thing noteworthy was that he had no longer been practicing psychology. Rather, he had been writing about it and lending his insights as a "consultant" to companies looking for financing. Megan figured there was more money in industry than private practice — but investing? She was also surprised to see he only had a Master's Degree and not a PhD. An impressive set of secondary institutions to his name — but he lacked the terminal degree for many psychologists. Maybe collecting from insurance companies proved too difficult, necessitating the switch to business? Otherwise why end a practice that had been his lifeblood for so long?

Megan toggled back to Paul's LinkedIn

page. Nothing there indicated why Paul left private practice. One thing on his LinkedIn site did catch her eye. He'd listed himself as an investor and noted that he was looking for small businesses in which to invest. That seemed quite a switch from private practice as well.

Megan rubbed the back of her tired neck with one hand. She took a few deep breaths, trying to quiet her cluttered mind. Gunther changed position, providing a momentary lull in his snoring. In the quiet, Megan heard the wind blowing against the old window panes, she heard the water gurgling through the house's ancient radiators. She heard the sound her blood made as it pulsed through her veins.

And then she heard the unmistakable screech of glass shattering.

Megan flew down the stairs behind the dogs, her fingers dialing 911 as she ran. Gunther was using his big boy bark and the noise awakened Bibi, who was standing in the hallway looking dazed.

"What's happening?"

"Break in. Go back in the parlor and close the doors. Stay out of sight."

"Megan —"

"Bibi, please." The 911 operator answered

and Megan explained what was happening. "We need a car to this address. Hurry."

She heard another of Gunther's deep barks, then a high-pitched scream. Bibi and Megan looked at one another. Megan recognized the voice — and clearly Bibi did too.

"I don't know if she's alone," Megan whispered. "Or why she's here." Megan handed her grandmother her cell phone. "Call King. His number is on speed dial." When Bibi looked at her blankly, Megan took the phone, quickly hit the digits, and handed the phone back. "Just press the green button."

"But what will you do if she's violent?"

Megan heard one of Gunther's warning growls, followed by a whimper. "I don't think we need to worry about that."

Once Bibi was back in the parlor with the French doors closed, Megan made her way down the hall, toward the kitchen, where the sound was coming from. She flipped on a light, her heart racing. The first thing she saw was Gunther. He was standing over someone with the fur on his back raised and his ears back. Warning posture — but not threatening. Sadie stood behind him, and she looked as perplexed as Bibi had. With a quick glance, Megan saw that someone had shattered the glass to the door leading into the kitchen. Shards lay on the floor, and small dots of blood speckled the old flooring.

The sound of weeping pushed her forward.

Becca Fox sat against the kitchen counters, her knees up against her chest and her palms forward toward Gunther. Her hair was in complete disarray, a cacophony of curls circling her reddened face. She wore blue and gray flannel pajamas and dirty white slippers. Her right hand was bleeding — probably from breaking the glass — but she didn't seem to notice.

"Becca," Megan whispered. "Are you alone?"

Becca didn't respond, and Megan asked again, more sharply this time.

"Yes," Becca muttered. Her face was shiny with tears. When she looked up, Megan saw wide eyes and the unmistakable glaze of terror.

Sirens wailed in the distance.

Megan placed a hand on Gunther, letting him know to stand down. He did, although he stayed close to Megan's side. Sadie edged close enough to Becca to lick the distraught woman's face. Becca wrapped her arms around the dog and buried her face in her fur, her sobs shaking her entire body. Sadie stood there, stoic.

Megan knelt down. "Becca, you're bleeding. Let me see your hand."

Becca shook her head. She looked up. Streaks of mascara had laid tracks on her ivory skin. "I'm next. Don't you get it? He's after me. I'm next."

"Who is he?"

"I'm next."

"Who is he, Becca? Tell me."

"My father."

"Your father is dead. He can't hurt you."

"I'm next. I know, I know, I know . . ." Her "knows" trailed off in a set of high-pitched wails.

Megan was no psychologist, and clearly Becca was terror-stricken, but there was something more going on. A psychotic episode? Bibi rushed into the room and Megan asked her to retrieve a blanket. A few moments later, they managed to release Sadie from Becca's grip and they wrapped the fleece around Becca's shoulders. They were just cleaning up her hand when Bobby King arrived.

He and two uniformed officers — one male, one female — entered formally, hands on their holsters.

"No need for that," Bibi said. "It's Becca Fox." Bibi walked closer to the police officers. "She's in a state," she said softly. "She needs help."

King nodded, and the female officer removed a set of handcuffs.

"I don't think you need them," Megan said, alarmed. "She's distraught and scared. I don't know why she broke in, but clearly she was in a panic. She needs help." When the officer came closer, "I'm not pressing charges, Bobby. She needs an ambulance, not a cell."

"We have a paramedic on the way. They're meeting us at the station."

Bibi moved protectively in front of Becca, who was looking at the ground, holding her injured hand, and whimpering. "Bobby King, this girl needs a hospital, not the police."

King took an audible breath. His beefy face looked lined and haggard. His blond hair was mussed, his clothes rumpled. He clearly hadn't been asleep when Bibi called him. It looked like he hadn't slept in several days.

"Megan, Bonnie . . . we were in the process of arresting Becca when she ran. She absconded with her aunt's car and apparently came here."

Megan peeked out the window. Merry's Volvo sat half on the driveway, half on a

165

small snow bank. Megan questioned King with her eyes.

"We arrived at Merry's with a warrant. She refused my officers entry. Then she sprinted outside and left the premises." King clenched a hand by his side. "I have two officers at Merry's house now with a search warrant. We'll see what they find. But the fact remains — she ran from the law, Megan. We'll get her treatment once she's in custody. She's under arrest, though, and she's coming with me."

Sixteen

Megan wasn't the least bit surprised to find Merry Chance in the farmhouse kitchen the next morning when Megan came in from chores. She *was* surprised to find her deep in conversation with Bibi, who was clutching a wad of tissues and who looked as though she'd been watching the Hallmark channel again.

"Good morning," Megan said on her way to the sink. She scrubbed her hands and dried them, cognizant of the sudden silence. "Merry, how is Becca?"

Bibi and Merry exchanged a glance. "Megan, Merry needs some help."

After the previous night's drama, Megan was expecting Merry to ask for the name of a good local lawyer. Or maybe information about jail procedures.

Instead, Bibi said, "Merry wants you to talk to Bobby. She thinks he's going to charge Becca for the murder of her father."

Megan sat down, hard. This didn't surprise her. She wished it did. "He found something at your house?"

Merry dabbed at her eyes with a fresh tissue Bibi had placed on the table. "I guess. He wouldn't tell me anything. But when I inquired this morning, he said they are holding her temporarily. And that she needs a psychiatric evaluation."

Another non-surprise. "I don't imagine he can tell you much else, Merry."

"He can tell her how long they plan to hold Becca. And what she's being charged with." Bibi crossed her arms over her brown "Winsome Blues" concert sweatshirt. "The girl has issues. They can't keep her indefinitely without charges. I know that from *Murder, She Wrote.*"

"Yeah, well, Winsome is starting to feel like Cabot Cove," Merry murmured. She turned her attention to Megan. "Becca is on medication for some mood issues. She has been ever since Blanche died. Her mother's death was hard on her. Hard on everyone, but especially Becca. I had hoped . . . well, I had hoped this love potion business would be the boost she needed to make a fresh start. I'm afraid, though, that The Love Chemist was her undoing with the police."

168

"They found chemicals?"

"I don't know what they found, but they hauled a lot of stuff from her room. Along with her computer." Merry seemed to melt into the chair. "First her father goes, now this. Everyone will think we're *that* kind of family. It's my fault. If only I'd stayed out of it. And Luke . . . he's like a caged animal right now. Pawing at the earth, angry." Talking about Luke seemed to lend Merry strength. She sat forward, white knuckles grasping white tissues. "Please get to Bobby before Luke does. Luke is protective of his sister and not completely rational right now. Tell Bobby that Becca is innocent. She hated her father, yes — but she would never, ever have done something so heinous."

"I can tell him, Merry, but he's the Chief of Police. He has to investigate the murder and if his evidence led him to Becca —"

"That's just it, Megan. Of course it will lead him to Becca. She hated her father, and she made no attempt to hide it. But that doesn't make her guilty. And while he's sniffing around my niece, the real killer is getting away, quite literally, with murder."

She had a point. Assuming Becca was innocent. "Your niece seemed very distraught when she broke in here last night. She kept saying she was next, seemed to think her

169

father was after her. She looked almost crazed. Is it possible someone was after her, Merry?"

In a soft voice, Bibi said, "Tell her why you're so sure she's innocent, Meredith. Tell Megan. Go on."

Merry turned toward Bibi. She seemed about to say something but stopped. Instead, she stood up and walked toward the door that led onto the porch. She reached one hand out and touched the window that had been broken last night, tracing the outline of the cardboard and plastic Megan had secured to keep the cold December air out.

"I can't," Merry said finally. "You tell her whatever you want."

With that, Merry pushed open the door and left.

"She has problems," Bibi said once the door was closed. "Adjustment issues. Has ever since Blanche died."

"I figured that. Her unhealthy obsession with her mother's death. Her insistence that her father is the culprit. But why is Merry so certain she can't be the killer?" Megan's eyes narrowed. "And what were you two talking about? I felt like I'd interrupted something deep."

"I never was a big fan of Merry's. Too gossipy. But family is family, as you know, and we do stuff for family because we have to. Because it's proper. That's all Merry's doing right now — looking after her own."

Megan knew this was headed somewhere she wouldn't like. Whenever Bibi started with the "family protects family" speech, it meant someone had done something stupid.

Megan sat down. "What was Merry so reluctant to tell me?"

"She lied to the police."

"Oh. Great."

"Because of a man."

"Merry told me last time she was here. She's afraid Becca is making poor relationship choices. What does that have to do with lying to the police?"

Bibi shook her head. "No, no. It turns out the man is not a boyfriend. Merry overheard a phone conversation between this man and Becca the night Paul was killed. She heard Paul's name mentioned over and over again. Becca seemed distraught. She left the house."

"Doesn't that lend credence to the fact that Becca could have hurt Paul? She had motive, and if she left the house, she may have had opportunity.

Bibi shook her head. "Merry followed her.

She saw her go in the direction of town. The opposite direction of Paul's rental house. She saw her meet with this guy. Then she lost them for a very short while — maybe twenty minutes, not enough time to get to Paul's rental in that snow. Next thing she knows, Becca is back at the house. So you see? She didn't kill her father."

"Did Merry hear what they were talking about?"

"Only that it had to do with Paul. And that whatever this man was doing or not doing was upsetting to Becca."

"Did she get a look at the guy?"

"No. Not really."

"Bibi, you realize that even if Becca didn't physically kill Paul, she could have been an accomplice. This doesn't necessarily prove Becca's innocence. And she could have done something later, after the encounter."

"But the existence of this other man calls into question her guilt. It means there's another possibility."

Bibi had a point. Megan was quiet for a moment. "She needs to tell Bobby this herself."

"She can't."

"Why, Bibi?"

Bibi looked torn. Her bright eyes danced, deciding, Megan knew, between what felt

172

right and what *was* right. "Because she lied to King. Before you get too lawyerly on me, at the time, he asked her if she could confirm Becca's whereabouts for that night. She'd told him Becca was upstairs in her room, reading or working. She didn't tell him about this because she was afraid it looked suspicious and she thought it was nothing. But now she's afraid to go back to him. He'll think she lied about other things."

"And he would be right to think that way."

"You know Merry better than that. She's a nosy neighbor but not a liar. He'll wonder if she's hiding something. That maybe she'd covered for Becca one of the nights before he died."

One of the nights when he was being slowly poisoned, Megan thought, understanding.

"Is there anything else Merry didn't tell him?" When Bibi shook her head, Megan rubbed her own face with her hands. She wanted a glass of wine — and it was only nine in the morning. "Bibi, I'm not getting involved in Merry's mess. I feel badly for her and Becca, but Merry needs to tell Bobby the truth. He's not a bad man, just young. The more we can help him do his job the right way, the more likely there will be a just outcome."

"What would you do if this were me, Megan? If I could be in trouble and you were certain I hadn't done anything."

That was easy enough to answer. Hadn't she been there before after Simon Duvall died in their barn? "I would do everything in my power to find the real murderer."

Bibi looked at her, a faint smile of pride tugging at the corners of her lips. "Maybe we can help Merry. You and me. I've watched Angela Lansbury. I read Agatha Christie. And you're young."

Megan stifled a laugh. "That's all I have going for me? I'm young?"

Bibi stood. The action took some effort and she winced when she moved. "When you're my age, you realize what a huge advantage youth is. It's like anything, really. You don't appreciate what you have until it's gone." Bibi made her way to the sink, where she started washing dishes. "What are you waiting for?"

"What exactly do you want me to do?"

"Start with Sarah, Megan. She knew Paul Fox well. Better than she's letting on."

The book. The argument in Merry's parking lot. "Okay. If she'll tell me anything."

"Tell her I sent you. That we're here to help."

174

■ ■ ■ ■

Megan didn't go directly to Sarah's house. Instead, she ran upstairs and grabbed Sarah's novel, *To Kill Again*. She donned her hat, some thin gloves, and a thick wool blanket. With Gunther and Sadie behind her, she snuck out of the back of the house and made her way to the goat enclosure.

Heidi and Dimples were sleeping but rose when she came in. Megan spread the blanket in their heated pen and sank down on the ground. The dogs lay next to her, and after two unsuccessful attempts to eat the book, the goats soon settled as well.

Megan read.

She didn't stop until the very last word.

SEVENTEEN

Aunt Sarah agreed to see her that evening. "Come for dinner, Megan. I'm no Alvaro, but I make a mean bowl of spaghetti Bolognese."

And so Megan drove to her aunt's after finishing her farm chores and dropping greens and onions off at the café. Sarah lived several miles from Winsome, and as Megan pulled onto her property, she was once again reminded of its storybook charm. An English cottage in the woods, and now the cottage sat in a fluff of white amidst snow-covered pines. It was dark outside, but with light flurries coming down from a moonless sky, the house looked warmly lit and inviting. Or would have felt inviting were it not for the ropes binding Megan's gut.

Megan knocked twice before Aunt Sarah opened the front door. She wore her usual attire — loose-fitting brown pants, a deep plum kaftan, and a string of colorful beads. The frames of her readers picked up the color of her shirt; the glasses hung from a brown rope around her neck.

"Good to see you." Sarah leaned in and kissed Megan on the cheek. "Come. I've been waiting for you."

The house smelled of garlic and roasting meats. Megan handed her parka to her aunt and followed her into the kitchen.

"I thought we'd eat in the dining room tonight," Aunt Sarah said. "I lit a fire and moved the books off the table. Nice to have company for a change."

The lights in Sarah's home were kept dim, and the fire in the fireplace crackled brightly. The table was set for two. Two plates of appetizers had been set at one end next to a bottle of Sangiovese wine, a half-full decanter, and two wine glasses.

"Would you care for some wine?"

Megan nodded. She took the glass gratefully.

"Sit. Get comfortable. Dinner will be ready in a half hour. We can chat until then."

Megan sank down on an upholstered armchair, white with blue flowers, a shabby chic contribution to the cottage room. Aunt Sarah sat across from her in a blue armchair, lifting the chair's current occupant — an orange tabby — and placing the cat on her lap.

"You read my book? I assume that's why you wanted to come over."

"Right to the point?" Megan smiled. "Yes, I read it. And I want to talk about it. But that's not why I'm here."

"Oh?"

"Bibi sent me." Megan explained portions of her earlier conversation with her grandmother. She watched Sarah's reaction and was disappointed when the older woman's face remained neutral. "You don't seem surprised."

"I'm surprised it took you this long to show up. Bonnie knows I had a history with Paul. The police know because I told them." She took a long sip of wine. "Hell, Megan, with the way gossip flies around this town, for all I know by now all of Winsome knows."

The cat yawned and stretched. It eyed Megan with disdain before returning to its nap.

Megan said, "What kind of history?"

"He was my therapist. And then he was my lover."

Megan stared at her aunt, taking in her news, swallowing her surprise. "He was your lover while he was your therapist? Or afterwards?"

"Do you want to know whether he was breaking his therapist code of honor? The answer is yes. Do you want to know if he was a cheating sonofabitch? The answer is yes." Another swallow of wine, her face a practiced blank. "If you want to know whether I killed him, that answer is a resounding no."

"Why would I think you killed him?"

"Just putting that out there. After the grilling I received from King, I thought I would handle the question up front. Thankfully I had an airtight alibi for the entire damn week or I think I'd be spending the night at Hotel Lockup."

Megan took a sip from her own wine glass, trying to hide her surprise. The liquid was thick and dusky, a little bitter for her taste. "Tell me about Paul. What happened between you?"

Sarah stood. "Come with me. I need to pull dinner together. I'll tell you in the kitchen."

Sarah stirred the contents of a large pot with more vigor than was needed. She turned off the gas and poured the pasta through a colander in the sink. Steam clouded the window over the counter.

"I was obviously much younger," Aunt Sarah said as she worked. "I'd recently been through a messy divorce. My first books were out, but I wasn't making much money yet. Bill — that's my ex — had left me emotionally and financially drained. And of course your grandfather had all but disowned me. I had no one, really. Except your mother." She threw an apologetic smile at Megan over her shoulder. "She never wavered in her support."

Well, I'm glad she was there for someone, Megan thought. "So you went to see Paul?"

"Yes. He was recommended to me by Denver's aunt, Dr. Kent. Eloise had recently hired Paul to provide counseling at her office for kids and their parents — victims of trauma. I trusted her opinion, plus there just weren't a lot of choices around here back then."

The pasta was still steaming in the colander. Sarah poured it into a large pasta bowl and sprinkled on parmesan cheese. She ladled thick, meaty sauce on top. "Right back," she said, disappearing into the dining room with the bowl of pasta.

When she returned, she pulled a salad out of the refrigerator. "Shall we eat?"

"Sure, but please continue with your story. I want to hear what happened."

Once settled in the dining room, Megan took a small portion of pasta and a large helping of the Caesar salad and placed them on her plate. Sarah watched her approvingly.

"You eat like your mother," Aunt Sarah said.

"Please don't. I don't want to hear comparisons. It's not fair."

Sarah looked away, her expression pained. "You're both important to me. Sometimes . . . sometimes I forget. Your grandfather is still waiting, you know. He's ready, I think, to see you again. If you'll agree."

Thinking of October, of nights spent wondering what was going on, Megan said, "Bully for him." Megan recoiled at the reproach in Aunt Sarah's eyes. More gently, she said, "Paul?"

"Ah, yes." Sarah forked a piece of lettuce and studied it. "My sessions with Paul helped at first. He was an attentive listener, as he should have been, I guess. He asked questions, probed, always wanted more details, urging me to disclose the most painful parts, the most sordid aspects of my experiences, of my marriage." She sighed. "I was so hungry for attention, for someone to hear me, that I amplified Paul's good qualities. I made him into some psychological warrior fighting battles on my behalf."

181

"And he wasn't."

Sarah laughed. "No, clearly he wasn't." She popped the lettuce into her mouth, chewed, and swallowed, then drained her wine glass before continuing. "On session five he grabbed my hand during a particularly painful disclosure about sex with my former husband. On session seven he hugged me platonically before I left. By session twelve he was kissing me. We had sex during session fifteen."

Megan sat there, absorbing her aunt's admission. "He was married."

"And the father of two."

"Yet you slept with him."

"I did."

The words hung there between them. It was clear from Sarah's tone that this was something she had come to terms with years ago. That the guilt had been weighed and measured, and whatever penance required had been performed.

"At some point you ended it?"

"There was never a session sixteen. I knew the moment I walked out that office door that what had happened was wrong. I allowed him to manipulate me. I felt dirty and exposed and very, very vulnerable. It wasn't until later that I understood the full gravity of what had happened."

Megan put down her fork. "What do you mean?"

Sarah tilted her head, her eyes thoughtful. "The sex was very intense. I felt like he was devouring me. His eyes bore into me the entire time we were together. He was rough. I felt violated; that's why I never returned. Years later, after I spent time with a real therapist, I came to understand something about Paul. He was a sadist in the most basic sense. He consumed my stories the same way he consumed me sexually. The trauma I had been through, the sordid details . . . they fed him. They excited him."

"That's disgusting."

"I know." Sarah put down her own fork. "I wish I could say I was sorry to see him go."

"Did you report him?"

"I tried." The orange tabby jumped up on the table and Sarah shooed him off. "Sorry. Buttercup's not used to visitors." She bent down to pet him, soothing his fragile ego. "I called Eloise and let her know. I suppose I should have done more, but I was pretty depressed at the time." She shrugged. "Not that that's an excuse."

"Is that why Denver's aunt fired him? Because of what happened with you?"

"I don't know — maybe. Remember, I

183

didn't live here full-time. I still used my ex-husband's apartment in New York, and after that happened I returned to the city. I heard later that Paul and his family had moved out of town. To somewhere in New York, I think."

"So there was never a scandal?"

"About me?" Sarah looked confused by the question. "No, of course not. Not back then. I mean people knew something had happened, I'm sure, but I didn't go screaming from the rooftops. And I don't think Eloise would have told many people. The fact that he worked for her would have made her look bad."

Megan placed more pasta on her plate. It was good, and she was hungry. "I'm just looking for the connection to your book, *To Kill Again.* I thought maybe if your fling was public, someone might have used that book against you."

"Just because I didn't make a big deal about it doesn't mean other people didn't find out. Blanche could have told her sister or a friend. And who knows, maybe Paul told someone — bragged about his conquest."

"What about the parking lot? That day at Merry's? The two of you were arguing."

Sarah nodded. "He was afraid I was going

to go public with what happened. Seemed suddenly paranoid that I would. As though after all those years I'd try to get revenge that way."

"It does seem odd." Megan twirled spaghetti onto her fork. It resisted, slipped off, and she caught it with a spoon. "Does Becca know about the two of you?"

"I didn't tell her."

"But she could have learned about it on her own?"

"Anything is possible."

Truer words, Megan thought, and downed some more wine.

Megan helped Sarah clean up. They worked side by side in a comfortable silence. Megan caught herself wondering if this is what it would have been like with her mother. Whether this was what her mother had shared with Sarah.

Before she left, Sarah handed her a Tupperware container. "For Bonnie. I know she loves spaghetti."

"Thank you."

They headed toward the front door. "What did you think of my book?"

"I devoured it," she said, recognizing the echo of the words Sarah had used to describe Paul not an hour ago. "It was excellent. I had no idea whodunit until the end."

"Did you see the parallels?"

"The phosgene, the room, the taped windows? Yes. That's where the similarities ended though. The killer was a drunk ex-husband. The victim an abused wife."

"But the means were the same."

Megan slid her coat over her arms. "And the house in which the crime was committed even sounded eerily similar. An older Cape Cod in a rural area. There must be a connection. Or someone got their ideas from your book."

"Neither thought is comforting."

Megan hugged her aunt and thanked her for her time and the dinner. "It rivaled Alvaro's," she said.

"You flatter me so." Sarah smiled. "Don't be a stranger. Please."

"I won't. I may have more questions about the book. About Paul."

Sarah nodded. She held Megan's gaze for a long time, her own uncharacteristically maternal. "I wonder about Becca," Sarah said finally. "Paul's desire to feed off pain. His need to dominate and possess. It could not have been easy growing up in that household."

"You think she may have more mental scars than what we see?"

"I think the damage is lasting and deep. Paul's biggest casualty could be his daughter."

Sarah's words echoed the things Merry had said about Becca Fox. The thought unsettled Megan for the rest of the night.

EIGHTEEN

The café was unusually crowded the next morning, a phenomenon fueled, Megan figured, by the upcoming holidays and Paul's untimely death. Clover had done a great job creating a holiday atmosphere, and despite the charged tension, Megan enjoyed the smells and sounds of Christmas. The scents of coffee, cinnamon, and cloves wafted from the kitchen, and instrumental Christmas music played softly in the background. Clover had set up a wreath stand outside the storefront using wreaths purchased from a nearby farm, and a line of customers waited to pay for their decorations.

Megan should have felt happy. Their first real Christmas with the farm and café running, and things were really coming together. Yet Megan couldn't get her conversation with Sarah out of her mind. Or Bibi's request that they help Merry. Megan glanced around as she headed back toward the café. She nodded at people she'd known her whole life, people who rallied around her grandmother when her mother left, when her grandfather died. People who sent cards and gifts and made phone calls when Megan's husband was killed in Afghanistan. This was small town living.

And once again there was a sore festering amongst the good people of Winsome.

Roger Becker stopped Megan in her tracks. He tugged gently at her elbow and pulled her aside. The new zoning commissioner was gaunt and balding, and he looked down at Megan over wire readers. A Santa hat covered his scalp, and a red and green Phillies tie mostly hid the coffee stain on his white shirt. "Do you have a minute, Megan? I need to speak with you."

"Sure, Roger. Although I promised Alvaro —"

"This will just take a minute. I promise." He led her back to a quiet corner of the store, next to the paper goods and organic pet food. "It's Merry. She didn't show up to last night's Historical Society dinner. She *always* comes to the meetings and the dinners. *Always.*"

"I think she's been preoccupied, Roger.

189

With Becca and what happened to Paul and all."

Roger pressed thin lips together, shook his head. "I know, but she always comes. The Historical Society is what roots her, feeds her mojo. When Blanche died, she still came. When Simon was murdered, she still came. When she had an emergency appendectomy, she called in to that night's meeting and participated by conference call, for goodness sake." Roger's face was quickly turning red. "And last night she neither showed up nor called in. She didn't even call to let me know she wasn't coming."

"Did you swing by her house to check on her?"

"Of course." His eyes narrowed, his nostrils flared. "I went first thing this morning."

"And?"

"She was in bed."

"Okay, so maybe she doesn't feel well."

Another firm headshake. "Her nephew Luke said she'd been in bed all night and all morning. He said she wasn't feeling well. That she was having a hard time accepting Paul's death and Becca's possible role in it. That she needed time."

Megan leaned against the shelf and took a deep breath. She made a mental note to refill her stock — it really was getting low. Pulling her cluttered mind back to the conversation at hand, she said, "Roger, I feel awful for Merry. She came by the farm yesterday and seemed quite upset, so I'm not surprised she's feeling this way. I don't think it's easy for her to lose her brother-in-law and then have her niece stand accused. You know Merry."

"Yes, yes, she's image conscious. We all know that, Megan. But that's just it. Merry would get out ahead of this. She'd tell people what was going on, demand justice. Control the message." He pressed his glasses against the bridge of his nose. "This isn't Merry. I've been working with her for years, and I'm worried."

Megan nodded. "I can see that. What would you like me to do?"

Roger looked momentarily relieved to be asked the question. "Go visit her. Send Bonnie over. Something. I'd feel awkward going into her bedroom to talk to her, but she likes you and your grandmother."

"Surely there's someone on the Historical Society she'd rather see? Or maybe Anita?"

"No, no," Roger said. "Historical Society members would be seen as a threat to her privacy. Her sense of decorum would kick in. Same goes for Anita. They get along, but it was Blanche my wife was close to. No, it needs to be a Birch woman. Merry has known Bonnie forever, and she likes you."

Megan nodded. She had some other errands related to Paul Fox to deal with today. She'd add this to her list.

Roger leaned in. He sniffed. "You smell good, Megan. I hope you don't mind me saying that." He placed his hand on her shoulder affectionately. "It was nice to see you."

Megan smiled. She'd worn Becca's pheromones today, figuring it couldn't hurt. She wanted information from people. If they liked her — for whatever reason — it could only make her job that much easier.

Dr. Eloise Kent lived on a sprawling horse farm not far from Denver's bungalow. Megan drove down the long paved driveway and saw Eloise's horses were outside wandering around the partially cleared pasture. The house, a stately white Colonial, wore its best holiday finery. Wreaths decorated the barn and the fence posts. A manger scene had been arranged by the front of the house, its baby Jesus missing from the straw bed. The day was sunny, and despite the cold air and the snow on the ground, the warmth added to a sense of hopefulness.

Megan pulled into the driveway and killed the engine. Eloise was expecting her. Denver had made the arrangements.

Megan found Denver's aunt in the barn. Like her nephew, she was fond of animals, and in addition to three horses, the barn housed a number of barn cats, two of whom scattered when Megan walked inside.

"Megan." Eloise nodded. The sixty-something-year-old was cleaning a stall. Petite and neat in appearance, she somehow managed to make jeans, a thick parka, and a pair of tall plaid rubber boots look fashionable. "Denver said you would stop by. How is my nephew? I haven't seen him in weeks."

"He's well, although I haven't seen him for a while either. I'm heading there next to surprise him with dinner."

"How nice." Her tone said the jury was still out on whether that was, indeed, nice. "How can I help you?"

Megan picked up a shovel. "Would you like a hand? I have some experience with farming."

Eloise cracked her first smile. "No, that's okay. I'm almost finished. Our trainer couldn't make it today, and I wanted some fresh air."

Megan nodded. She watched tidy Eloise do this distinctly untidy chore and used the time to collect her thoughts. "I'd like to discuss Paul Fox."

"Paul?" She glanced at Megan under arched eyebrows. "What about him?"

"He worked for you years ago."

"He worked *with* me years ago. I contracted with his office for him to provide services to my patients."

"And you subsequently let him go."

Eloise stopped what she was doing and leaned on her pitchfork. "He's dead, Megan. Why dredge this stuff up now?"

"It might help lead to the killer."

"That's a job for Bobby King and his people."

Megan didn't say anything. She didn't need to. Eloise — the whole town — knew about Megan and Denver's role in the last incident that occurred in Winsome. It shouldn't surprise anyone that Megan was asking questions.

Nevertheless, Eloise said, "I don't like to speak ill of the dead. What happened with Paul was years ago. I doubt it has any bearing on this case." She returned to cleaning, her stabs at the soiled hay strong and sure.

"Did you know his daughter is being held? The police suspect her of his murder."

No response. Eloise turned her back and attended to something at the other end of the stall. Megan waited.

"Becca has some emotional problems. Perhaps as a result of Paul."

Eloise propped the pitchfork against the barn wall. She bent to pick up a bucket that lay to the side of the enclosed space, then grabbed the bucket and the pitchfork. She moved past Megan hurriedly, her face a twist of conflicting emotions.

"Dr. Kent —"

Eloise stopped and turned around. Megan couldn't tell if the high color in her cheeks was from exertion, the cold, or anger.

"Paul's departure sparked a lot of questions. There were concerns . . . about his behavior, about what he may or may not have done while in the company of my patients. I am a doctor. I took an oath. I will not . . . cannot . . . reopen those wounds."

"Not even if his daughter's freedom hangs in the balance?"

"If I thought I could change things for Rebecca Fox, I would. But nothing I say will help her now."

"Aye, she's a stubborn lassie when she wants to be." Denver placed another log in the tipi wood stove. He'd become fond of the contraption, putting off its donation, and insisted they come out for a nightcap after dinner. He settled in next to Megan. "I'm not a bit surprised she won't tell ye what happened back then. She never talks about it."

"She seemed angry that I was asking."

"She's afraid she did something wrong in hiring him — or not firing him soon enough. If he hurt one of her patients, it would be on her shoulders. Not something ye want to relive if ye don't have to."

"You're right, of course." Megan put her head against Denver's shoulder. They were lounging against a few large pillows atop a thick blanket. As usual, the dogs had joined them, and all but the Golden were asleep by the stove. The Golden Retriever had placed a tennis ball in front of them and was looking at them and the ball with a tilted head and a baleful expression.

"Go, ye daft creature," Denver said. But he tossed the ball in the small space and watched with affection as the dog brought it back. "All she wants to do is play ball. A stranger showed up the other day, and this beast brought him a bloody ball." He gave Megan a hard look. "You're going to chase this one down, aren't you, Megs?"

"I don't really want to be involved. But Bibi and Merry and Becca . . . if I can help,

I feel like I should."

Denver nodded. He took her hand in his own and caressed her fingers with his work-calloused skin. "Some people are toxic. They spread anxiety and unhappiness wherever they go. Have ye met someone like that, Megs?"

She nodded. Of course she had. She could think of a few off the top of her head. Often these people worked through passive aggression, undermining self-confidence or creating an atmosphere that demanded constant sensitivity to their feelings.

"My sense is that this Paul Fox, he was that type of person. Spreading misery wherever he went. With people like that, the suspect pool may be bottomless."

"Perhaps, but those with opportunity would not be endless. Bobby King knows that, and he's doing what he can. But he needs to look more broadly. Slow down and observe. He's in a rush to solve this, and he's perhaps jumping too quickly to conclusions."

"Maybe. But I don't want to see you or Bonnie get hurt."

"We'll be smart about it." Megan teased him with a smile. "I have you to remind me."

Denver's eyes darkened. He leaned in to

kiss her, his lips warm and soft against her own. "I think I'm falling for you, Megan," he whispered. "This may very well be love."

"Are you just realizing it now, Dr. Finn?" Megan teased. "I've known how I feel about you for quite some time." She kissed him back. Her cell phone rang. She ignored it. A moment later, it rang again.

Reluctantly disengaging from Denver's embrace, Megan glanced at the caller name. Roger Becker. "Hold that thought," she said to Denver.

But the spell was broken.

"Yes, Roger?"

"Have you seen Merry yet?"

"No, not yet. I'll head there next."

"Promise? She's still not taking my calls. It's very unlike her, Megan. Very unlike her."

"I promise."

With an apologetic smile, Megan got to her feet. "I'm afraid I need to go. I have to stop by Merry's, and then I have some stuff to do at the store after it closes."

Denver looked at his watch. "Want me to come with you?"

"You're on call tonight. I'll be fine. Get some rest."

Denver nodded, his face a study in concern. "Text me when you get home."

"I will."

"Better yet, call me."

Megan laughed. "Seriously? I'm a big girl."

"You said yourself, Megs — neighbors look out for one another. I'm just being neighborly."

He stood and took her hand to walk her back through the snow-covered yard and out to her car.

"Well, if that's all it is, fine," Megan said. But the words he'd spoken just a few minutes before, his first mention of love, had already wrapped their strong fingers around her heart. Surprisingly, what she felt wasn't apprehension. Or even guilt. Rather, Megan felt light enough to soar.

NINETEEN

The downstairs lights were on when Megan arrived at Merry's home, but unlike her last visits, the Christmas lights were not shining, and even the electric candles in the windows had been turned off. That was strange — perhaps as strange as Merry not showing up for the Historical Society dinner.

Megan rang the doorbell. When no one answered, she banged on the front door. It was only 8:12, too early for the night owl to be asleep. She pulled out her phone and called Merry's number. No answer. Now she was getting worried too. Megan was mulling over whether to contact King when the front door opened. Luke Fox was standing in the doorway, his expression friendly but noncommittal.

"Hi, Megan. What can I do for you?" Luke tucked his hands in the pockets of his jeans and rocked back and forth on his heels.

"Are you looking for my aunt?"

"I am, Luke. Is she here?"

Luke nodded. "She's asleep."

"It's kind of early for her to be in bed. Is she feeling okay?" Megan strained to see beyond Luke, feeling just like a nosy neighbor. Oh, how the tables had turned.

"Not great. She's been like this since last night. She doesn't want to be disturbed. Some guy has called multiple times. She just turns him away."

Roger Becker. That didn't sound like Merry. Not one bit. "Would you mind if I come in? I'd really like to check on her. You know, woman to woman."

Luke moved back into the center hall. "Of course, where are my manners? Do you want some tea? Maybe a glass of wine?"

"Ice water," she said gratefully. "If you don't mind."

"Not at all. Why don't you go see Aunt Merry and I'll get some water."

Megan left him and found her way up the steps and into Merry's second floor. It wasn't hard to figure out which room belonged to Merry. It was the only one with a closed door.

Megan knocked. After a moment, a sleepy voice said, "Luke, tell them I'm asleep."

"It's me, Merry. Megan."

"Oh."

"Can I come in?"

"The door is unlocked." Merry's voice sounded weak.

Merry's room was suffocatingly hot, perfumed by a cloyingly sweet smell. It was not altogether unpleasant — like dried roses or a shriveled orange. She immediately saw the culprit: a basket of dried up flowers and fruit on a table by the window.

"Merry, are you okay? Everyone is concerned. You haven't been responding to phone calls, you didn't show up at the Historical Society dinner." Megan moved closer to the bed. The lights in the room were dimmed. Megan saw a dog-eared romance novel by the pillow. The television was on, tuned to a game show, its sound muted. Clothes sat on a chair by the closet, unfolded. A glass of water and a vial of pills were propped next to a notebook, and a stack of Hollywood rags on the bedside table.

"I'm fine. I just needed time to myself."

Megan took a hard, long look at the woman on the bed. Her hair was unwashed and the strands, left to their own devices, stuck up at odd angles from Merry's head. She seemed to be wearing an old-fashioned dressing gown, its high neck tied near her collarbone. Her covers were pulled up mid-chest despite the overwhelming warmth in the room.

Megan sat on the edge of the bed, uninvited. "You need to get out of bed. You're not helping anyone, least of all Becca."

"This whole thing started because I tried to help Becca. Look where that got her."

"Merry, none of this is your fault. None of this is likely Becca's fault. But unless you get up and help the police, things will get worse."

Merry yawned. Her face was registering understanding, but her eyes drooped as Megan spoke.

"Have you been sleeping?"

"It's all I do."

"I don't mean lying in bed. I mean sleep. Have you had real sleep?"

"I don't know. I guess." She struggled to sit up in the bed, clutching the bed covers to her amply-covered chest. "What else am I supposed to do? The police don't want to hear that Becca is innocent, and even Becca won't see me at this point." She sat back with a huff.

"Is Becca all right?"

"Luke was there today. He said she seemed better. More coherent."

"Does she have an attorney? A psychologist?"

"Luke arranged for a lawyer. The lawyer will get her the right services. I gave Luke some names."

Megan was relieved that Becca had a lawyer at least. "Have you told Bobby about the night Paul died? About the stranger you saw with Becca?"

Merry's face flushed. "Not yet. I was hoping Bonnie would talk you into doing it.

Megan considered whether Merry's sudden issues could be guilt related. Maybe it would help her if Megan was the messenger. "Do you still want me to be the one to tell him?"

Merry didn't hesitate. "Would you?"

"Yes. But he will likely come to ask you more questions. Are you up for that?"

Merry looked around the room. She seemed to really see the environment she'd created for herself — the sickroom atmosphere, the sense of hopelessness. Her eyes widened. "Yes, yes. I'll get up, get showered."

"Promise?"

"Yes. If you'll talk to Bobby."

"I will." Megan considered the conversation she'd have to have with Winsome's police chief. "Merry, do you have any idea

204

who the man is? The man Becca was talking to that night?"

"At first I thought it was a . . . a man friend. But the conversation seemed to be about Paul and only Paul. Whatever was said — and the man was doing much of the talking — it made Becca very upset."

"How do you know it was a man?"

The scarlet tone on Merry's face darkened. "Didn't Bonnie tell you? I may have listened. But only for a moment." She squeezed her eyes shut. "I heard Becca crying and wanted to make sure she was okay. There's nothing wrong with that. Tell me there's nothing wrong with that."

"It's fine." Megan pressed Merry gently back down onto the mattress. "Does Luke know this guy?"

"He says he has no idea who Becca's been talking to."

Megan remembered the holiday First Friday in Winsome, the tall man she saw with Luke. Same guy? Worth the question. Megan stood.

"When I call tomorrow, I expect you to answer. And to be up and showered." Megan smiled to offset the stern tone of her words. "Or else I will send Bonnie over here."

"No, not that."

They both laughed. The action seemed to

take the remainder of Merry's steam. She closed her eyes.

"Get some sleep, Merry," Megan said.

Merry was already breathing heavily.

When Megan reached the landing, she saw Luke walk out of a bedroom down the hall.

"She okay?" Luke asked. He'd exchanged his slippers for a pair of hiking boots and his hair was neatly combed.

"I think you were right. She's feeling a little overwhelmed and depressed."

"I told her to get some sleep. Maybe that would help. She's definitely been acting oddly." Luke bounded down the steps. At the bottom, he paused to wait for Megan. "Still want that water?"

"Sure."

Luke seemed surprised. "Okay," he said. "Just give me a second."

"Are you heading out?" Megan pointed to his boots. "I don't want to hold you up."

"Just meeting a buddy for a drink. But that's okay. I have some time."

Megan followed Luke into the kitchen. It looked slightly worse for the wear than it had when Merry threw the perfume party to introduce Becca's line. Dishes on the counter. Appliances not put away. A stack of unread mail on the island. A pair of muddy snow boots by the back door.

Luke smiled sheepishly, highlighting bright baby blues. "Consider it my own personal trap. If she doesn't get out of bed soon, her entire house will look like this." He handed Megan ice water garnished with a slice of lemon. "You've known Aunt Merry for a long time?"

"Yes and no." Megan took a sip of water, enjoying the tart bitterness of the lemon. "I grew up in Winsome, and I knew your aunt then. I left for college and law school, lived in Chicago for a while, and now I'm back." Megan shrugged. "Merry has been a staple in my life, like so many people in Winsome. But it's not as though we spent tons of time together."

Luke's face hardened into a frown. "We lived here too for a while. My dad had a practice, my mom got to spend time with her sister. It was nice. I remember those as being some of our better days as a family."

Megan tried to reconcile that with what Aunt Sarah had told her the day before. "I don't remember your family from when I was young."

"You wouldn't. It was probably during the period you were away. Dad was never good at staying in one place for too long. Restless."

"You were close to your father."

Luke nodded. "In our way."

Megan wanted to ask about Becca but something held her back. Instead she asked about the stranger she'd seen Luke with the week before.

"Tall? Dark haired?"

Megan nodded.

"I've been meeting with lots of people, looking for investment opportunities near Winsome so I can be closer to my aunt. But that sounds like my buddy Kyle. The guy I'm meeting tonight." Luke made a show of looking at his watch, a not-so-subtle reminder that he had to go soon. "He lives in New Hope."

"So it wasn't the man Becca was arguing with the night your father was killed?"

A cloud of emotion passed over Luke's eyes at the mention of his sister and a man. "What do you mean?"

"Didn't Merry tell you?" Megan relayed the bare bones of the story Merry had shared. "They argued, met up, and then who knows. Merry and I are both thinking he may know something about your dad's death."

Luke walked quickly away from the island and grabbed his coat from the hook by the back door. But Megan saw the look of pain that crossed his features before he turned away. Pain — or fear? She wasn't sure.

"I told you before, my sister has issues. She acts impulsively, has ever since she was a kid. The guy could have been a friend, a former boyfriend, a disgruntled customer. How would I know?" He turned back around to face Megan. "That's why I wanted to search your barn. Sometimes Becca doesn't make the best decisions. She always needs an escape route. Men often give her that escape."

"Merry said she and this man were talking about your father. That doesn't sound like a boyfriend."

"Aunt Merry was eavesdropping again? That's just great. Happy to see she's up to her old tricks too." The boyish charm and good manners were gone now. "I have to go, which means I need to lock up. As you saw, Aunt Merry's not in a position to do it herself."

Megan nodded. She put her glass in the sink, taking her time as she did so. She slipped on her coat and walked outside beside Luke. His agitation felt palpable, his concern about his sister obvious.

"Should you tell your aunt you're leaving?" Megan asked. "She may worry."

"She'll be out for the night," Luke said

before turning toward his car. "She always is." He slammed the car door and drove away without another look in Megan's direction.

It was only a little after nine when Megan arrived at the store. Most of the shops along Canal Street had closed by then, and the café closed at seven after serving its usual light fare dinner. The Washington Acres store portion was open until eight, though, and Megan was hoping to catch Clover before she left for the night. She was too late. Her shop manager and her cook were both gone and the store was locked up and dark.

Megan unlocked the front door and flipped on the lights. She secured the door behind her. A quick inventory proved that Clover had already restocked most of the shelves. Megan grabbed a pad of paper from behind the counter and walked from aisle to aisle, taking note of what was needed. That done, she sorted through the pantry and the storeroom in the back and replaced missing goods with whatever she had available. She was woefully short on many things, especially dairy and baking products and paper goods, things that tended to go when the weather forecasters predicted snow. Suddenly everyone in Winsome wanted to drink milk, bake, and clean.

Megan moved on to the refrigerator section. She noted vegetables and other items she needed to send to the store with Clay during his morning run: microgreens, spinach bundles, onions, garlic, potatoes, and eggs. A quick check of the kitchen stores and the note Alvaro had left for her alongside his proposed menu for the following week told her those same vegetables would be needed in the café. Plus bok choy and arugula from the greenhouses. Her chef was in love with arugula, which was beautifully mild when grown in the cool of the greenhouses during the winter months.

Megan glanced at her phone. It was nearly ten o'clock. She called Bibi and, when her grandmother didn't answer, left her a voicemail. She'd be worried. Megan should have called sooner to tell her where she'd be.

Megan unlocked the door and headed out into the cold night air. Canal Street was empty. The new period-style outdoor lamps cast pools of weak light onto the cobblestone, but beyond the pools lay only deep shadows. The snow that remained underfoot squeaked when she walked. Megan could feel her heart beating, could see her breath.

Anxious to get home, Megan was just

opening her car door when an object banged into her back, pushing her forward. Her head hit the truck. Something slammed into the back of her knees and she lost her balance, sliding down the side of the vehicle and onto her hands and knees. Her head was spinning, her back ached. Panic rose in her throat.

She tried to stand but was pushed down again. Before she could turn, she heard squeaky footsteps quickly retreating. Out of breath, her voice gone, Megan fought to keep herself under control. A kid. An attempted mugging gone wrong. A thug.

She reached for her phone, pulling herself up as she did so. She got into the truck hastily, locking the doors, just as the 911 operator answered. She explained what happened, where she was, her voice sounding far away.

As she described the mugging, her gaze settled on something outside the truck. A package left just outside of the pool of light. Not a package. A book.

Megan looked around. She grabbed a heavy metal flashlight from under the truck seat and held it, handle out. She pulled off her hat and grasped it with her other hand. With the 911 operator still on the phone, she left the relative safety of the truck and went back out into the night. Her stomach roiling, she grabbed the book with her hat, careful not to touch it with her fingers.

Once more in the truck, she locked the doors and started the engine, waiting for the police to arrive.

She opened the hat and looked at her bounty. Her breath once again caught in her throat.

The Killing Time by Sarah Estelle.

Sarah Estelle. Sarah Birch. Another mystery written by Megan's aunt.

TWENTY

Megan found herself back at the farm with Bobby King. He'd arrived alongside his patrolmen to take her statement. He took the book in case they could pull prints, and directed his officers to see whether any of the local security cameras had caught the perpetrator on tape.

When the formalities were over, he said, "I'd sure feel better if I could see you home, Megan."

"You know I'll be fine. I've dealt with far worse than this."

"Well, maybe *I'd* feel better if we had some time to talk."

"Are you thinking a piece of Bibi's raisin crumb pie might help you feel better too?"

King smiled. "Sure wouldn't hurt."

And so they ended up in the Birch kitchen, drinking Kahlua and decaf coffee and eating large slices of Bibi's pie. Neither said a word until the last crumbs were gone and even the dogs had a taste of the crust.

King leaned back in his chair and placed his hands over his burgeoning belly. "No one makes pie like your grandmother."

"That's true. Want any more, Bobby?"

"No. I should go soon or Clover will have the police out looking for me." He laughed lightly at his own joke. "Truth is, this case has me stumped."

"But you have your suspect."

King stared at his empty plate, silent.

"The books?" Megan asked. "They're bothering you."

"The girl, the books, tonight . . . best I can tell, someone is playing with us." His eyes darkened. "And tonight you got hurt."

"I got bruised, but nothing terrible. Whoever did that wanted to leave me the book. Maybe they hoped to place it on my car while I was in the shop and panicked when they saw I was already at the truck." Megan shrugged. "Maybe the murder and this joker aren't even related and it's all one giant coincidence."

"Do you believe that?"

"I don't know what to believe." Then, more quietly, "No."

Gunther rose from his spot next to Bobby and lay on the floor with a loud doggy sigh. Sadie, sensing the futility of more begging, followed suit. Together they formed a canine yin-yang symbol.

"I don't think Becca did it, Bobby. She certainly didn't attack me tonight. You have her locked up."

"I know that. But she could have had an accomplice."

"What do you have on her that makes you so certain she was involved?"

King rubbed his eyes. "That's just it. Maybe not enough. There's the fact that she's a chemist and should understand how to get or make phosgene."

"Did you find actual phosgene? Or attempts to procure it?"

"Not yet."

Megan waited for him to continue. He seemed uncomfortable, perhaps realizing as they talked that he didn't have a strong case.

King said, "We found some incriminating stuff on her computer, mostly diary entries about her dad and how much she hates him. There were also some files containing information about her dad's former patients that gave us pause."

Megan sat up straight. "His former patients? Like what?"

"Names and phone numbers mostly."

"How many former patients?" When King didn't answer, Megan said, "She hated her

216

father, Bobby."

"Like we didn't know that." His tone dripped with sarcasm. "So?"

"So why would Becca have her dad's files?"

"Blackmail?" When Megan nodded, he said, "Blackmail whom? Her father?"

"Why not? Did you ask her why she had them?"

King nodded. The pie and alcohol had kicked in and he looked worn and cross and sleepy. "We grilled her — with her attorney present, of course. She claims she was contacting former patients in the hopes they'd sue her father."

"Sue him? For malpractice?"

"She claims he was inappropriate with patients. That he used their pain to fuel his own sense of power."

"She may not be far from the truth. There's a reason my aunt's books were chosen. I'm sure of it. You talked to Aunt Sarah. You know she believes Paul was an unethical therapist at best, maybe even a criminal."

King met Megan's gaze. "Sarah is on the list of former patients. It's another thing linking Becca to the crime. She knows Sarah through Merry. It's not that far-fetched to think she'd know about the books."

"Is Becca the one who told you phosgene matched up to a Sarah Estelle novel?"

"No. Becca never mentioned it." King hesitated. "That was Merry. Seems she's read every masterpiece Sarah has ever written."

Megan toyed with whether to tell Bobby about Merry's omission now — or wait. She decided he needed all the cards laid out in front of him so he could get a clearer sense of the big picture.

Reluctantly, Megan said, "There's something else. Merry wasn't one hundred percent honest with you about the night Paul died." Megan shared Merry's story — the overheard snippets of conversation, Becca's departure. "Now perhaps Becca's phone conversation makes more sense. At first Merry thought it was a clandestine boyfriend, but then she realized it was about Paul. But there is an alternate explanation."

"You think she was talking with one of Paul's former patients?"

"It would explain the heated argument. Some of these people don't want to be reminded of whatever brought them into trauma therapy in the first place. Perhaps Becca was trying to convince this guy to go after Paul."

Bobby's eyebrows shot up. "You think

Paul was that unethical? That he was that much of a target?" He shook his head. "You think Becca would stoop that low?"

"People see therapists when they're at their most vulnerable. Think about it. Messing with someone who is at a low point in their life is pretty despicable. And if he was sexual with Sarah, maybe he took advantage of other patients." Megan was thinking of Eloise Kent and her refusal to talk earlier that day. Her patients — children already affected by trauma — were the ultimate victims. "People see therapists for a reason. Usually not a happy one. If he was abusing patients — well, there is no statute of limitations on that type of criminal behavior."

"As usual, you make a good point. Maybe my people need to look deeper into Paul's past. If he was shaking it up with his patients — or worse — it may be motive to kill."

Megan agreed. "Just go easy on Merry. She's having a tough time of it."

"She'd be having a tougher time if I decided to throw an obstruction offense her way." He stood, wobbled, and caught himself by grabbing the table's edge.

"Whoa. I think you'd better stay here tonight. Between the Kahlua and your exhaustion, you need a good night's sleep."

Bobby smiled. "What will the neighbors think?"

"We don't have neighbors. I think you're safe."

With Bobby tucked into the guest room and Bibi fast asleep, Megan hunted for *The Killing Time* online, the book her mugger had left on the street. The police had confiscated the novel as evidence, but this was a newer Sarah Estelle novel, just published three years ago, and she was able to get an electronic format to download immediately. By midnight she was tucked in bed, reading the mystery on her laptop.

She couldn't put it down.

It wasn't simply the setting: a small Pennsylvania town.

It wasn't simply the victim: a thirty-something shop owner.

It wasn't simply the season: the winter holidays.

It was also the way the victim died: a carjacking outside her own shop.

Megan saw no parallels to Paul's death. The parallels here were much more personal. Someone was trying to scare her. Or draw a connection. Or, more likely, warn her off.

TWENTY-ONE

Friday night was supposed to be the café's Night with Santa event. Megan had Denver lined up to be a very handsome Scottish Santa, and Bibi had kindly agreed to play the role of Mrs. Claus. Alvaro had reluctantly offered to make a dessert spread straight out of *'Twas the Night Before Christmas,* including sugarplums and homemade eggnog, and Clover was anxious to play her array of Christmas tunes over the café's new stereo system. Megan found herself thinking about the Night with Santa event all Friday morning. How could she not? The scents pouring from the kitchen were a constant reminder. She was both looking forward to the distraction and dreading the festivities. Mostly Megan didn't quite feel up to a party, especially because the victim in *The Killing Time* was murdered right after a similar event.

Not the jolliest of Christmases. At least

Merry seemed better.

A phone call around eleven had proven fruitful. Merry was out of bed and showered, and while she didn't quite sound her normal haughty self, she seemed to be on the mend. Some good news, at least. Nevertheless, Aunt Sarah's books and their odd connection to the happenings in Winsome troubled Megan.

"You're singlehandedly ruining the holidays for me," Megan told her aunt over lunch Friday afternoon. They were sitting at the far end of the booth at the café, enjoying curried butternut squash soup and watching Alvaro berate Clover in the kitchen.

"Not me you need to blame. Tell King to get a move on and find this person."

Megan swallowed a spoonful of soup. "How many mysteries did you write?"

"Nineteen."

"Damn." She smiled, but she didn't mean it and Sarah wasn't fooled. "Seriously. Can you think of any link, Aunt Sarah? Any reason someone might be using your books to terrorize people in this town?"

"I'm as stumped as you." Aunt Sarah's blue eyes squinted in Alvaro's direction. "Did King have any luck with the local security cameras?"

"Not so far. But his officers have to go through a fair amount of footage. Last I heard, they were still reviewing what they had."

"You didn't see the person at all?"

"Not so much as a shadow. He came at me from behind."

Sarah's eyebrows shot up. "He?"

"Just a hunch given the force used to push me down. Truth is, could have been a man or a woman."

Sarah took her time finishing her soup. The afternoon rush had thinned, and with Clover and Emily helping at the café and store, respectively, Megan had some rare downtime. She cleared her dish and Sarah's and returned with two pieces of homemade gingerbread smothered in whipped cream.

"If I keep eating like this, I'll be able to play Santa Claus," Sarah said.

They both laughed. The sound was brittle, forced.

"How did your grandmother handle what happened last night?"

"Okay. I spared her most of the details. Focused on the book."

Sarah frowned. "You could get hurt in all of this, Megan."

"Now you sound like Denver."

"Denver is a smart man."

Megan stabbed a forkful of gingerbread, moist and richly scented. She debated how much to tell Aunt Sarah. King had made it clear every former patient on that list was still a suspect — including Megan's aunt. She didn't want to tip any hands.

Behind her, a child laughed and talked excitedly about Santa. Megan leaned in toward Sarah. "Did Becca try to contact you?"

Sarah looked surprised by the question. "Paul's daughter? No, why?"

"Just curious. But Paul did?"

Sarah nodded. "He called me when he arrived in town. Came to the house under the guise of a friendly visit. But as with everything Paul does, he couldn't maintain the façade." She rubbed her wrist absentmindedly.

"Did he hurt you?"

Sarah looked away, toward the family with the little girl. "He came on to me."

"And he hurt you."

Sarah bit her bottom lip, her bright blue eyes heavy lidded with disgust. "He pushed me up against a wall and kissed me. Or tried to kiss me." She sneered. "It was a hollow ploy to manipulate me. Make the old woman feel wanted so she'll stay quiet. He was banking on his charm being enough."

"Assaulting you doesn't sound very charming."

"It's all in the way he did things. As though he was passionate and couldn't control himself. I didn't see through it then. I did — do — now. Rejection made him angry. He grabbed my wrist, twisted. Told me I'd better stay quiet."

"Or?"

Sarah picked up her mug and stared at drops of coffee dried on the side, brown stains against light blue ceramic. Quietly, she said, "There was no 'or.' "

Sarah was an award-winning mystery writer. She knew as well as any cop that admitting to an "or" was tantamount to providing a motive. If Paul Fox had threatened her life, her livelihood, she would have reason to kill him. If there was an "or," she wasn't trusting Megan with it, a fact that gave Megan pause. Perhaps her aunt didn't trust her yet after all.

Perhaps she simply had something to hide.

Becca Fox was released from police custody later that day. Megan received a call from Bobby a little after two to let her know — and to ask that she keep her ear to the ground at the café. "People talk. Maybe you'll overhear something that will be a lead in this case."

Megan agreed. "I guess you didn't have enough to hold her?"

"She's still a person of interest, but most of it was circumstantial."

"Have you had any luck looking into Paul's former patients?"

"We're going through Becca's list, one by one. There are a lot of people on that list. It'll take some time. We're hoping to find someone who lives around here. Someone with access to Winsome."

Megan was washing pots in the kitchen. She finished rinsing the large stock pot and turned it over to dry. With a glance around, she snuck into the pantry and closed the door. "I've been thinking about Sarah's books, Bobby. I keep coming back to the same question: what relationship does the killer have to Sarah?"

"If any."

"If any, true. And what does the killer think these books show."

"He's committing crimes based on the crimes in those books. The phosgene, the attack at your car."

"Maybe." The pantry was lined with canned and dry goods. On the floor was a stool that Alvaro used to reach the highest shelves. Megan sat on the stool, relieved for a moment's rest. She'd been on her feet all day. "But what if there's more to it. What if the books aren't just reflective of what's already happened? What if the killer is playing with you, taunting you?"

"Giving us clues."

"Yes. Exactly."

"You asked about the killer's relationship with Sarah, Megan. What if there is one? What if the killer knows something we don't about your aunt?"

"Or is obsessed with her for a reason we haven't figured out."

"Right." King was quiet for a moment. Megan heard a door open, the sound of hushed voices. Soon he was back on the line. "Forensics came back positive for phosgene, Megan. So we know that much for sure. What we don't know is where it came from."

"You haven't found a source?"

"Nothing tying Becca — or anyone — to an industrial amount of the chemical."

Something clicked and Megan sat forward on the stool, her mind racing. "Did you know paint thinner can turn into phosgene gas when heated? I saw that back when I was researching phosgene."

"Paint thinner? So? What does that mean?"

"It means whoever killed Paul didn't necessarily have to have access to large amounts of industrial phosgene. They could have produced it on their own."

"Our expert effectively said the same thing — that the poison can be manufactured on site. He didn't elaborate though." A moment of silence. "So paint thinner, huh? That sure expands the number of possible suspects. Anyone could have done it."

Megan rubbed the tension from her neck with hard, biting strokes. "If by anybody you mean someone with some basic knowledge of chemistry, a beef against Paul Fox, and a penchant for crime fiction, yes, we could be looking for anybody."

King said something that sounded like "shit."

"There's a bright side, Bobby."

"Oh, yeah, Megan? I'm not seeing lemonade being made out of these lemons."

"Whoever your killer is wants to keep playing this game. Killing Paul wasn't enough. I think whoever did it wants credit for the kill. Hence the book last night."

King snorted. "So he or she will keep going. How is that a bright side?"

Megan stood, stretching. "Because sooner or later your killer will get cocky and show their hand. And that's when *you'll* swoop in for the kill."

The more Megan considered the book angle, the more she believed she was right. While scrubbing the kitchen for that night's event, she found herself thinking about Aunt Sarah's novels, especially *To Kill Again.* What about that novel had spoken to the murderer? The means of death? The setting? Or something about the character, plot, theme? The only real similarities that stood out were the phosgene, the locked room, the duct tape.

The desire for revenge.

Megan headed back to her office, where she booted up the ancient computer she used to order stock for the store, and searched the rest of Sarah's novels. Suspicions confirmed, Megan called King back. He didn't answer his cell, but rang her back twenty minutes later.

"Check the libraries, Bobby. See if anyone has been requesting Sarah's books."

"Good idea. We're checking the local libraries and local bookstores."

"*To Kill Again* is out of print. It would be a special order, especially for a bookstore."

"You don't think whoever did this had their own copy?" King sounded out of breath. "An old time fan?"

Like Merry. "Maybe. Or maybe someone set the murder up to mirror what happened in the book." Megan paused, realizing this next statement would sound goofy to someone like Bobby. "There are two things that bind the two books together — *To Kill Again* and *The Killing Time.*"

"For one, the word 'kill' in the title."

"Yep, that's number one. I did a quick search of Sarah's books. Four titles contain the word kill. In addition to the two we know about, there are *Love Kills* and *The Killing Spree.*"

"That last one isn't promising."

"Neither of them are." Megan waited until Bobby caught his breath. He seemed to be outside, moving quickly. When his raspiness subsided, she said, "The second thing that binds the two books is the motive. In each of these novels, the killer murders out of a need for vengeance."

"So we have two books with the word 'kill' and both focus on getting revenge?"

"Yes."

"And let me guess. The other two books — *Killing Spree* and the other one — they also deal with revenge."

"Yes."

King sighed. "What a twisted way of seeing the world. Okay, so we need to read the other two books."

"On it already. I ordered one, and I'm trying to find the other. I'm going to have Bibi read them too. She has the time and she's an avid fiction reader."

"An avid fiction reader," King repeated. "They never mentioned that as a necessary skill at the police academy."

Megan laughed. "I don't imagine they did."

"So libraries, bookstores, and reading those two books. What else?"

"If we're right about the motive — revenge — then it helps narrow the scope of your investigation. Someone wanted to get back at Paul Fox for something. Figure out that something and you have your killer."

"You make it sound easy."

There was a knock at the office door. "Megs? Santa's here," came Denver's deep voice.

"I have to go, Bobby. Let me know what you find and I'll report on these books."

"Okay." King sounded skeptical. "But Paul sounded like a pretty awful guy. The number of people seeking revenge could be quite large."

"This killer has a showman streak. This is no quiet revenge killer. Think like him, Bobby. What would he do next?"

"*Killing Spree,* huh?" Bobby's voice sounded tight. "I don't like this at all."

TWENTY-TWO

Denver made a fine Santa. A little on the thin side, perhaps. And with a recognizable accent that had all but the youngest of the café visitors saying "Is that Dr. Finn?" But he had fun doing it, and Megan had fun watching him with Winsome's children. He was funny but gentle, firm but caring. And everyone walked away from his lap with a package of Alvaro's "Mrs. Claus" cookies and a dog or cat treat for any pets at home.

"You shouldn't be asking me to do this next year," Denver said afterwards, when he was no longer incognito and could enjoy a café mocha and a piece of gingerbread with the rest of Winsome's residents. "I don't think the kids appreciated a Santa who called them 'laddie' and 'lassie.' "

"You were wonderful." Megan kissed him on the cheek. "And very patient. I don't think I could be that patient, especially when Millie Donovan's son bit you on the shoulder."

"What's a little bite when you're wearing a thick layer of Santa suit? And as for patience, once you've sat up all night waiting for a cow to birth one calf, waiting for Ben Donovan to end his endless list of wants is nothing."

"Dr. Finn," a voice behind them said. They were at the café counter, near Clover and the eggnog, and Roger Becker was returning for a refill. "Nicely done."

"Thank you, Roger. It's my new calling."

Roger ladled more eggnog into his cup. Megan watched as he topped it off with a nip of brandy from a flask in his pocket. He returned the flask to its hiding place and joined Megan and Denver by the counter, seemingly unaware that he'd been caught.

"Where's Eloise tonight?" Roger asked Denver.

"She couldn't make it, I guess. You know my aunt. She's not always up for social engagements."

"True, true. Come to think of it, she wasn't at the Historical Society dinner either." Becker turned to Megan. "And how about Merry? I don't see her here. Were you able to check in with her?"

"I did, Roger. She seemed a little out of it, but okay. She promised she'd get herself

234

out of bed and back to her routine and she has."

Becker frowned. "Then I would have thought she'd come tonight."

"Don't forget, Becca was released today. She may be spending some time with her niece."

Becker brightened. "You're right. I'm sure she's busy with Becca, poor thing." He squinted, the expression on his long face conspiratorial. "I don't believe for a moment that her perfumes are love potions. Fantasy, at best. That girl has . . . issues. I applaud Merry for helping her."

"Helping her in what way?" Denver asked casually.

"Why, every way. It was Merry who gave her the money for The Love Chemist. Silly idea, if you ask me, but Merry wanted Becca to have something of her own. And then bringing her here to jumpstart the business. And the open house. And of course, the emotional support over the years."

Denver took a long sip of mocha, looking at Roger over the rim. "I never heard her mention her niece until recently. You, Megan?"

Megan shook her head. "No. As a matter of fact, I didn't know Merry had a niece until I picked her up on the side of the road."

Roger looked from one to the other, trying to determine, Megan figured, whether they were somehow insulting Merry. Seeming to decide they were not, his face relaxed. "You don't remember the family because you'd already left for college when the Foxes arrived, Megan. And they were here only a few short years. Not even two, I don't think. This is the first time Becca and Luke visited Winsome since."

Roger glanced at Denver. "And you would never have had the opportunity to meet the kids. But Eloise knew them. My wife, Anita, knew Merry's sister quite well. They were close friends."

Megan was about to respond when the older man slammed a hand down on the table, surprising them. "Speak of the devil!"

Megan and Denver looked up at the same time. They saw Becca and Merry enter the café. Each wore a red coat over jeans. Becca, her hair tamed into a pair of braided pigtails, looked like a little girl. Merry, her hair washed but still unkempt, looked like she'd aged a decade.

Roger smiled. "Thank goodness she's back up and around. You have no idea how much Merry does for the Historical Society,

Megan. She's a one-person action committee."

As he walked away, Denver leaned in to whisper in Megan's ear. "Merry's a one-person judge, jury, newspaper . . . you name it."

Megan was swallowing a giggle when she saw Becca making her way in their direction.

"If you're nice to me," Denver whispered to Megan, his facial hair tickling her ear. "I'll let you sit on Santa's lap."

Megan play swatted him and pulled away, sitting up straight when Becca arrived.

"You've been wearing the pheromones, I see," Becca said. She gave Denver an appraising glance. "Are they working?"

Megan did have the perfume on. She liked the floral scent. "Yeah, Denver, what do you think? Is it working?"

Denver glanced from Becca to Megan and back again. "I think this is a loaded question and I can only get myself into trouble. The truth is, I always find Ms. Sawyer a pleasant lady to be around, whether she smells like flowers, as she does now, or goat, as she does on occasion." His dimpled face barely held back a grin.

Becca seemed not to know how to take this, so Megan said quickly, "It's working,

Becca. Clearly the love potion is working."

Denver kissed Megan on the cheek. "Aye, it's working." To Becca, "Ta, lassie. The men of Winsome are most grateful." The look he threw Megan as he walked away said *this one is all yours.*

Megan watched Denver head over to Bibi, who was holding court in front of Mona Desai and Geraldine Keller, the women who owned the local sewing shop. All female eyes followed his progress, but the vet seemed oblivious to their attention — or how sexy he looked in his thermal shirt, his hair messed and curled from the Santa wig.

"He's a good-looking man," Becca said. She, too, was watching Denver, who was now sitting with Bibi, who gazed at him with affection. Bibi had dabbed on some of the pheromone perfume too, although it seemed to be working in reverse. "You're lucky."

Megan turned her full attention to the younger woman. "How are you, Becca? I know it's been a rough few days. Are you getting along?"

"I'm mostly embarrassed."

"There's no need to be."

The corners of Becca's mouth turned up on the ends, but her eyes remained hooded in sadness. "Oh, I disagree." She pushed a stray hair behind her ear, her gaze wandering to Merry, who was standing by the store counter talking with Clover. "I got you involved in this mess."

"Who says I'm involved?"

"My brother. He said you came by. You were asking questions about my father."

"Did he also tell you that I was there to check on your aunt? That she seemed to be in some sort of funk?"

Becca nodded. "He said you were worried about Aunt Merry."

Megan mulled over her next words. She decided to be direct. "What happened, Becca? You came smashing into our house claiming that someone was following you, that someone was after you. You seemed genuinely terrified."

Becca hung her head. "I'm sorry."

"What happened?"

Becca looked up. Again her eyes searched for Merry. "I don't know. I remember reading at the house — research for my pheromones. Next thing I know, I heard a knock at the door. The police were there. And then . . . something else. Someone else." She probed Megan's eyes for understanding. "I had this overwhelming need to escape to somewhere safe. I grabbed Aunt Merry's keys and ended up at your place."

She shrugged. "I guess it's the first place I thought of." Becca shook her head. "I wasn't thinking straight."

"I understand the police confiscated your computer. That you had lists of your dad's patients on it."

Becca squirmed on her stool. "So?"

"So, why did you need that?"

"I was hoping they would sue my dad. Come forward with their allegations of abuse."

"What makes you think they had something to come forward with?"

"How do you know a dog barks, a duck quacks? Experience." She stood suddenly, pigtails swinging. "I promised Aunt Merry I would mingle. Make sure people knew I was fine. That the business is fine." She marched away, a little girl in a grown woman's shell.

Cleaning up took almost two hours, mostly because the small group that stayed behind to clean drank the rest of the eggnog and chatted while working, which slowed them down. Clay had joined them around eight, and he and Denver were doing the brunt of the bulky work: tucking away folding tables and chairs, putting shelves back in place, moving Santa's heavy wooden chair. Clover and Megan were reorganizing the storefront while Alvaro and Bibi cleaned up the kitchen. Despite everything, it had been a pleasure to see the people of Winsome come together for a warm evening of camaraderie. For Megan, it was even nicer to spend the rest of Friday night with this group, her makeshift family.

"Alvaro, those were the best sugarplums I've ever tasted," Clover said.

"You've never had sugarplums," Clay said. He popped a chocolate chip cookie into his mouth and grinned. "Now the chocolate chips, on the other hand. I've had many in my life, but none like these."

Megan could see Alvaro's mouth turn down from her vantage point at the counter. She could also see the pleased twinkle in his eye.

"And how about Roger Becker?" Clover said. "He and Anita were the life of the party. Once Merry arrived."

"He'd been worried about her," Megan said. "She hasn't been herself." Megan didn't say "since Paul died," but she knew she didn't have to.

"I learned something interesting tonight," Bibi said. She was scrubbing the last of the baking pans and she put it down to come out into the front of the store. "Blanche had threatened to divorce Paul the month before

241

she died."

Megan looked at her sharply. "Really? Who said that?"

"Anita and Roger Becker. Anita remained friends with Blanche even after the Fox family left town. Roger said their marriage was a troubled one, which we knew. Paul was unfaithful. There were some incidents, they moved a lot. I guess Blanche had enough."

No one, not Becca, Luke, or Merry, had mentioned divorce. Did it matter? Megan wasn't sure.

"There's more," Bibi said. She lowered herself onto one of the café chairs and fanned herself with a brochure that someone had left on the table. "Becker also said Paul was carrying on with a woman who lived near him. A woman named Sherry Lynn Booker."

"Should we know of her?" Clover asked.

"No, but according to Roger, she lives in northern New Jersey." Bibi threw Megan a probing glance. "Not far from here. And there's more."

"Bibi." Megan sighed. "Just tell us."

"Sherry Lynn had been Blanche's best friend. Blanche found out just weeks before she died that Sherry Lynn had betrayed her."

"That's horrible!" Clover smacked a hand

242

over her mouth. "Talk about backstabbing."

"That is pretty awful," Megan said. "I wonder if Becca knew."

"So this Sherry Lynn would have known something about the family dynamics," Denver said. "Insight into how Becca was as a child, whether her accounts of Paul's behavior were accurate."

"And maybe information about how Blanche died," Megan added. "Or another suspect." She thought about this. If they were looking for clues about Paul, who better to ask than his mistress — and his wife's former BFF. "Who wants to take a road trip to New Jersey this weekend?"

"I will," Bibi said. She tilted her head to the side. "Who is more likely to be a trustworthy person, someone you want to spill your guts to, than a little old lady?" she asked with a devious smile.

"Yeah, a little old lady who knows how to wield a gun," Clay said.

"Exactly." Bibi clapped. "Bonnie Birch, undercover agent. Tell Sarah to put *that* in one of her novels."

TWENTY-THREE

Sherry Lynn Booker lived on a quiet street corner on the edge of Breakwater, New Jersey, a small blue-collar town about an hour west of New York City. Her house was a faded green one-story with freshly painted white trim. A new Honda Accord sat in the driveway. Two gray tabbies perched on the porch, one on a weathered white wicker armchair, the other on a matching end table. The cats watched Megan and Bibi with mild curiosity.

"You know the drill," Bibi said. "I'm Becca's aunt and I'm worried about her. You're her cousin. We're trying to find out where Paul is."

"You really want to lie?"

"I want to find who killed Paul before someone else in Winsome dies," Bibi said. "I want to help Merry before she comes looking for eggs one more time and I kill her." She straightened her elastic waist beige skirt. "God will forgive the lie." She glanced at Megan. "Do I look the part?"

Bibi was wearing the beige skirt, an oversized white blouse tied at the neck with a bow, knee-highs, the elastic bands showing right beneath the skirt hem, and thick-soled walking shoes her podiatrist had prescribed two years ago that she'd never worn.

"I'd say you look the part," Megan said, holding back a smile. Bibi pulled a cane out of the truck and Megan shook her head. "Going all out on this one?"

"Just having some fun. It's for a cause."

As they climbed the three steps to the door, the cats scattered. Megan was about to raise her hand to the doorbell when the front door flew open. A woman stood before them, her hand held to her mouth. She looked momentarily hopeful before her face fell.

"Yes?"

"I'm looking for Sherry Lynn Booker. Can you tell me if I have the right house?"

The woman stared at her, then at Bibi. "What do you want?" Sultry voice, low and mellow, with just a hint of Southern accent. She had long, full, dyed-blonde hair, a set of fake double Ds, and wore enough gold to support a developing nation. Her heavily lined eyes were red, and her skin looked mottled from crying, something even thick pancake makeup couldn't hide. "Why are you here?"

Bibi had made it up the steps. She leaned on her cane, breathing hard. Or pretending to. "Are you Sherry Lynn?"

"Yes —"

Bibi moved forward, toward the door. "I sure could use a glass of juice or something sweet. Maybe some maple syrup if you don't have juice? It's my hypoglycemia. You know how that is, don't you?" Bibi waved the cane toward the interior of the house. "I'm Becca's aunt. Well, more of a great aunt. You know Meredith? Blanche's sister? Of course you do."

Bibi kept moving slowly, using that cane to clear away Sherry Lynn's resistance. Sherry Lynn moved backwards and let them in.

"I wasn't expecting company," she said.

"Oh, we won't stay. Just a glass of juice and then maybe you can help us. You see, we're looking for Paul."

At the mention of Paul's name, Sherry Lynn stopped moving. Not just her legs, her entire body. Her face froze mid-syllable, her hand froze mid-air, even her fingers froze mid-wave.

"Dear, are you okay?" Bibi asked.

"I'm fine," she said finally. "Y'all are here about Paul?"

Bibi nodded. "We're worried about his daughter, Becca. We know you were close friends with Blanche, God bless her soul. We thought maybe you could help us."

Sherry Lynn nodded absently, her mind clearly elsewhere. "Please. Sit. I'll get you that juice."

The interior of the house was clean and cluttered with bric-a-brac. It was the home of a woman with banal taste, a midsize budget, and the desire to impress. Lots of shiny brass, lots of cut glass, lots of knock-off knick-knacks. Megan sat on a brown micro suede couch. Bibi lowered herself down on an upholstered beige armchair. She put the cane in front of her, between her legs, and leaned on it, displaying her knee highs, which had now rolled down to her ankles.

"Laying it on a little thick," Megan hissed.

Bibi pretended not to hear her. "Hummels," she said pointing to a cherry wood curio cabinet. "They're not cheap."

"Those aren't real. You just forgot your glasses."

Bibi gave Megan an exasperated look that morphed into a gracious smile when Sherry Lynn reentered the room.

"Here's your juice." Sherry Lynn handed Bibi a glass of red liquid. "No orange juice, but that's sweetened cranberry. I hope that will do."

"Thank you, dear."

"I brought you some ice water," she said to Megan, handing her a tall glass.

Megan thanked her. "We'll only take a minute of your time. As my aunt said, we're worried about Becca. It's our hope you can give us some information that might give Becca some peace."

"You want to know where her father is."

"Yes." Bibi smiled warmly. "If you know."

Sherry Lynn's eyes narrowed. "I don't know. I haven't seen him in weeks."

"Weeks?"

Sherry Lynn nodded. "He took off for a business trip. He was very secretive about the whole thing. I thought for sure I would hear from him, but he hasn't returned my calls. Nothing." A moan escaped her. "It's been twenty-six days."

"There, there." Bibi reached over and patted Sherry Lynn on the back. "You and Paul are in a relationship." It was a statement, not a question.

The woman nodded. "We've been together since . . . since after Blanche passed away."

Bibi gave Megan a look; Megan matched

248

it with a warning look of her own. Don't push or confront, it said.

Bibi ignored her. "I heard Blanche thought you and Paul had started a relationship before . . . perhaps while they were married."

"She wanted a divorce." When Bibi didn't say anything — and Megan had to hand it to her grandmother, she managed to keep her expression blank — Sherry Lynn continued as though the thoughts had been building without release for some time. "They had an awful marriage. Awful. Paul's a strong man. Virile, smart. A visionary. Blanche didn't see that. She didn't see his potential."

Bibi nodded. "He had trouble with his career?"

"Only because of her!" Sherry Lynn shot forward. "I'm sorry to yell, but she never believed in him. She emasculated him by doubting him, making him doubt himself."

Megan said, "You were her friend, Sherry Lynn. Surely she shared her version of things?"

Sherry Lynn answered Megan with a bewildered stare. "I guess. But Blanche was depressed so much of the time. She often didn't have the energy for me or him. They hadn't had sex in over two years. Two

249

years." Sherry Lynn's eyes begged for acceptance, some sign of understanding. "She didn't have the energy for me either. That's how we got together. I guess both of us felt rejected."

"Is that what he told you?" Megan asked. "That Blanche had rejected him?"

"What would you call it when a wife ignores you? Refuses to sleep in the same bed, much less make love? Paul felt rejected."

"Becca, my niece, keeps insisting Paul hurt her mother. Could there be truth to that, Sherry Lynn?"

"Becca has been saying that since Blanche died."

"You don't believe it?"

Sherry Lynn's eyes shifted to the window. "No, of course not."

Bibi pushed herself up using her cane. "Well, if you see Paul, tell him to contact his daughter."

"I thought Becca hated her father. Becca and he fought since I can remember. But I'm sure you know that."

"Becca says her father was emotionally abusive." Megan kept her tone light, as though she didn't quite believe that.

Sherry Lynn looked at her sharply. "Of course he wasn't."

"We just want Becca to reconcile with Paul, but that can't happen if we can't find him." Bibi gave her a knowing look. "She needs peace in her life. Blanche's sister, Merry, wants that too."

Sherry Lynn said, "Don't we all?"

As they headed back outside, Megan said to Sherry Lynn, "So Paul is on a business trip?

Sherry Lynn nodded. "He's meeting with investors. People who could put money into a new company he's supporting."

"We heard he'd recently switched from private psychology practice to investment consulting." Megan watched as Sherry Lynn's eyes darkened. Megan added, "Do you know why he changed course?"

"Tired of dealing with whiny patients and their whiny parents? Counseling can be a draining occupation. He'll make more in the financial industry."

"And what exactly does he do?" Bibi asked. "It sounds fascinating."

"Stuff. Match businesses with investors. That's all I know." Sherry Lynn shrugged and smiled coquettishly — the epitome of the little woman who didn't need to know what her man was up to. "You know, businessman stuff."

"Oh, it's best to mind your business when

251

it comes to that hard stuff, right?" Bibi's gaze was warm. "And what do you do, dear?"

"I'm a bookkeeper."

"Is that how you met Blanche?"

Sherry Lynn smiled. "Blanche never worked outside the home once Paul was established in his career. Paul had strong feelings about that. He still does. When we marry, I'll probably quit too. Can't wait."

Megan did her best to keep her eyes from rolling into the back of her head at the tone of Sherry Lynn's voice, and her misplaced faith in a dead man. "How did you meet Blanche?"

By now they were back on the porch. It was a sunny day, and the sun was melting the mounds of dirty snow that had collected in piles along Sherry Lynn's street.

"We took a class together. It was a silly class about home repair. As a single woman, I thought maybe I'd meet someone there." She shrugged. "At worst, I'd learn how to fix my leaky faucet. Which I did learn, by the way. I'm pretty handy around the house."

Bibi frowned. "And what about Blanche? That sounds like a funny class for her to take."

"Paul thought she was taking a cooking

252

class. When I finally told him the truth last year, boy did he get angry. I don't think I've ever seen him so mad."

"Then why did she take it?" Megan was curious.

"Money. Paul made her ask for money — every cent, to hear her tell it. If something broke and she could fix it herself, she didn't have to bother him. Or she could fix it herself and tuck the funds away. She never admitted to doing that, but that's what I think she did. Lied and then kept the money."

Bibi looked around the front entry. "You have a lot of beautiful things here. Is that how he is with you, Sherry Lynn?" Bibi asked. "Frugal?"

Sherry Lynn blushed. "He buys me presents all the time." She held out her arms, shaking the gold bangles. "I think Blanche must have had a money problem. He was helping her. She needed the help in order to learn to be disciplined."

"You think that was it?" Bibi asked sweetly. "It was her fault?"

"I'm certain." Sherry Lynn's voice had gotten an octave higher.

Bibi studied her. Then she turned to Megan. "Can you get the truck warmed up, dear? These old legs can't take the cold anymore."

Megan knew a hint when she heard it. Or more like an order. She nodded her agreement and went out to start the truck.

"So what did you say to her?"

Bibi was back in the truck, and they were pulling away from the curb. Sherry Lynn was standing on the porch, watching them leave.

"I told her that men don't change their feathers. If a man is mean to one woman, he will be mean to the next."

"Just like that? You told her that nicely?"

"I may have told her not to be a fool."

That sounded more like Bibi. "But Paul's dead."

"With women like her, there will always be another Paul."

True. Megan hit the gas and drove through an intersection just as the light was turning yellow. "Bibi," she said, "do you think Sherry Lynn could have had something to do with Paul's murder?"

"I don't know."

"She acted as though she didn't know about Paul's death. The tears and all."

"Quite the act." Bibi frowned. "A pretty good cover up if you were the killer."

"But then she could have known we were lying."

"Or she may have thought we didn't know he was dead. I wouldn't cross her off our list. We need more information. Like who will inherit Paul's estate?"

Megan laughed. Her grandmother was pretty good at this. "You did well."

"Think Angela Fletcher would be proud?"

"If she were a real person, Bibi, I think she would be very proud."

TWENTY-FOUR

When they got back to Winsome early Saturday evening, Megan had to feed the goats and the chickens. She let Sadie and Gunther out and watched them chase each other around the yard, enjoying the thick snow that blanketed the hillside. With his heavy white coat and undercoat, Gunther, a Polish Tatra Sheepdog, was made for the winter weather. Sadie, a rescue who'd long ago rescued Megan, looked like a cross between a Golden, a Collie, and a hamster. She wasn't quite as fond of the cold and soon asked to go inside.

So Gunther made the rounds with Megan. He enjoyed the goats almost as much as he enjoyed his adopted sister, and he allowed them to nibble his collar and butt him in the chest. Megan could have watched them play all night. But she had work to do — year-end accounting and internet holiday shopping. She called Gunther and headed back to the farmhouse.

She found Bobby King sitting on the porch step, waiting for her.

"People are actually going to talk, Bobby. They're going to think *I'm* under suspicion."

"What makes you so sure you're not?"

"The amount of pie you've eaten in our kitchen. Way I see it, it looks pretty bad if you're taking food from a suspect."

Bobby smiled. "Can I come in?"

"Of course. Bibi's inside. You could have gone in."

"I saw you up by the barn. I figured I'd take a minute to clear my head."

"The farm does that — helps you clear your head." Megan smiled. "I was going to call you anyway."

Bibi was in the kitchen kneading bread dough. She'd changed out of her "disguise" and was wearing jeans and a gray "Winsome Warriors" sweatshirt. She nodded when she saw King. "There's apple pie in the refrigerator, Bobby. Megan can heat you up a piece if you want."

"Bonnie, I'm getting fat." He rubbed his stomach. "Clover put me on a diet."

Bibi shook her head. "You're letting that girl push you around, Robert King." She slammed the dough onto her marble slab and pummeled it with her small fist. "You're getting soft."

"Yeah, well. I like this one. I don't want her to run away because I'm letting myself go."

"I'm sure she knows what she has in you." Bibi punched the dough into a round ball and placed it back in the bowl. She laid a cotton dishtowel over the bowl.

"You missed Bibi's big performance today," Megan said.

"What was that?"

"Come in the living room. I'll fill you in, and you can tell me what you wanted to say."

In Bibi's parlor, Bobby sat on the couch. Megan stood by the fireplace, her back against the mantle.

"What were you and your grandmother up to today? I looked for you at the café. Alvaro said you had an errand in New Jersey."

Megan explained their road trip to King. "Bibi was wonderful. I don't think I could have gotten Sherry Lynn to open up at all on my own." When King's eyes darkened, she added, "We didn't interfere with police work. We didn't tell her Paul was dead — didn't even mention Winsome."

"You should have told me you were going."

"I figured you have your hands full. We didn't even know if what Roger told us was true."

"That was up to me to decide."

He was right, and Megan said so. "In the future I will."

Megan's refusal to argue seemed to deflate the police chief. He placed one foot over his knee and his hands behind his head. "So what did you learn?"

"For one, Paul was unfaithful. Roger gave us Sherry Lynn's name and town and we found the address on our own."

"What did you learn from Sherry Lynn, Megan? Anything else of note?"

"Much of it was stuff we knew already. Blanche and Paul had a rocky marriage. In fact, Blanche had been planning to file for a divorce right before she died."

King put his arms down. "That's news."

Megan nodded. "No sex for two years, according to Sherry Lynn. And Blanche — again, according to Sherry Lynn — emasculated Paul. Made him feel unworthy."

"Hurt his male ego? Interesting, perhaps, but I'm not sure that provides any new insights."

"What was interesting was hearing her take on the family. She denied flat out that Becca was emotionally abused, blamed

Blanche for the marital problems, even found a way to dismiss Paul's cheapness."

"Cheapness?"

"Apparently Paul ruled the bank accounts as well. Made Blanche ask for household money. Sherry Lynn told us that she met Blanche during a class. A *home improvement* class."

"So?"

"So Blanche supposedly died when there was a gas leak. A mechanical mistake, one that doesn't happen often in this age of scented gas and detectors. According to Sherry Lynn, Blanche was quite handy. She knew how to fix things well enough that she didn't need to hire contractors, which meant she didn't need to ask Paul for money." Megan met King's gaze. "Does that sound like a woman who would miss a gas leak?"

"You think the fact that she was handy means Paul murdered her? That Becca is right?" King's eyes squinted with doubt. "Sounds like a stretch."

Megan sat on Bibi's recliner. She tucked her legs under her and stared at the police chief, her emotions roiling. What did she think? What did she believe at this point? "I think Paul and Blanche had a terrible marriage. I think Paul was a sadistic ass who played on people's emotions and made a lot of enemies. But to hear Sherry Lynn talk, Paul was a genius, a visionary, a misunderstood man." Megan shook her head. "Becca hated him, his son was close to him. Merry thought he was an upstanding gentleman, a good addition to the family. Eloise Kent can't even talk about him — and her distaste for the man is palpable. My Aunt Sarah? Well, you can ask her yourself. You'll get no kind words there."

"None of that means he killed his wife."

"He controlled Blanche's every move. What she could do, what classes she could take, the money she had. How do you think he would react when he learned she was leaving her, Bobby? I think he wanted to make sure she couldn't reject him yet again."

Bobby put his head back against the couch. "Even if he did kill his wife, what does that have to do with recent events?"

"Revenge."

"Are we back to Becca then?"

"I don't know. And that's the truth. I just don't know."

King nodded. "I don't know either." He studied Megan for a moment, then turned his attention to the afghan Bibi was working on. It sat in a basket atop yarn and Bibi's knitting needles. "I came to see you about something else. My officers watched the security tapes from the night you got attacked. They saw the person who attacked you."

Megan's eyes widened. "And?"

"Well, let me back up. We saw your attacker's body. Their face was hidden by a hoodie and every attempt by our experts to hone in on some physical characteristic was thwarted by that piece of clothing and grainy photography. All I can say for certain is that whoever slammed you into that truck was wearing black from head to toe."

"Surely you saw something? Body shape? A piece of jewelry?"

"I'm afraid not. It was dark. We have a police artist doing sketches to try and get a general sense of build, but I don't think there's much there."

"You came just to tell me that?" Megan waited. She knew Bobby King would not have wasted a trip to tell her the news was no news.

"We did see something else, Megan." Bobby glanced toward the parlor's French doors. Almost instinctively, it seemed, he raised a hand as though to ward off the implications of what he was going to tell her. "Whoever your attacker was, he or she had been watching the store for days."

"What do you mean?"

"The footage showed the same black-clad figure standing in the shadows between your business and the alley. Night after night. Just watching the shop, watching whoever was closing up."

Alarm bells were ringing in Megan's head. Her pulse raced — for her staff's safety as much as her own. "You're saying we're being stalked?"

"I'm saying someone's been watching you. Probably the same someone who attacked you."

They sat across from one another in silence. It was Megan who broke the spell. "What are we going to do?"

"I've assigned an officer to patrol the area. If he sees someone who meets this description, he'll pick him up. If he sees anyone just hanging around the store, he'll stop them."

Megan nodded. What else could they do? "I need to tell my staff. Maybe institute a buddy system for now."

"That's probably a good idea."

Megan refused to give voice to her next thought: if they had a stalker at the store, did they have one at the farm too?

"You have the dogs," King said as though

reading her mind. "And I'd make sure Bibi isn't coming and going alone after dark. Just in case."

Megan nodded, swallowing a groan. They'd both been down this road before.

Megan couldn't sleep again that night. She cracked open a window hoping some cold air would cool the demons holding court in her head, but that didn't work. Even Sadie's rhythmic breathing wasn't enough. Finally, worn out from worry, she turned on her laptop and began reading her latest Sarah Estelle novel, *Love Kills.* This book she'd read before, years ago. She found herself instantly pulled into Detective Margaret Lewis's world.

At 3:26, Megan closed her computer, too tired to read the last fifty pages. No matter. She remembered how this book ended. The motive was indeed revenge, but not by a jilted lover, as the name might imply, but by a teenage son. A son who finds out his father had multiple wives. A son who finds out his father is cheating on his mother and had been for years. The murder weapon? A shovel. It was a terrifying plot, one that would echo in the head of any parent. Despite Megan's now heavy eyelids, she still couldn't sleep.

Becca Fox. A girl with a troubled past who hated her father. Luke Fox, the favorite child. Paul Fox. A terrible husband. A terrible father. An unethical therapist. A killer?

No one would be surprised if Becca sought revenge. Only she was locked up when Megan was attacked. Just as Megan drifted off to sleep, her mind latched on to Merry's story of the night Paul was murdered. Becca, having a heated conversation on the phone. Becca, meeting a man under the cloak of night.

Could it have been Becca all along? *Could* Becca be working with an accomplice as King originally thought?

Megan's final image before sleep was of Becca Fox sitting on her kitchen floor, head in her hands, a deranged glow burning in her intelligent eyes.

Denver's words came back to her: "Bees that hae honey in their mouths, hae stings in their tails." Perhaps Becca's sweet, open attitude hid something much darker.

TWENTY-FIVE

Megan announced the shop's new protocol the next morning before the store and café opened, while Alvaro was prepping for the morning church crowd and Clover was assisting him.

Both of her employees eyed her as though she were daft.

"Buddy system?" Alvaro sneered. "I served my country. I'll be fine."

"Bobby told me to be careful already. I have pepper spray. I'll carry that with me."

Megan didn't feel particularly comforted by either response.

Brian Porter had ridden with her to the café that morning. Brian was Megan's farm hand. He worked part-time in the winter and full-time in the summer, and his sullen attitude masked a strong work ethic and an even stronger back. It was Clay's day off, and Alvaro had requested potatoes, onions, eggs, and other food from the farm's stores.

Brian, who'd been looking for extra hours, had agreed to go through the vegetables remaining in the root cellar and Cool Bot and help Megan carry them in. Now he listened to the conversation with a stony glare on his young James Dean face.

He remained stormy silent.

"What's wrong?" Megan asked once they were back in the truck. "You seem especially upset by what I told Alvaro and Clover. There's no need to worry. I just want them to take precautions.

Light flurries were falling from the heavy gray sky. Megan put on her wipers and turned to Porter. "Well?"

"I saw someone here. I didn't think anything of it at the time. Just some stupid kid, at least that's what I figured." Porter's jaw clenched. A former soldier, Brian had anger management issues, ones he'd self-medicated for years with copious amounts of alcohol. He was clean now, but Megan worried about his temper — and about a relapse. "I didn't say anything because I didn't think it was anything."

"When was this?"

"A few days ago. Looked like a guy to me, but I couldn't tell. It was dark, person was wearing all black. Face was covered by a hoodie." Porter looked out the window. His profile, like his body, was lean and slightly grizzled for his age. "I was driving through town with Sarge. Sarge didn't even growl. I thought nothing of it at the time. Now —"

"The truth is, if you had mentioned it to me or even the police, it would have been dismissed as irrelevant."

"Why is it relevant now? Paul's murder?"

"That, and —" Megan hesitated. She never quite knew how Brian would react to news, especially news that involved people he cared about. And he had come to care about her and Bibi, a fact he often tried to hide. "I was attacked outside the store."

Porter's neck snapped around. "By whom?"

"We don't know. Someone in all black."

"Damn." Porter punched one hand with the fist of the other. "Damn, damn, damn, Megan. I'm sorry. I should have said something."

Megan turned down Fine Road toward Merry's nursery. Bibi wanted another wreath for the barn door, and they needed some supplies for the greenhouses and hoop houses.

She said, "I wasn't hurt. There is no need to apologize. I never saw the person coming, so honestly, even if you had said something we would have thought nothing of it.

But now we know."

But Porter had crossed over some surly threshold. He brooded for the next few minutes. Finally, tired of the silence, Megan touched his arm.

"It's not your fault, Brian. But if you see anything else, tell us. And maybe you could drive by the farm now and again to check on Bibi."

That seemed to calm him — the thought of something to do, some way to help. "Did your friend ever contact you?" he asked, his voice a tad lighter.

"My friend?" Megan glanced at him. "What friend?"

"I ran into a friend of yours at Otto's Brew Pub. Tall guy, dark hair. We started talking, I told him where I worked, and he lit up. Said he'd been hoping to reconnect with you."

"How old was he?"

Porter shrugged. "Maybe late thirties, early forties." When Megan didn't say anything else, Porter said, "That wasn't your friend, was it?"

"I don't know. No one has contacted me."

"Unless the guy I met was the guy who's stalking the café."

Megan had been thinking the same thing. "Could you describe him to Bobby's police artist? He may not be anyone relevant to this case, Brian. But it may also be a breakthrough. Call King, please? For me?"

Brian stared straight ahead, his jaw set, his mouth a tight, angry line. "Yeah, of course."

"You would have had no way of knowing."

Porter didn't respond. The fists clenched in his lap did that for him.

Merry's nursery was closed. Normally she opened from nine to two on Sundays, and during the holidays she typically opened the doors earlier and stayed open even later. It was 9:17 and the doors were locked, the parking lot empty.

"That's odd," Megan said. She noticed a piece of paper taped to the double glass doors. "Brian, would you mind hopping out to see what the sign says?"

Brian was back a few seconds later. "It just says 'Closed Sunday.' "

Merry promised to get her butt out of bed, Megan thought. But perhaps a promise wasn't enough to overcome whatever emotions Merry was battling.

"One more errand?" Megan said to Brian.

"Of course. I feel like I'm spending Sunday with my grandmom."

That was as close to a joke as Megan had

ever heard from Brian Porter. And he'd loved his grandmother — the one constant in his tumultuous life. In that, they were soul mates.

"Well, then, buckle up. We're going to Doylestown."

"Why?"

"We need the wreath and farm supplies. And their bookstore has the best selection of Sarah Estelle novels in stock. Ever read Sarah Estelle?"

"No, who is she?"

"My aunt, Sarah Birch. She writes mysteries. And right now they seem to be the key to solving Winsome's latest crisis."

Like a good grandmother, Megan bought Brian a book. He wanted *The History of NASCAR,* and Megan figured any reading was good for him. They returned to Winsome with a haul they couldn't really afford: five mysteries by Sarah, plus Porter's book, along with the other sundry items Bibi had sent them to get.

"Why didn't you just ask your aunt for the books? I'm sure she owns them if she wrote them."

"I don't want to alarm her. Plus, I don't want to be swayed by her thoughts. So mum's the word."

Porter agreed. He helped Megan bring the purchases into the house.

"Coffee?" she asked.

"Nah, but thanks. I have to get home to Sarge."

Sarge, Porter's hundred-pound German Shepherd, was Porter's emotional support dog. Denver had rescued the Shepherd and then asked Porter to take him. It was another case of who had saved whom.

So Megan said good-bye to Porter and put away her stash of books. All except *Killing Spree*. This one she took into the parlor. With Bibi at the café and the dogs surrounding her on the couch, Megan spent the afternoon with Margaret Lewis and the townsfolk of fictional Kennedy, Wisconsin. She read quickly, looking for anything that resonated with the current case. Again, the only constant was revenge — this time as retribution for a business deal gone wrong.

Megan took notes. The killer was a business colleague. The victims, employees.

No real parallels there. Or were there? Hadn't Merry set Becca up in business? The Love Chemist had been funded by Merry Chance. And Sherry Lynn said Paul was away on a business trip. Had he lied to her? Had Sherry Lynn been lying? Or was there a business connection — and a connection to the book?

Megan kept coming back to the books. The only connection she could think of was Sarah's former relationship with Paul Fox. Who would have known about that relationship? Who, living today, would have cared?

The mysterious stranger? Who was he? How was he involved — if at all?

Sarah? Hard to believe she would use her own books as a blueprint for murder. Plus, she already said she had an alibi for the night Paul was murdered — for the entire week, she'd claimed.

Eloise? While she may have had reason to hate Paul, and she would have known about Sarah and Paul, it seemed a stretch to think she'd exact revenge all these years later. She'd let him go from her practice — despite the fact that she didn't admit it, it seemed pretty clear. But Eloise was hiding something — what?

Merry? She had been acting strangely lately. And she had a great deal to lose.

Luke? He seemed closer to his father than his mother — but it was possible.

Sherry Lynn? What would be her motive? Revenge seemed unlikely. Greed?

Becca? She had motive, opportunity, and the chemistry knowledge to make it work. And with her sense of loyalty toward her mother, exacting revenge like in *Love Kills* seemed imaginable.

Oh, Becca, Megan thought. Why does it keep coming back to you?

TWENTY-SIX

Monday brought another half a foot of snow, closed schools, and a big headache in the form of a fallen tree branch. The tree branch had landed on one of the chicken tractors placed on the edge of the property, by the woods. Thankfully no chickens were hurt, but Megan and Clay spent the morning calming fragile chicken nerves and fixing the shelter.

"Great day for this," Clay said as wind whipped snow into his eyes.

Megan nodded. Her head was throbbing from the cold and change in pressure, and it was all she could do to keep working. Her eyes stung from the pellet-like snow. She pulled a scarf up over her mouth and murmured her agreement.

"Were you expecting Bobby?" Clay said a few minutes later. He pointed toward the house, where Winsome's police chief was making his way up the hill. Despite no hat and no scarf, he seemed impervious to the wind and snow buffeting his face.

Megan stopped hammering. She placed her tool on the ground and turned to King. "What's going on, Bobby?"

"Can we talk?"

"Of course. Inside?"

King looked around. He nodded at Clay. "Here's fine." The wind picked up as though on cue, and the trees around them wailed against the assault, their branches rubbing together in unison. "Okay, maybe the barn — out of the wind. This won't take long."

Clay stayed behind to finish the tractor repairs while Megan led King down the hill and into the barn. Closing the heavy doors behind them, she turned on the lights, happy to be out of the wind.

"You look shaken, Bobby. Did something happen?"

King nodded. " 'Fraid so. It's Eloise Kent. She was attacked this morning."

"Eloise?" Megan covered her mouth in surprise. "Why would someone attack Eloise?" Only Megan already knew the answer.

King didn't bother responding.

"Is she okay?"

"We don't know yet. She was in the barn with the horses, feeding them. I guess her farm hand was late because of the snow.

Someone came in and struck her in the head with a shovel, of all things. Her farm hand arrived and found her unconscious on the floor, the shovel beside her. She'd lost some blood from a wound on her scalp, but the biggest issue is possible brain damage from the blow."

With a shovel. Megan's head spun. Just like Simon Duvall in the Washington Acres barn. Hadn't Becca been asking about Simon's murder? In fact, hadn't she displayed an unhealthy interest in what had happened in the barn?

A shovel. Just like in *Love Kills.* What a horrible thing to endure.

"Were there witnesses? Fingerprints? Footprints?"

"Nothing usable so far. Somebody took great pains to be careful. And the snow has erased any footprints."

Megan thought of Eloise's reticence to speak against the psychologist. Clearly she had information. Was someone trying to keep her quiet? Or trying to make her talk? Poor Denver.

"Does Denver know?"

"I called him just before I came here. He was on rounds. His answering service is trying to track him down." King leaned against the edge of a work table. His blond hair was wet from the snow, and a day or two's worth of facial hair made him look more man than boy. "I had an officer follow up on what you found out about Blanche and Sherry Lynn Booker. Sent someone there yesterday to tell Sherry Lynn about Paul's death, gauge her reaction."

"And?"

"Officer said Sherry Lynn was upset, almost histrionic. Went on and on about how Paul had been the love of her life, blah, blah, blah." King let out a huff. "We found out she stands to inherit Paul's entire estate. She doesn't know that, but I'm sure it will quiet her crying."

So much for Bibi's intervention, Megan thought. "Did she give you any more information?"

"Not really. As with you, she blamed most of the marital problems on Blanche. Paul was an angel in her eyes."

"Most?"

"She alluded to some . . . male problems. Said Paul had suffered from impotence on occasion. He blamed Blanche, but she said it happened with her sometimes too." He shook his head. "Thought maybe he had overdosed on Viagra."

"Oh, wow."

"Oh, wow is right. We talked with the

county staff psychologist. We don't have a formal profile, but the doc felt Paul had sociopathic tendencies, perhaps suffered from Antisocial Personality Disorder."

Megan said, "That makes sense. The sadism, the lies, the need to be in control, the lack of regard for consequences."

"And the impotence could be part of that too. Either he needed to be in control to feel aroused, or maybe he was attracted to things others would find off-putting. At least that's what the doc said."

"His unethical interactions with patients could be part of his profile too. One person described him as feeding off details, getting aroused by accounts of others' pain. Some therapist. Speaking of which, did Brian Porter contact you?" She told King about Porter's interaction at the brewery. "I was hoping your sketch artist could create a composite drawing. We can see if Becca recognizes him. Or if he's the same guy I saw talking with Luke outside the café."

"Brian called. He's supposed to meet with our artist later today. We found a few additional allegations of impropriety on Paul's part. He moved the family quite a bit, so my officers are checking in with precincts up and down the East Coast. Some articles about unpaid debts, allegations of fraud.

Chances are good more of the patients on Becca's list will match up with places they've lived — and will have stories to tell."

Megan nodded. Continued transgressions fit the picture she had of Paul Fox. A charmer when you first met him. After that, always lying, always running from the messes he caused, nothing ever his fault. "Did you talk to Sherry Lynn about Blanche's death?"

"She clammed up at that point. Asked if she needed a lawyer."

"Interesting. Maybe Paul's death made her nervous?"

"Sure seems that way." King straightened up, focused his blue eyes on hers. "Megan, I came here to tell you about Eloise. I thought you should know, both for your own safety and in case you see Denver. She's been taken to the trauma center in Doylestown. I can give him the details if you have him call my cell phone."

"Thanks, Bobby. I'll find him and let him know." She waited, sensing there was more.

"We found something else, but this you need to keep quiet. I mean that. No Bonnie, no Merry. No one. At least for a day or two."

"Okay . . ." No information that started that way was good.

"After you and I talked, I had my officers run some reports on Paul's history. Where he was born, school records, that sort of thing. It seems Paul was quite a liar. He didn't go to Penn, as he says on his website. Well, he went to a cognitive psychology seminar program, but he never actually attended graduate school there. He has an associate's degree from a community college in New York. That's all we could find."

Megan whistled. "He got away with that for a long time."

King nodded. "He convinced a lot of people he was legitimate."

Megan felt stunned. She thought of Eloise. Could that have been what she was hiding? The fact that she allowed this man to work with her most troubled patients without a sufficient background check? Megan could see how it could happen. He was Merry's brother-in-law — Eloise would have taken him at face value. Until it was too late. Other employers and patients would too. When was the last time she'd called an older employee's school to confirm graduation dates? Never.

And diplomas could be forged.

Megan said finally, "Fits the sociopath angle. Could also explain why he stopped counseling. Maybe someone was on to him."

"Like his daughter. And the list of patients she'd put together." King seemed to be weighing his next words. "He was also married before, Megan. Blanche was his second wife."

This was news. Eyes wide, Megan said, "Who? When?"

"Her name was Nancy Brown. She was from Bennington, Vermont. And she died eighteen months into their marriage."

"How? How did she die?"

"She fell down the steps."

Megan let that sink in. "An accident?"

King chewed on his thumbnail, already torn to the quick. "You tell me."

"Seems suspicious."

"Vermont police thought so too. In the end it was ruled an accident. No proof."

Megan thought about her conversations with Becca. Surely if Becca had known she would have mentioned it.

"From what we can tell, no one knew about Nancy," King said. "They married at twenty-one, she died when he was twenty-three, he met Blanche seven years later."

"Two wives, two accidents. Two coincidences?"

King nodded. Megan knew he was thinking about Becca, about more reasons for revenge. But with dawning horror, Megan was suddenly thinking about something else.

"I read two more of Sarah's books this weekend, Bobby. Including *Love Kills*. In it, a son kills his father for betraying his mother. With affairs. And multiple wives." She frowned, thinking of the storyline. "And the weapon used? A shovel. Just like with Eloise."

King's face paled. "I guess I'll be having another conversation with Becca Fox."

"Her brother too." She thought about Sherry Lynn, all she had to gain when two wives were out of the way. "And maybe Paul's mistress."

King nodded, his mind already elsewhere. "Pray that Eloise makes it. Otherwise, we'll have another murder on our hands."

TWENTY-SEVEN

Denver reacted with rage Megan hadn't anticipated. "She's my only close relative, Megs. Eloise was there when my own parents weren't. Other than my sister, she's all I have left." He slammed a hand down on his SUV, eyes narrowed to slits. "A week before Christmas. What bastard does something like this?"

And so Megan spent Monday night at the hospital beside Denver. Eloise had been transported to Penn and was in the ICU, so they could only see her during defined periods. The rest of the time they sat in the family area, holding hands, mindlessly watching a muted Christmas program on the television overhead. Denver's worry was palpable. There was nothing Megan could do but be there, and so together they waited.

Sometime around midnight, the doctor, a young black man with a tight smile and tired eyes, told them she was in an induced coma and would stay that way for several days. "Go home. Get some rest," he said in accented English. "We will contact you as soon as there is a change."

The drive home was quiet. The snow from earlier in the day had subsided, and the roads were mostly clear except for drifts along the sides of the road and the patches of black ice. Denver drove, his focus on the road, his eyes straight ahead.

As they neared Winsome, Denver said, "Come home with me, Megs." He looked at her, his bright eyes searching her own.

"I'd like that." Emily was staying with Bibi, and it was well after two. Too late to go home without waking everyone. Although the truth was, Megan wanted this. She wanted to awaken in Denver's arms. She wanted to get up and see his face before her day even started.

They pulled into his driveway at 2:39.

By 3:17 they lay next to each other, naked, spent, limbs entwined, and sound asleep.

Bobby King woke Megan up at eight. She answered the phone groggily, her free hand searching the bed for Denver. His side was empty. The scents of coffee and bacon told her where Denver was and what he was doing.

"What's up?" she asked Bobby, trying to wipe the sleep from her voice.

"I think we have a match on your stranger. His name is William Dorset. Does that ring a bell?"

"No. Should it?"

"He was one of Paul's patients when they lived near Syracuse. Youth record is sealed, but I'm guessing Fox was treating him for behavioral issues. Now Dorset lives in Norristown. Has a record, which is why we identified him so quickly. And a few café patrons reported seeing him on Canal Street. One person even recalled seeing him leave news clippings at the café."

Megan told King about Alvaro finding clippings before Paul died.

"Which may link him to Paul and prove that he was here in Winsome and had opportunity." King paused. "I'd like you to come into the department and see if he matches the guy you saw talking to Luke."

"Have you asked Becca or Luke about him?"

"Not yet. We wanted to see your reaction first."

Megan agreed to be there by ten. She climbed out of bed, donned one of Denver's pajama bottoms and a navy blue Colorado State t-shirt, and headed downstairs. She found the veterinarian drinking coffee by the window, his gaze on the snowy horizon.

Megan wrapped her arms around his waist from behind. "Good morning."

Denver pulled her gently so that she was in front of him. He leaned down and kissed her softly, then more intently. His eyes still looked bruised and tired, but his dimpled smile was genuine.

"I made you some French toast, bacon, and coffee."

"You're the best. Thank you."

Megan started toward the coffee machine, but Denver held her back with a light tug.

"It feels right having ye here, Megs."

"It was nice to finally stay."

"It doesn't have to be a one-night thing, ye know."

Megan kissed him, long and hard, knowing exactly what he was proposing. Her hands traveled the length of his strong arms, his solid chest. She loved his virility and his gentleness, his sense of humor and his intelligence. He was a study in contrasts, and she loved *him.* But she loved her life on the farm too.

When Megan didn't respond with words, Denver disengaged. He walked to the coffee machine and poured her a mug of coffee, adding cream until it was just the color she liked.

"Denver," she said.

He swung around. He looked so hopeful just then, hopeful and sexy. Megan wanted to reach out and touch him. She ached to give him what he wanted. What she thought he wanted. Instead she said, "Have you heard from the hospital?"

"Not yet. I'm going down later today, after appointments."

"I'll come with you."

"Ye have your own stuff to do. I'll be fine. Another time."

He didn't sound upset or rebuffed, but Megan took it that way. She drank her coffee slowly, inviting the sting on her tongue and the heat in her throat. Why did love always have to hurt? She wondered. No matter how right it seemed to be.

"That's the man I saw. I'm pretty sure." Megan squinted at the photo of the stranger Porter had met. He was dark-haired, looked to be in his early forties, and had a large, heavy brow. His mouth was his most distinguishing feature. It was full and small, with corners that turned down. When Megan had seen the man on Canal Street, he was in profile. But this picture looked close enough

288

to be a hit.

"William Dorset, huh?" Megan glanced at King, who was standing to the side, away from the drawing. His cramped office smelled like Italian hoagie and Lysol. Megan noticed a picture of Clover on his desk. He had another on his credenza, one of Clover doing a handstand by the canal. Other than that, his office was institutional ivory. "I only saw him that one time. Do you think he's the guy who's been stalking the café?"

"I can't say for sure, but if I were a betting man, I'd say I have my mark." King rubbed his face. "Why would he want to know about you? That's what's throwing me off. Eloise had a history with Paul. It's possible she somehow knew about this William and he wanted to keep her quiet. But you? It's not like you, or even Bibi, had much to do with the Fox family."

"I gave Becca a ride into Winsome. Bibi and I have been talking with Merry. Maybe he thought we were interfering."

"Maybe." King sounded skeptical. "And what about the books? How would this guy have known about Sarah?"

Megan had to admit, his involvement with Sarah seemed especially hard to explain. "Paul wasn't exactly professional. Maybe he mentioned Sarah at some point to other patients."

"Or somehow used her as a warning." King seemed to consider this. "It's possible."

"Well at least you have a name and a face. It will be interesting to see what Becca and Luke have to say about him."

King lifted the file that held the photo. "I'll call you later?"

Megan nodded. "Please do. I'm as anxious to find out as you are."

Megan was surprised to find Luke Fox at the farm, talking with Clay. The two men stood on the edge of the property, behind the barn, and were faced in the direction of the abandoned Marshall place. Megan made her way across the farm, Gunther at her heels. Even from this distance, she could tell Luke was upset. He was gesturing with two hands, his bearded face a mask of frustration. Clay looked his normal calm self, so it was hard to tell if they were arguing — or if Luke was venting.

They both stopped talking as Megan neared. Luke stared at her, eyes dark.

"Where's my sister?" he said.

"I have no idea." Megan stopped next to Clay. She threw her farm manager a questioning look.

"She came here last time, I thought maybe she did this time as well." Luke was staring at the Marshall property. He tucked his hands in his pockets and glanced down at his boots. He wore a heavy army green LL Bean field coat and a pair of snow boots. His beard was salted with flecks of snow and ice from the particles blowing off the trees. "We can't find her."

Megan said, "When was the last time you saw her?"

"The night before last. She went to bed early, said she was tired. She looked tired, so I didn't think anything of it. When Aunt Merry came down for breakfast yesterday she asked where Becca had gone. Said her room was empty." He held Megan's gaze with a fierceness that shook her. "You can imagine how distraught my aunt is."

"You need to call the police," Clay said. "They'll fill out a missing persons report. Put out an APB."

"They'll also assume she ran because she's guilty. No thanks."

"Luke, think for a moment." Megan kept her voice low and steady, the tone she used for spooked animals and irate customers. "The police have an ongoing investigation into your father's death. For all you know,

Becca is hurt. A victim of the same person who hurt your dad."

Luke's eyes widened. His mouth moved beneath his beard.

"Let's call now." Megan dialed King's number. He didn't answer, and she left a message for him to call her back. Megan turned toward the house. "Why don't you come down to the house? Have some tea. Talk with Bibi. We'll hear from Chief King soon."

Luke nodded reluctantly. His body pulsed with an invisible energy. Megan could feel his restlessness, his worry. "I heard someone else was attacked yesterday," he said finally. "Dr. Kent. The woman my father worked with in Winsome."

Megan nodded, unsure how much was public.

"Becca always blamed Dr. Kent for up-rooting our family. She liked Winsome, especially being near Aunt Merry. They were always close. When Dr. Kent broke my dad's contract, we had to move again. It was hard on my sister."

"Do you think Becca went to Eloise Kent's house?" Clay asked. Megan understood the underlying meaning of his words. *Do you think your sister hurt Eloise Kent?*

"I hope not," Luke said. He glanced back

at the Marshall property. "But I just don't know."

While Luke was in the kitchen with Bibi drinking chamomile tea, Clay pulled Megan aside and into the front parlor.

"I found Luke at the old Marshall property. He seemed upset, was banging around over there. Kept insisting his sister was hiding in that dilapidated house. When I confronted him, he became agitated." Clay glanced toward the French doors as though waiting for Luke to come barging in at any moment.

"Think about it. He lost his dad, and now his sister is missing. And everyone in that family is under suspicion. From what I can see, Merry's not holding it together too well either. I don't particularly care for his methods, but I can understand his angst about calling Bobby."

Clay nodded. His tight jaw indicated that he didn't agree with her, but he didn't argue. His head tilted at the sound of knocking coming from the direction of the kitchen.

"Sounds like Bobby's here," Clay said.

"Good. He can talk to Luke." Megan turned her focus onto Clay. "Are you okay? You don't seem yourself."

"Just frustrated. Another murder in Winsome? And now Eloise?" He shook his head. "I can't help feeling like the Fox family brought this here. That Paul's reconciliation attempt is at the root of the problem."

Megan had to agree.

Clay was heading out the door when he spun around suddenly. "I almost forgot. You got a call while you were out. Patricia Smith, that farm to table chef from Philadelphia. She was happy with the samples. She wants to order baby spinach and mixed microgreens for the restaurant."

Megan clapped her hands. Hallelujah. Patricia Smith had been passionate about buying only local, chemical-free ingredients, and out of everyone she'd met that day, the chef had seemed the most interested in giving Washington Acres' produce a try. Megan said, "I'm glad one good thing came out of that fateful snowy trip into the city."

"Given all that's happened since, I thought you'd appreciate that. It may just be the opportunity we need to get Washington Acres on the Philly map."

"I'll give Patricia a call later."

"I already let her know we could fill the order."

Something was banging into the wall in the kitchen. Megan sprinted toward the parlor door. "Never a dull moment around here."

Clay was right behind her. "Would you want it any other way?"

Megan stopped just short of the kitchen. She could see through the doorway that Bobby had things — things being Luke — under control. "Yes," she said in answer to Clay's rhetorical question. "I really, really would."

Twenty-Eight

"You're just upset right now. Sit down and stay down." King was looking at Luke Fox. He had his hand on his holster and a warning in his eyes. "I am not the enemy."

"You need to find Becca."

"And we will. But first I have a few questions for you. You need to come with me down to the station."

"You'll be wasting my time and yours. In the meantime, something could have happened to Becca."

"Luke," Bibi's voice broke in, "where's Merry?"

Luke looked momentarily confused by the question. "Looking for Becca. When I left, she was making calls."

"She didn't call me or Megan."

Annoyance flashed across Luke's face. "How should I know what Aunt Merry does or why? For as long as I can remember, it's been Becca and me. I need to find her and you need to help me." He looked pointedly at King. "Please."

King beckoned for Luke to follow him. "We may have a lead, but I need your input, okay? While you're with me, my officers will look for Becca. Do you have any idea where she could be?"

"Here. But we looked and didn't find her here. Otherwise, no."

King shot Megan a look of exasperation. He managed to maintain his professional composure. "Megan, Clay, Bonnie. Thanks for helping us out."

"They weren't helping you out —" Megan heard Luke say as they were leaving.

Once the door closed, Clay let out a long, low sigh. "He really is upset."

"Becca is all he has left," Bibi said. "Perhaps it's a case of like father, like son."

Megan looked at her, a thought taking shape. "Truer words, Bibi." She kissed her grandmother on the cheek, said good-bye to Clay, and walked toward the hallway.

"Where are you going?" Bibi called after her. "I want to know how Eloise is doing."

"No word yet," Megan called back, and closed her office door.

"Like father, like son," Bibi had said. Becca demanded so much attention, but Luke was their father's favorite. He seemed so different from his father in many ways — quiet, responsible, and lacking in the charm that had won Paul the affection of some. But maybe there was something in Luke's past, some connection to Paul or Becca, that could be key.

Megan did what free searches she could on Luke Fox, but she turned up empty-handed. Engineering degree from Drexel University, Master's Degree from RPI. According to LinkedIn and other social media sites, Luke had spent most of his career traveling for one consulting firm or another before starting his own. He helped start up factories in developing nations. Nothing telling or unusual in his background, and he was listed on alumni sites for his respective colleges. Megan couldn't find any indication of relationship status. And no obvious criminal activity.

And so Megan paid for a criminal search. She was sure the police had done this as well, but it never hurt to have fresh eyes, a fresh perspective. Only the criminal checks turned up nothing. Luke Fox was clean.

Like father, like son. Maybe the key existed in their relationship to one another. The competition Becca had mentioned. The testosterone-driven rivalry.

Megan found Luke's Facebook site. She studied his photos. A smiling man holding a fishing pole. A smiling man sitting with three friends at a bar in Mexico. A good-natured man wearing a sombrero next to a rather plain woman at a street fair in San Diego. A grinning man petting a large Labrador outside a museum in what looked like San Francisco. In every picture, Luke Fox looked like a confident, happy man. That wasn't the man she saw in her kitchen just now.

Luke did just lose his father, Megan thought. And his sister had been accused of murder. It was enough to make anyone a little crazy.

Megan scanned Facebook and other social media sites for pictures of Luke Fox in the hope that she'd find something more provocative. After a few minutes of viewing irrelevant photos, she decided to search for Sherry Lynn Booker. She finally found a few of interest on Sherry Lynn's Facebook page. Sherry Lynn with Paul — Paul was staring at the camera, Sherry Lynn was staring adoringly at Paul. Another of Sherry Lynn and Paul on a boat. It was sunset, and her long tan legs were stretched out on the deck, her bikini top just barely covering her ample breasts. Paul had his hand on her shoulder protectively, and she wore a grin that matched the price of the boat. The perfect couple. Or so one would think.

Another photo caught Megan's attention. It was older, and in this one Luke had been tagged. The photo caught Sherry Lynn, Paul, Blanche, and the Fox kids at what looked like a barbeque. It had been taken when Becca was in her late teens, maybe a year or two before Blanche died, during Fourth of July or some other summer occasion. Sherry Lynn and Blanche were standing near one end of a picnic table, holding Samuel Adams beers and smiling. Paul and his son stood on the other end. Paul had his arm around a grinning, baby-faced Luke. Both Paul and Blanche were looking at Becca. Sherry Lynn was looking at Paul. And Luke was staring at his father. Only Becca stood by herself, her wavy blonde hair tucked under a baseball cap, her fingers clutching a giant soft pretzel. Her eyes were dark angry orbs gazing straight ahead at the camera.

Blanche and Sherry Lynn. Paul and Luke. And Becca, all alone.

The phone rang. Bobby King. Megan turned off her computer, her concern for Becca Fox deepening with every second.

"It's a hit," King said over the phone. "Luke admitted to knowing him. Identified him as William Dorset."

"So that was the guy who I saw Luke with outside of the café."

"Looks that way."

Megan tapped the eraser tip of a pencil against the wooden desk, thinking. "How does Luke know William?"

"He says Becca contacted William as part of her plot to have former patients go after her father. Luke met William through Becca. Luke claims there is no acquaintance between him and William or between William and his sister beyond that."

Megan thought it odd that Luke knew William at all. He had told her that he didn't know who his sister was acquainted with. "Was Luke part of the plot to go after Paul in court? I thought it was only Becca who wanted to get back at Paul."

"Luke claims it was all Becca. He found out about it, confronted her, and she introduced him to William hoping to sway Luke to her side."

Megan had seen the early interactions between Becca and her brother, the way he tried to convince her to give their father a chance, the way Becca resisted — so that Megan could believe. "Does he think William could have anything to do with the murder of his father?"

"You mean like Becca stirred up a hornet's nest? Contacted this guy, reminded him of all the ways Paul had done him wrong, and suddenly he wants to kill Paul?"

Megan stood and walked to the window. She opened it a crack, letting the cold air wake her up. "I guess. I'm not sure I see William Dorset as a literary mystery reader though. So where would the books fit in?"

"He could be acting in tandem with Becca." King sighed. "But your question was whether Luke thought William did this. The answer is he doesn't know. Luke said William seemed angry and not terribly bright. That the thought of a lawsuit seemed to trigger visions of easy money. Maybe William went rogue and tried to blackmail Paul. Maybe Becca and William blackmailed him together."

"And Luke claims he knew about the lawsuit but had nothing to do with it."

"That's right."

Megan considered what King was telling her. "He knew his father had been murdered. Why didn't he come forward with this information?"

"Luke said he didn't want to implicate his sister. He didn't think this guy was a true threat, and he knew it would make Becca look bad."

That made a certain sense — although it didn't excuse the omission. "Did Luke know what Paul had done to this guy to make him think he even had a case?"

"He didn't know."

"Yet he went along with this anyway?"

"He says he tried to talk them both out of it."

Megan wasn't buying that. "Why wouldn't he have warned his father about Becca's plot? Tried to stop it?"

"Says he was about to do that when Paul was killed."

Megan shut the window harder than she intended and returned to her desk. Staring at the photo of the Fox family with Sherry Lynn, Megan said, "Do you believe Luke?"

King took a moment to respond. "He seemed sincere. That's the most I can say." There was a firm knock on King's door. Megan heard him answer it, and he was back a few moments later with, "Megan, I have to go."

"Is everything okay?"

"They found Becca." King's voice

sounded strained. "She's not well."

Megan could feel her heart begin to race. "Where was she?"

Bobby barked orders at someone in his office. In almost a whisper, he said to Megan, "At Emily's house."

"Oh, no —"

"I don't have time to explain now. If you want to help, find Emily. Bring her to the house. We may need her. But stay in your car until I get you. No matter what."

King's tone was starting to scare her. "Is it such a good idea to bring Emily over? She already has a lot of baggage tied to that house."

Megan heard more shouts, the wail of sirens in the background. A door slammed.

"Just meet me there, Megan," King said. "I have to go."

TWENTY-NINE

Emily was working at the spa and unable to leave right away. Megan was afraid of what Emily might see, so she arranged for Clay to pick Emily up after her shift and bring her to the house. Megan would meet them there.

"I'll call you and let you know what to expect so you can forewarn her," Megan had said.

Nothing had prepared Megan for this, though.

Fire engines and police cars surrounded the property. The right side of Emily's house was stained black from smoke. As Megan pulled up to the driveway, she could see part of the roof missing around the back side of the Cape Cod. Rafters stuck out like charred bones in an oversized skeleton. The gutters on the right side hung off the house, and the newly painted windows were gaping dark holes. Tendrils of smoke rose into the sky, melding with the gray sky above.

The house was all but destroyed.

It took Megan a moment to catch her breath. The air was acrid, and her chest felt heavy. She knew the smell was only part of the problem.

Megan had promised Bobby she'd wait in the car. She dialed Clay's number and explained what she saw.

"Oh, god," he said. "She'll be distraught."

"I know. You should tell her beforehand. Otherwise it will be too much of a shock."

"I'm heading over now," Clay said. "After I fill in Bonnie. We'll see you in about forty minutes."

Megan clicked off her phone and watched as an ambulance pulled away from the house. Had Becca been hurt? What was Becca doing at Emily's house in the first place? And who had set the fire?

"Where's Emily?" King asked.

Megan had climbed out of the truck when she saw King approaching. She leaned against the bed of the truck and watched the firefighters inspect the remains of Emily's house.

"On her way. Clay's picking her up from work."

King joined Megan. His gaze followed

hers. "Shame about the house. The inside is a shell."

"Where did it start?"

King turned to her. Megan saw streaks of soot across his forehead and down one cheek. "The downstairs bedroom."

Megan frowned. "Where Paul died?"

King nodded. "Where her father was murdered. Creepy, right?"

"I have a lot of questions, Bobby. But first, how is Becca? I saw the ambulance. Was she hurt?"

"Burns on her hands and arms, smoke inhalation, but she'll be okay. It's more her state of mind. She seems very out of it."

"She set the fire?"

"She says she did."

Megan cocked her head. "You don't believe her?"

King sighed. "There's little doubt she did it. We found her sitting outside, watching the flames, her hands and arms red from the heat. She had a gas can and a torch with her. She seemed mesmerized by the blaze. But without her lawyer present, and with her state of mind, I didn't want to ask too many questions." He shrugged. "Maybe everything has been Becca all along."

"Don't forget. I was attacked while Becca was being held."

"Becca plus one, then. It seems likely she didn't act alone."

"Speaking of plus one, have you located William Dorset?"

King made a sound like a strangled laugh. He unfurled his arm and waved it in the direction of the house. "We're a small-town department. I'm lucky I had enough human power to handle this, much less locate Dorset. But we're on it."

Megan smiled. "So no luck so far."

King's smile back was wry. "No, no luck so far."

"Have you told Luke?"

"Oh, yeah. Got an earful there. He's on his way now."

"And Merry?"

"I left a message."

Poor Merry, Megan thought. She tried to do a good thing — misguided, perhaps, but well-intended — by bringing them all together for the holidays. And then this happens. If she was disheartened before, this would only make it worse.

"I can stop by to see her," Megan said.

"You've been so good. I tell you more than I should perhaps. Next I'll be getting you on the payroll."

"A police consultant. Grows tomatoes, solves crimes."

"Sounds like a perfect profession for you."

Two of the firetrucks were pulling out of the driveway just as a new car was arriving — Clay's pickup truck. Megan and King watched as shock, then grief registered on Emily's face. Clay pulled to a stop and Emily tumbled out, her hands shaking, her face bunched in fear and frustration.

"I have to question her," King said. "And it won't be fun."

"Because she owns the house?"

"Assuming she has insurance, she stands to profit from the fire. We need her statement on record." His head turned to follow Emily's progress toward them. "Doesn't look like she's taking it well."

"Oh my god, Bobby. What happened? Is anyone hurt?" Emily cried when she arrived at Megan's truck. Tears streaked down her face. "I can't believe this."

Clay put a calming hand on her shoulder while King explained the bare bones of what they knew. Emily kept nodding, but her gaze never left the burnt remnants of her house. Megan reminded herself that Emily had lost her father just a few short months ago. This house had been his. Having a murder take place here, and now losing the house — devastating.

"If you could come with me, Emily, I'd

like to ask you a few questions. And then you'll want to get your insurance agent on the phone immediately. You do have insurance, right?"

Emily nodded forlornly. As she and King started to walk toward his car, another car pulled up to the site. Megan recognized Luke Fox's Mustang. She and Clay watched as Luke rolled down his window.

"Hold it, Chief!" Luke called from his vehicle. He climbed out and jogged over to Bobby King and Emily. Megan heard a few expletives and an "if you did your job" before King demanded that he quiet down.

After a few minutes of hushed discussion and flailing hand gestures, Luke marched away, leaving King to continue his discussion with Emily. Spying them across the yard, Luke turned and aimed for their direction.

"Oh, shit, here he comes," Clay muttered.

Before Megan could respond, Luke was by their side. He stared at the old Cape, mouth ajar. "Becca did this?"

"Looks that way."

"I told them," Luke said quietly. "I told them she needed help. I told Merry she needed help. When she came up with the idea to sue my father, I knew this wasn't going to end well." He turned slowly from the house toward Megan and Clay. "I know she paints herself as a victim, and my father wasn't nice to her, that's true, but this?"

"I'm sorry," was all Megan could manage.

Luke rubbed his bearded chin. Turning back toward the house, he took three steps forward into the snow. "Do you know where they took her?"

"Bobby should know."

"I'd like to see her."

"Why did she run in the first place?" Megan asked.

Luke reached down and picked up a handful of snow in his bare hand. He rubbed it between his fingers as though it were grainy sand. "The fire might have been worse if not for all the snow." His gaze traveled to the decrepit farm across the street, and then to the trailer behind the house. Seeming to remember that Megan had asked him a question, he said, "Why does Becca do anything? Because she can."

"She just set a house on fire," Clay said. "The woman I met at Merry's nursery selling love potions didn't seem like someone who'd commit arson."

Luke kicked at the snow beneath his feet. He met Clay's gaze, one eye half closed to ward off the bright sun. "Well, Clay, looks can be deceiving — can't they?"

THIRTY

Megan stopped by Merry's house, but no one seemed to be at home. She knocked, hit the doorbell, even yelled Merry's name — no response. Perhaps someone took her to the hospital to see Becca, Megan thought. She called Merry and left a message. Then she left one for Denver telling him she would take care of the dogs while he was with Eloise. Merry didn't call her back. Denver did.

"No need, Megs," he said. "I just fed them and let them out. I'm heading down to Philly now and won't be there for long. I just want to talk to her doctors and let her know I'm there." He quieted. "She can feel my presence, I think."

"I have no doubt." Megan considered bringing up the topic Denver had broached earlier that day. She decided against it. He sounded fine, and it really wasn't something that needed to be dealt with right now.

Instead she asked if he'd heard about the fire at Emily's house.

"Aye, word travels fast around here. So Becca set it?"

"Looks that way."

"I'm wondering if she attacked my Aunt Eloise." His words were iron. She understood.

"I don't know. I can't see it, but . . . I just don't know."

"I'm turning into the hospital lot now, Megan. I think I had better shut down the phone. Will you be all right?"

"I miss you."

Denver didn't respond right away, but Megan heard a catch in his breath. "Will I see you tomorrow?" he asked.

"If you'd like."

"It's hard to plan with Eloise down here. We'll play it by ear?"

"You can always come by the farm on your way home."

Denver laughed. "That won't be too much scandal for the good people of Winsome? Local vet makes house calls to young female farmer? I can see the headlines now."

Megan turned the truck's ignition. She pushed it into reverse and started backing out of Merry's driveway. "Considering all Winsome is dealing with, I'd say a house call from Winsome's handsome Scottish vet is the least of our town's worries."

"I saw Winsome mentioned in the Philly paper today. I'd say you're right."

Megan was at the café helping Clover and Alvaro with the dinner rush when Aunt Sarah showed up. Emily, understandably upset after what happened, had called out for the night, and although the crowds were light, the café needed all the help it could get.

Alvaro placed a bowl of Irish stew on the serving counter. Megan picked it up and set it before Roger Becker, who'd come in with a few other members of the Winsome Historical Society.

"Good stuff," Roger said. "Tell Alvaro it needs more meat."

"You tell him," Megan said. "I'm sure he'd love to hear your opinion."

Benny Rothman laughed. "I'd rather tell my mother-in-law I don't like her lamb. At least then I could justify my divorce."

The men laughed — all except Roger. He leaned in and asked Megan if she'd heard from Merry. "You know, since the fire incident."

Megan shook her head. Word did travel fast in this small town. "No, I'm sorry,

Roger. I stopped by but she wasn't home. You?"

He nodded. "Just briefly this morning. Before everything happened, though."

"How did she sound?"

"Well, she called me to say she wouldn't be at tonight's special meeting of the Beautification Board. At least she called this time. We're discussing which homes will be featured in the holiday light tour on Saturday."

"Isn't it a little late to be deciding that?"

"We had some recent entries. We want to be fair." Becker frowned. "Normally Merry would be all over that. She loves a good light show. Especially one that will raise money for the cause."

Clover walked by and refilled Roger's soda. She smiled at him, but he was still lost in the discussion and didn't smile back.

"As for how she sounded?" Becker continued. "Better, I guess. More chipper. She's been hit with a stomach bug, which is never pleasant."

Megan felt a sense of relief. While she didn't want Merry to be ill, it explained her conspicuous absence from work and the fact that she never called Megan back.

Clover came by a second time to refill glasses. She paused by Megan and whispered, "You have a visitor."

Megan turned. In the glow of the holiday lights, Sarah Birch appeared an apparition, hovering in the corner by the door. She wore a soft gray knitted cap, a soft gray coat, and charcoal gray gloves. When she spotted Megan, she waved.

"Excuse me, Roger," Megan said. "Clover, can you hold down the fort?"

"Of course."

Megan met her aunt by the front of the store.

"Get your coat and come for a walk with me?" Sarah asked.

Megan glanced back at the café. Only the Historical Society men and a few singles. Nothing Clover and Alvaro couldn't handle. "Sure," she said. She grabbed her coat and scarf from her office and followed her aunt into the cold.

Sarah was walking briskly, her arms swinging by her side. She turned left down Canal Street and headed for the canal bike path, a favorite with walkers, runners, and cyclists in the summer but deserted now. The air outside was crisp and cold, the night sky dark. Megan found herself watching for shadows out of the corner of her eye. Everything felt ominous.

"You look nice this evening," Sarah said.

It seemed an odd opener, especially because Megan was dressed in jeans and a plain black turtleneck sweater. Nothing special. She could smell her aunt's sweet scent from here, though, so she said the first thing that came to mind. "You smell nice. New perfume?"

"Love Potion. Rose scented. Is it working? The man at the deli didn't seem to think so. He barely glanced at me while slicing my Havarti."

Megan laughed. "I'm not sure that's the litmus test. Deli Hank can barely smell anything over the lingering stink of old salami."

Sarah chuckled. After a few more yards, she said, "How are things with the investigation into Paul's death?"

"Have you talked to Bobby King?"

"Not since he questioned me. He wants me to come down again tomorrow."

Megan stopped to re-tie her scarf. "Is that why you came by?" She sensed an agitated energy coming from her aunt. "To see what's happening before you speak with Bobby?" Megan felt a little hurt. It was Christmastime and she realized part of her hoped Sarah was here for another reason. More information about her maternal grandfather. Or better yet, news that her mother wanted to see her.

Even if Megan wasn't so sure she'd want to see her mother.

"Yes and no. I'm afraid I have a confession to make. I wanted to do it before I talk to Bobby in case you hear it from him."

Sarah spoke with her normal matter-of-fact directness. Megan had realized months ago that her great aunt was a woman for whom right and wrong were black and white. For Sarah Birch, even the gray areas could somehow be cast as absolutes. That sense of conviction lent strength to her writing, but it could be infuriating to someone like Megan, a lawyer who understood nothing was so simple.

Megan waited quietly for Aunt Sarah to continue. The canal path jogged right, then left beside a row of low hedges. The snow had accumulated two feet on top of the edges, and Megan strained to see beyond them.

Aunt Sarah said, "I told you that Paul visited me when he arrived in Winsome, right?"

"You did."

"And I told you that he became . . . physical."

"Yes." Megan kept her voice noncommittal, afraid where this was going.

"There was more to it, Megan. For one, I lied when I said I broke it off and never saw Paul again. I did refuse to sleep with him again — that part was true. But he continued to write to me, to call me after the family moved away. He said he loved me. That we had something special."

Megan stopped walking. "And you believed him?"

"Is it so hard to believe someone would love someone like me, Megan?"

Megan flushed despite the cold. "No, no. That's not what I mean. You're so savvy and he was such a . . . womanizer."

"Ah, but I didn't know that at the time. Remember, I was coming out of an ugly divorce. I was looking for affirmation, someone to care. As much as it pains me to admit it, I enjoyed the attention."

Megan resumed the walk. She needed something to occupy her hands, her feet. This wasn't quite the conversation she'd expected to have with Bibi's sister-in-law. How could two women be so very different? A large part of Megan admired her aunt's worldliness, her take-no-prisoners, make no apologies attitude toward life. The other part of her just wasn't sure what to do with this information.

"That's it?" she said finally. "You kept in touch with Paul?"

"For years."

"For years? As in —"

"On and off since he left Winsome." Seeing the expression on Megan's face, Aunt Sarah followed it quickly with, "We weren't friends, by any means. But we did maintain contact. Often that meant Paul complaining about Blanche, his gout, the ways in which the world was treating him unfairly. Over time it became rather fatiguing and I actively discouraged it." Sarah quieted. "I see in your eyes that you don't understand. But this is all just context for what came next."

This time, it was Sarah who stopped walking. They stood on the far side of Canal Street, near Roman's Bakery. Sarah glanced at a bench by the path, but seemed to think better of it. Megan was glad. It was too cold to be still for long.

"I'm convinced what Paul *really* wanted was money."

That surprised Megan. "What makes you say that?"

"He asked for it."

Megan started to laugh and Sarah soon followed suit. "That's what you didn't want to say? That Paul asked you for money?"

"Think about it, Megan. Who do you ask

for money? People you're close to. If I had told you or Bobby or anyone that Paul came into town, hit on me — that part was true, by the way — and then hit me up for fifty grand —"

"Fifty thousand dollars?"

Sarah nodded. "I know."

Megan sat on the bench, cold be damned. "What did he need the money for?"

"An investment. That's all he'd tell me. He tried to convince me I'd make money off the deal."

Megan remembered seeing the investor information on his professional website and LinkedIn account, the conversation she'd had with Sherry Lynn. "That was his new profession. Investment consulting or some such nonsense."

"Yes, he told me. I knew he was expanding his career options, as he put it, but this was still unexpected."

"You should definitely tell Bobby tomorrow. It may mean something, fit together with something else King has learned. Maybe Paul needed money to pay off a loan shark or someone else who ultimately came after him." Or maybe he needed the cash to pay off a blackmailer, Megan thought, but kept that to herself.

The wind picked up and Sarah hugged

her coat tighter around her chest. Her long hair blew across her face, and Megan got a glimpse of the girl she might have once been.

"You look like Charlotte," Sarah said.

The comment, made when Megan's guard was down, made her fumble for words. "Oh," is all she managed.

"Your mother was a beautiful girl. Now she's a beautiful woman. Inside and out. Like you, Megan." Sarah reached a hand out to push Megan's hair away from her face.

It was a gentle touch, full of warmth and concern. Megan couldn't help it; she flinched.

"I'm sorry if I made you uncomfortable," Sarah said. She stood abruptly and, turning back toward the Washington Acres Cafe and Larder, started walking. "It seems I keep doing that," she called over her shoulder.

After a full minute of uncomfortable silence, Megan said, "I'm sorry. Talking about my mother makes me feel angry and sad at the same time."

"I'm sorry for bringing her up. You're not ready."

Megan pressed her lips together in a bid to stay quiet. It wasn't up to Sarah to decide when she was ready. She might never be ready. But it was her choice.

Not wanting to fight, Megan said what had been on her mind since she left Emily's ruined house hours ago. "Did you ever write a novel about arson?"

Sarah frowned. "Several. Why?"

"There was an incident today. I'm sure you heard about it — with Becca?"

"No, I didn't hear anything. What about Becca?"

Megan explained how Becca had been missing, and that she had been squatting in Emily's house. How she set fire in the room Paul had died in. "I didn't see Becca before she was carted off to the hospital, but Bobby said she was in a bad way. Mentally. I know it's a long shot, but I thought maybe it fit in with the books."

Sarah turned to Megan. She placed a hand on each of Megan's shoulders and leaned in. The scent of rose love potion was overwhelming.

"A young woman went to an abandoned house and lit the place on fire?"

"Yes. Becca went to Emily's house. She broke in and started a fire from the room in which Paul was killed."

"Full circle," Sarah muttered. Her face looked ashen, the skin under her eyes bruised under the unforgiving glare of the streetlamps. "Full circle."

Megan shook her head. "I don't understand."

"I wrote a novel originally called *Full Circle.* In it, a man is murdered by his family. It was an honor killing, done in retaliation for certain transgressions. The man's daughter returns to his abandoned house and attempts suicide in the room in which he was killed. Suicide by fire."

Megan let that sink in. While nothing indicated Becca had been trying to harm herself, the setup certainly echoed the crux of what had happened. "I didn't see a book titled *Full Circle* when I searched your list."

"You wouldn't. My publisher changed the title to *Killing Honor.*"

Megan put a hand to her mouth. There was another book with the word "kill" in the title. "How did I miss that?" she asked. "I didn't see that when I searched."

"I'm not surprised. We've been haggling over deadlines. After they changed the title, they decided to give advance reader copies to those who'd signed up for my newsletter during a certain period. The book doesn't actually release until late next year."

"So other than your publisher, agent, etc., the only people who would know about that information should be fans who've signed up for your newsletter?"

"During the months of October and November. Yes." Sarah's eyes brightened as she realized what Megan was suggesting. "You think perhaps the police can use my list to track down the killer."

"Or at least see whether any of the suspects are on your fan list. Circumstantial, perhaps, and it's possible the killer used a fake name — but it's something."

"Something is good."

Megan nodded. Maybe they could pull some of these pieces together. "You'll tell Bobby tomorrow?"

"I'll do better than that," Sarah said. "I'll call him as soon as I get home."

THIRTY-ONE

Megan lay in bed unable to sleep. Every sound the old farmhouse made, every creak, every rattle, sounded like a car pulling into the driveway. It was after eleven when Megan finally gave up on Denver. He had his aunt to attend to and a practice to run — she understood. She just wished she had let his dogs out for him one more time.

The day's events played like a silent film in Megan's head.

Especially Emily's house. That house had been a horror from day one. The events of last fall would forever be tied to the property in her mind, and she knew in Emily's too. Still, to see it there, burned and hollow, made the events of the last few weeks all the more real.

The door to her bedroom opened and Gunther padded his way across the room. Megan held her breath, waiting for her oversized teddy bear to heft himself onto the bed where Sadie had already staked out space. Some people didn't believe in letting their dogs sleep in bed. She didn't much care what those people thought. On occasion, though, she imagined how nice it would be to have leg room.

Gunther's nose pressed against Megan's arm. She wiggled her hand out from under the blankets and pet him, thinking about comfort and warmth and her conversation with Aunt Sarah. It was hard for Megan to imagine Sarah with Paul Fox. It wasn't the age difference, which was less than a decade, it was the personality difference. She reminded herself that Sarah was not always the strong, confident woman she was today. She'd earned those stripes over time.

Had Charlotte Birch changed too? Would Megan even recognize her mother if she saw her today? Somehow she felt she would. Do you ever forget a bond like that?

Stop, Megan thought. This isn't helping you sleep. It's not helping with anything.

Megan made a mental list of things to follow up on tomorrow. She still needed a tree. It was their family's tradition to decorate it on Christmas Eve before a turkey dinner and a roaring fire. She hoped Denver would join them this year. Clover and Clay too. Maybe even Emily. She and Clay had seemed closer lately. Wouldn't it be funny if Becca's love potion was working after all?

Speaking of love potion, Megan still needed to shop.

Beyond the farm and café and holiday jobs, she wanted to get to the bottom of what was going on. No one in Winsome would be able to rest until this mess was solved. But how? And where to start? She couldn't shake the feeling that Paul's two wives had something to do with what was happening in Winsome.

Revenge.

The deaths of Paul's wives, and Sarah's imagination.

And money? Thinking of Sarah again, Megan wondered — could Paul's finances play a part in this too?

How all of these things intertwined was a mystery. One Megan hoped to solve before someone else in their small town met with Fox family misfortune.

Megan woke up to the sound of a text registering on her phone. She rolled over and glanced at the clock. 2:14. It was Denver asking if she was still up.

She texted him back: No, but I could be.

Twenty minutes later, he joined her at the farmhouse. Sleep came more easily then.

"Aunt Eloise is awake. She doesn't remember much about the morning she was attacked. The doctors said that's normal. She may get some memory back as the swelling subsides. Right now she's not really communicating. The doctors want her to rest."

Bibi had made pancakes and sausage for Megan, Denver, and Clay. Denver was eating his way through a tall stack and trying to wake up with a tall mug of black coffee. He looked worn and worried but content, despite getting only a few hours' sleep.

"I'm glad she's okay," Megan said hopefully. She didn't want to ask about lasting damage, but it was what was on her mind.

And Denver's apparently.

"We don't know if there is brain damage yet. She suffered quite a blow and the swelling was severe." His eyes darkened. "Only time will tell."

Megan poured herself another cup of coffee and refilled Clay's mug. Bibi was drinking tea this morning, and she smiled at Megan when no one else was looking. Bibi liked Denver, and although she might not have approved of finding him in her kitchen at five forty-five in the morning, freshly showered and carrying an overnight bag, Megan knew she'd tolerate it because she wanted Megan to be happy.

"What I don't understand," Clay said, "is why your aunt? If this is related to Paul Fox's death, what could she have to do with him?"

Megan and Denver exchanged a look, but it was Bibi who spoke first. "Eloise was the reason the Fox family left town. Sarah, my sister-in-law, alerted Eloise that Paul was not a very ethical therapist. Eloise had contracted with him to provide counseling for her patients who'd suffered some form of trauma in their lives. When Eloise heard, she did some digging into Paul's background. What she found was not savory. She let him go."

"Is that common knowledge?" Megan asked.

"I don't think Eloise advertised it, but it didn't take much to put two and two together."

"How did Eloise's dismissal force Paul to leave Winsome?" Clay asked. He placed another four-stack of pancakes on his plate and drizzled warm maple syrup over the top. He cut into the stack as he said, "He must've had other work."

Bibi replenished the pancakes with a fresh

batch. Looking over the table to ensure everyone was fed, she said, "He'd been unfaithful to Blanche and many people knew it. On top of that, being let go from Dr. Kent's office was humiliating. It's a small town now, but smaller back then. People talked."

"So you think Paul blamed Eloise?" Denver asked. "Paul is dead, so clearly he couldn't have attacked my aunt."

"But Becca could have." Bibi glanced at Megan. "Right?"

Megan nodded reluctantly. "Becca went missing the morning Eloise was attacked, Denver. Her brother and Merry couldn't find her." Seeing Clay's look of disbelief, Megan added, "There are other possibilities."

"Such as?" Denver asked.

Megan tried to put her thoughts in order. "Well, there is a missing man, a former patient of Paul's named William Dorset, who Becca approached about suing her father. Bobby thinks perhaps the man became enamored with the idea of money and didn't want to wait for a lawsuit."

"So he was blackmailing Paul?" Clay put his fork down. "And then killed him?"

"It's possible." Megan told them about Paul's request for money — leaving out the other sordid aspect of her aunt's encounter with the victim. "Maybe he was requesting the money to pay off his blackmailer."

Bibi looked thoughtful. "That doesn't explain Eloise. Becca could have had a beef with Dr. Kent for ruining her family life. That's how a child might perceive it. But this William?"

Denver said, "Could he have been a patient of Eloise's practice, someone Paul victimized and now he is looking for revenge?"

Megan shook her head. "I don't think so. Bobby said William is from New York. Paul worked with him after he left Winsome. That said, if he's not working alone, if he's paired up with Becca, it's possible they were blackmailing your aunt. Maybe she refused to pay."

Denver stared at Megan mid-bite. "Do you think Aunt Eloise did something wrong?"

"I'm not saying that at all. I did speak to her — remember that? — and she was less than forthcoming. I got the sense she didn't want to talk about any of this. At the time I chalked it up to regret. Painful to think you'd exposed patients who were afraid to trust to someone so untrustworthy, but now I'm wondering if it's not more than that.

Maybe they'd already approached her and she was feeling the pressure."

Denver pushed his plate away. The thought of his aunt's involvement seemed to weigh heavily on him and he shook his head back and forth. "My aunt is a very ethical person. Not always friendly, I know, but she would never do something to endanger her patients. If they thought they had dirt on her, they were wrong. I just don't see it." He met Megan's gaze. "Becca makes more sense. She had reason to be angry if her life went downhill after they left Winsome. Like a child, she may have blamed my aunt."

"And Sarah." Bibi's voice was low. "She may blame Sarah too."

"Sarah was included on Becca's list of potential victims. She must have known something," Megan said. "It could explain the books."

They all turned to look at Megan and she realized Clay and Denver weren't aware of Sarah's novels and the role they seemed to play. She gave them a quick summary. "From what I can tell, it's the books with 'kill' in the title. They seemed to be linked with the concept of revenge. But in every book there is some detail that relates to a crime committed here. In *Love Kills,* a teenage son kills his father because his father

333

had multiple wives and was cheating on the boy's mother. He uses a shovel to hit his father on the back of the head."

"So the shovel used against Eloise comes from that book?" Denver looked skeptical.

"And it turns out Paul had been married before Blanche. When he was very young." Megan paused. "And his young wife died accidentally. She fell down the steps."

Bibi's eyes widened. She sat down at the table and looked at Megan. "Paul was married before Blanche?"

Megan nodded. "Bobby found that out. They lived in Bennington, Vermont at the time. He said the police ruled it an accident. I was asked to keep it quiet for a few days."

Denver asked, "Have you seen the death certificate?"

Megan shook her head.

"If it's true, I don't think Blanche knew that. I certainly don't think Merry knew." Bibi shook her head. "That's a very big thing to hide."

"And it calls into question Becca's accusations that Paul killed her mother. Two dead wives?" Bibi's face said she was searching for the right words. "Gives more credibility to the claim. Especially if he had been hiding one of them. A lie of omission, if you ask me."

Megan nodded. "Paul also lied about his education, and this goes back to your aunt, Denver. He never got a graduate degree in psychology. He didn't even graduate from undergrad. He had an associate's degree from a community college. The folks suing him? They could have had a case."

"He lied about his schooling too?" Bibi's face had paled. "How did he get away with that?"

"Not everyone checks," Megan said. "Especially when the person seems to have such good credentials."

"And he moved around a lot," Denver said. "Probably left a place before they could catch on. Unless someone contacted a school to confirm, they might never know."

Bibi shook her head. "Merry was so proud to have a distinguished therapist in the family. We heard about it for months after he and Blanche married. Paul this, Paul that. Poor Merry. If someone could lie about such fundamental things, it does make you question everything else they've told you."

Merry. Megan looked at her grandmother, the wheels turning. Merry had a stake in all of this too. She'd lost her sister. A lawsuit, if it went through, would drag her family through the mud. She'd been acting odd lately. Antisocial, unresponsive. Could there be more than a stomach virus going on?

"And then there's the brother," Clay said. "I don't like him and I don't trust him."

"He can be abrasive," Megan agreed.

Megan considered Luke. His alibi for the night of Paul's death was also Merry. The family seemed tangled up with one another. Was one of them involved . . . or all of them?

Clay stood and put his dishes in the dishwasher. He went around the table clearing plates until Denver rose to help him.

"The fact remains that it was Becca who set fire to Emily's house. Not Luke. Not some prior patient of Paul's. Not Sarah or Eloise. Becca." Clay rinsed the coffee pot, his voice raised over the sound of the spigot. "Becca."

"An incident that could be unrelated," Denver said.

"But it, too, seems connected to the books." Megan went on to tell them about *Killing Honor,* Sarah's upcoming novel, and the connection to her fan base. "Given everything else, I doubt that's a co-incidence."

"Becca," Clay said. "I can't believe I'm saying it, but she makes the most sense."

Denver nodded. "And she has the chemistry background. Poisoning her father would not have been a stretch."

"Remember that anyone with basic knowledge — or an internet connection, for that matter — could have produced the phosgene," Clay said. "It's not hard. People get sick from it more often than you'd think."

Megan agreed. "But Becca does make sense." Maybe too much sense? "I can't stop thinking about the novels. Whoever is tying these incidents to the books has a message for us. At first I thought it was a blueprint for murder, but the connections are more tentative, less linear. And all seem to revolve around the concept of revenge."

"Becca," Clay said again.

"Or someone who wants it to look like Becca," Bibi said. "Someone very, very clever."

"Or very, very sick," Megan said.

THIRTY-TWO

"We need to make an arrest, and soon. This is in the national press now, and my boss is breathing down my neck." King rubbed his chin. His eyes were shadowed, his face moonlight pale. It appeared he hadn't slept in days.

"Bobby, did you talk with Sarah Birch?"

King nodded. He had stopped by the café looking for Clover and Megan pulled him into the back office. He straddled her extra chair, his long legs stretched out across her cramped quarters. "She called me at home last night."

Megan felt relieved. "So you'll look into the financial angle?"

"You mean the money Paul wanted to borrow?"

Megan nodded. She could hear Alvaro barking orders at Bibi in the kitchen, and Bibi's biting remarks back. She would have laughed had the situation in Winsome not felt so dire.

"Right now we're building our case against our prime suspect. So yes, we'll look into Paul's finances. We have already, in fact."

"And the email list for Sarah's newsletter?"

"That could take weeks to decipher, even with computer assistance. We need the warrant, and then we need to try to match email addresses, some of which will be tied to fake accounts —"

"But if you know what you're searching for, that shouldn't take as long. And you may be able to get Sarah to turn over the information voluntarily."

"Will still take time."

Megan frowned. "It sounds like you've made your decision, Bobby. That Becca is your man, so to speak."

King didn't respond. Megan felt a tug of sympathy. She knew he was under duress, and that he wanted to do the right thing. She also knew that he had two real issues to put to bed: Paul's murder and the attack on Eloise. The rest — the books, the Canal Street stalker, Blanche Fox's death — was all noise. Unless it helped make an arrest. And at this point, to King, it probably sounded too far-fetched to be useful.

"Have you talked to Merry?" Megan

asked. She heard the weariness in her own voice. "She also has something to lose here."

"Merry has been sick in bed for days. Her nephew confirmed that. And yes, I did go by the house to talk to her. She was pretty out of it. I told Luke to call a doctor."

Megan nodded. King stood. He edged closer to the door, clearly looking for escape.

"You know Becca couldn't have perpetrated the attack against me, Bobby."

"It could have been wholly unrelated."

"The book. The perpetrator left the book. Clearly it was related."

Bobby sighed, hand on the doorknob. Laughter from the kitchen wafted in, along with the scent of cinnamon scones. "We're still looking for William Dorset. But that doesn't change anything regarding the murder."

"You really think you have the right person?" Megan asked.

Bobby's eyes searched hers, but only for a moment. He opened the door and disappeared back out into the café.

It was nearly eight before Megan arrived home. By then she'd gotten word that Becca had been arrested for Paul's death. Megan's head was pounding. It felt as though the entire town was going mad. Merry still wasn't taking her calls, and Luke was actively petitioning for his sister's release. Even Bibi was charged up. She met Megan at the door with a string of complaints regarding how the young police chief was handling the situation.

"He's caving to pressure from that commissioner," Bibi said. She was wearing her "Welcome to Winsome" sweatshirt, and she'd tucked her hair under a bright red beret.

"Where are you going?"

"Bridge."

"It's eight o'clock."

"We have an emergency meeting."

Megan hung her coat on the hook by the door. "An emergency meeting of bridge? I didn't think there was such a thing."

Bibi buttoned her own coat. She added a red scarf and red mittens. She looked adorable, and Megan resisted the urge to hug her.

"It may be our holiday party, Megan, but we're using it as an emergency meeting to talk about what's been happening in Winsome."

"What do you think that will accomplish?"

Bibi held her keys in one hand, sharp key up between two fingers, the way she learned in self-defense class at the senior center.

She paused at the door. "We're all worried. We're worried about our safety, and we're worried about Merry."

Megan could understand. Only she was worried about her eighty-four-year-old grandmother driving around at night. "How about if I drive you?"

Bibi smiled. "I know you're worried about me. I'll call when I get there, and I'll call when I'm on my way home."

When Megan didn't say anything, Bibi opened the door. "If I can't do something as basic as bridge, then I've really lost my freedom."

Megan nodded. She was right, of course. "Just call me."

Once Bibi had pulled safely out of the driveway, Megan set up her laptop in the kitchen. She started poking around the internet, searching for anything related to Paul Fox. Specifically, she was looking for financial information. But after an hour's worth of searching, she still hadn't found anything new.

Frustrated, she decided to look around his family's social media sites again. Becca's business had a Twitter account dedicated to The Love Chemist. She had almost twelve thousand followers and what looked like many ardent fans, but Megan couldn't find anything personal or telling on the site. Luke had that Facebook account, but all she'd found were innocuous photos. Only Sherry Lynn's account had any real accessibility — and that was limited too.

Nevertheless, Megan returned to Sherry Lynn's site. She paged through selfie after selfie of the fifty-something-year-old woman, searching for anything that might provide a clue. Megan's brain searched sideways, looking at pictures and seeking connections.

Nothing clicked.

And then one photo caught Megan's eye. It was of Sherry Lynn. She was sitting on a dock, the sun was setting behind her, and across a narrow band of water sat a pink two-story house, unremarkable except for its color and the American flag that flew above the first floor. Sherry Lynn wore a black bikini top, a pair of terry cloth shorts, and sunglasses, the mirrored lenses of which reflected the edge of the dock, the sun-dappled waves, and the woman holding the camera.

Megan's heart pounded. She recognized the location. And she recognized the woman taking the photo.

Bibi was home by twenty after ten. She

came into the house bearing two shopping bags' worth of gifts. She placed the bags on the table with a huff. "Two hats, three scarves, one Christmas stocking pin, and a mug full of Hershey Kisses from the new teacher at the elementary school. I'm pretty sure she re-gifted." Bibi started pulling things out of the shopping bags. "And enough cookies to feed Cookie Monster for a year."

"How did the emergency meeting go?"

Bibi paused while putting away the shopping bags. "Everyone is on edge, as you would imagine."

"Did you glean anything? Any insights?"

"Only that Merry is a mess. We all think she's simply hiding out at this point. Ashamed and worried. And everyone seemed relieved that Bobby made an arrest."

Megan studied her grandmother. "You don't look so relieved."

"I think Bobby is young. Like I said earlier, he's caving under pressure."

Sadie rubbed up against Megan's leg and Megan reached down to pat her. "You don't think Becca is guilty?"

"She may be. That's not for me to decide." Bibi placed the mug of candy in her special treat cabinet with a furtive glance at Megan.

"But I would feel better if I thought Bobby was considering all of the facts. Not looking at them selectively."

Megan nodded her agreement. "Are you up for a road trip tomorrow?"

"You know I'm always up for a road trip, Megan."

"Back to see Sherry Lynn Booker."

"Oh?" Bibi questioned her with her eyes.

"We need clarification on a few things. Thought you might enjoy donning your beige skirt again."

Bibi laughed. "Don't forget my cane. And it doubles as a weapon."

THIRTY-THREE

Wednesday morning was dark and overcast with wind chills in the teens. It was the kind of morning that invited hot coffee, warm baths, and created the aching desire to stay tucked under layers of blankets. But after finishing their morning chores, Megan and Bibi made their way across the Pennsylvania border and into New Jersey, driving north-east until they reached Sherry Lynn's green one-story. As with the last time they arrived, Sherry Lynn was home, her Honda parked in the driveway. The car was running and the lights were on.

Bibi started to open her door. Megan stopped her.

"Let's wait and catch her when she comes out. Now that she knows Paul died, she may realize we weren't honest with her last time and she may refuse to see us."

Bibi nodded. "Good idea. You should back up then. Stay out of sight."

Megan re-parked the truck and they waited. Two minutes later, Sherry Lynn came out of her house. She was wearing a black full-length parka with puffy horizontal sections and carrying an overnight bag and a purse.

"She looks like the Michelin Man," Bibi whispered.

Megan had to agree. "Ready?"

"Let's go."

Sherry Lynn was hidden behind the open trunk, putting away her bags, so Megan took advantage of the opportunity and approached while the woman was unaware. "Be careful," Megan whispered to Bibi. "There's ice on the sidewalk."

"I'm only pretending to be old and unworldly. I can still see, Megan."

Megan left Bibi to walk down the sidewalk on her own. She skipped ahead and was waiting behind the trunk when Sherry Lynn closed it. Sherry Lynn stared at her, recognition slowly dawning in her eyes.

"What do you want?"

"To talk to you."

Sherry Lynn's gaze wandered to Bibi, coming down the road with her cane out in front of her. Sherry Lynn rolled her eyes. She walked around to the driver's seat and opened the door. Megan stuck her foot on the runner. The two women stared at one another.

Sherry Lynn looked good. Her skin was clear, her cheeks flushed. She'd carefully applied makeup to her face, and her blonde hair had been touched up and blown straight around her shoulders. Other than the giant coat, her bearing seemed more regal, her posture straight. In short, Sherry Lynn hardly seemed the same forlorn woman they'd talked to just days ago.

And she hardly seemed to be a woman in mourning.

"I'm not talking to you," she said. "No way. Paul is dead. You must have known that."

"I'm sorry for your loss," Megan said. "But we really are trying to help Becca."

"Why?" Sherry Lynn's stare challenged her. "She's a spoiled brat who will finally get what she deserves."

"A life in prison?" Bibi asked. She moved closer to the car so that she was standing directly in front of Sherry Lynn. She'd dropped the granny pretense and was holding the cane across her front with two hands — a senior citizen Charlie's Angel. "You were friends with Becca's mother once. Surely you want better for Blanche's daughter."

Sherry Lynn grabbed the car door and pulled. She stared at Megan's leg, which continued to block her entry. "Move, or I'll call the police."

Megan shifted her weight to get better balance against the car. "Tell us about Paul's financial issues and we'll go."

Sherry Lynn stared at her in surprise. "What financial issues?"

"Insolvency? Debt? Why was Paul trying to borrow funds?"

Sherry Lynn's face scrunched in what looked to Megan like genuine confusion. "Paul was a wealthy man. We'd just purchased the shore house, he said his business was taking off. He was in the best financial shape of his life. There were no *issues.*"

"And who stands to inherit that now?" Bibi asked.

"Are you insinuating that I harmed Paul?"

"I'm simply asking you who stands to inherit his money?"

"How the hell would I know?" Sherry Lynn's voice screeched, her eyes fluttered closed with each syllable. "I just found out he was dead a few days ago, remember? I have no idea who he left his money to."

"I do," Megan said. "You."

Sherry Lynn stood dead still. "Me?"

Megan nodded. "You didn't know that?"

"We never discussed it. I assumed it was his kids."

Sherry Lynn pulled her sunglasses out of her leather bag. With a glance toward the gray sky, she put them on. They were the same mirrored glasses she'd worn at the beach. Which brought Megan to her second topic.

"Merry joined you at your beach house last summer."

"Please move your foot."

"Why was Merry there?"

Sherry Lynn frowned. "Because she's family. Why else?"

"I didn't think she and Paul were that close," Bibi said.

Sherry Lynn let out a cross between a sigh and a snort. "She adored Paul. I think she would have moved in with him had he shown the least inclination to let her do so."

It was Megan's turn to feel confused. She glanced at Bibi, who looked equally perplexed. "She knew about you two?"

"Of course." Sherry Lynn looked back and forth between Megan and Bibi. "Don't kid yourself into thinking Paul was ever faithful to Blanche. If it hadn't been me it would have been someone else. Maybe even Blanche's own sister." Sherry Lynn pushed at Megan's booted foot with her own.

"Please. Leave."

Megan backed away. Sherry Lynn pushed past her, slamming Megan into the closed back door of the sedan.

"Hey —" Bibi repositioned her cane so that she was holding one end up.

"It's okay, Bibi," Megan said. As Sherry Lynn climbed into the passenger seat, Megan straightened up. She was moving away from the car when something in the back caught her eye. A large black leather computer case lay on the seat, its zipper side up. A stack of papers and a book stuck out from the opened compartment. Megan could make out what looked like a lease. And on top of it, a book. The title was unreadable, but Megan could see the distinctive scroll that signified its famous author.

Sarah Estelle.

As Sherry Lynn pulled out of her driveway, she stared angrily at Megan and Bibi. She rolled the window down before she drove away and yelled, "Next time you come here, I will call the police and request a restraining order."

Megan watched her leave, still thinking of the book.

"Well, that was a waste of time," Bibi said.

"I'm not so sure about that," Megan

351

responded. "This trip may have been just the thing we needed."

Megan called Bobby on their way home on the truck's speakerphone. "Sherry Lynn was reading Sarah's book."

"Did you go see Sherry Lynn Booker again, Megan?"

"Bibi and I went. We wanted to ask her a few more questions about —"

King cut her off. "Megan, we've made an arrest. We have our person. Leave it alone."

Megan merged onto the highway. A silver Audi tried to cut her off and Bibi reached over and slammed on the horn. Megan said, "Did Becca confess?"

"You know I can't talk about that."

"This is Bonnie, Bobby King," Bibi shouted into the speaker. Megan smiled to herself. Her grandmother had never quite gotten the hang of speakerphones. "Did Becca confess or not?"

"You don't need to yell, Bonnie. I can hear you just fine." King's tone softened. "She hasn't. In fact, she won't talk at all."

"Not even with her lawyer?"

"I don't know what's been said between them, but I imagine it's much the same. She's been transferred to the psych ward. She just sits there, staring, and won't speak.

It's not like she's not coherent. She looks at us, is alert. Just . . . silent."

Megan and Bibi exchanged a look. "I'm not so sure you have your killer, Bobby."

"The book in Sherry Lynn's car?"

"The book. The way Sherry Lynn acted — not at all like someone overcome with grief. And Merry."

"Merry?"

"I was on Sherry Lynn's Facebook page last night. I saw a photo from last summer. Merry wasn't in it exactly, but Sherry Lynn wore aviator glasses with mirrored lenses. Merry was the photographer. I confirmed that with Sherry Lynn today."

"I'm sorry but I don't see the significance, Megan."

It started to flurry. Megan put her wipers on. "Merry was at Paul's shore house with Paul and his girlfriend, a woman who was his mistress before Blanche died. Blanche's former best friend. Don't you think that's odd?"

King sighed. "Maybe she didn't know about Sherry Lynn. Are you trying to say Merry is Paul's killer?"

"I think she's trying to say there's more here than meets the eye," Bibi shouted. "Merry never mentioned spending time with Paul last summer, and God knows that woman brags about everything. Is she ashamed? And where is she now? A stomach flu? Seems awfully convenient."

"Has she been to see Becca?" Megan asked.

"Come to think of it, no. I called her, of course, to let her know what was going on. She sounded upset, as I would expect."

"But you haven't seen her there?"

"No. But she may just be ill and depressed. Blaming herself."

"Exactly," Bibi said. "Guilt. But for what?"

"Your imagination is working overtime, ladies. I have to go. I'm finally going to be off duty for a few hours, and Clover is making me what promises to be a downright awful meatloaf. But I'm going to enjoy it and her company and not think about the crazy Fox family for a few hours."

Megan didn't want to let King off the phone. She knew he deserved some downtime, but he was feeling pressured and exhausted and not looking at the big picture. "The book, Bobby. Sherry Lynn had Sarah's book."

"Which one?"

Megan hesitated. "I don't know. I couldn't make out the title."

"So she could just be a fan of Sarah Estelle's novels. Again, your imaginations are working overtime. Becca killed her father and attacked Eloise. Case closed."

King hung up. Neither Bibi nor Megan spoke for a while, each lost in their own thoughts. Finally Bibi said, "You're not done with this, are you?"

"Not by a long shot. You?"

Bibi shook her head. She picked up the cane and placed it closer to her lap. "One thing I've learned in my four score plus years is to pay attention when people act oddly. Merry is acting oddly. That woman Sherry Lynn acted oddly. And Becca Fox?" Bibi slapped the cane for effect. "Oddest of all."

Megan arched her eyebrows. "Something wicked this way cometh?"

"It's cometh all right. But I'm not so sure it's going anytime soon."

THIRTY-FOUR

Megan lay in Denver's arms in the glow of the tipi's small heater. She snuggled in closer, enjoying the warmth and the scent of his musky aftershave. Her shoulders were bare, as were his, and the feel of skin against skin felt intoxicating.

Denver shifted, looking down at her. "I feel like a teenager sneaking away from the parents to have a feel with a bonnie lassie." He smiled. "And ye do look bonnie, Megs."

Megan hugged him tighter, not wanting to let go. She needed to leave, and he needed to get down to the hospital in Philly to see his aunt. They'd stolen an hour in the tipi in the early evening, rushing across the snow like two children. Megan supposed as silly as it seemed, the tipi felt like neutral ground. Somewhere safe from the demands of the farm, his busy practice, and the events taking place in Winsome. Their own little escape. Denver had even set up a tiny

Christmas tree near where the dogs liked to lay, and its white lights twinkled in the dim light.

"Eloise still has no memory of what happened?" Megan asked.

"No, nothing, I'm afraid. She's still a bit out of it. I dinnae when she'll be one hundred percent. The doctors don't either."

Megan sat up. She reached for her clothes, feeling suddenly self-conscious. "You should go to her."

"And where are you going?"

"To see Anita Becker."

"Roger's wife? Why?"

"Because she knew Blanche Fox."

"Still looking for patterns, Megs? I guess you don't agree with Bobby that Becca is the culprit?"

Megan looked at Denver, who was studying her with an almost fierce intensity. She felt the familiar pull of affection and a longing to rejoin him under the blanket. He was on his side, propped up on one elbow. The thick tartan comforter covered him from the waist down, but his chest, muscular and broad, reminded her of his power. So like her late husband Mick in many ways — his kindness, his generosity, his love of life. Megan took a deep breath. She realized she could think about Mick in Denver's presence without feeling disloyal. It didn't mean she loved Mick any less. It just meant she loved Denver as well. The realization felt freeing.

"I just want to tie up a few loose ends." She told him about their trip to see Sherry Lynn. "I'm not sure what I was expecting to get out of her, Denver, but the interaction was odd. The first time we saw her, she was this doormat of a woman — all about Paul and the life they had together. This time she seemed stronger, more together. And then there was the book."

"Maybe she realized he had been a cheating bastard."

"She knew all along."

"You think she could have killed him?"

"I don't think Bobby should dismiss her out of hand."

Denver pulled Megan down for a kiss. He stood, not nearly as self-conscious as Megan had been.

"She said Paul was in good financial shape, yet he asked Sarah for cash," Megan said. "He asked her to invest."

"In what?"

"She didn't know. They never got that far into the discussion. Once she said no, he became angry."

Denver pulled his jeans on, then tugged a

358

t-shirt over his head. He sat back down to put on his socks and boots. His intelligent eyes narrowed in concentration. "Maybe Luke would have some idea about his father's investments."

"But would he talk to me?"

"I heard he's making quite a fuss over his sister's incarceration. If it will help her, he might." Denver stood and took Megan in his arms. "It's almost four, Megs. I need to go to the hospital. Will ye swing by later and let the dogs out tonight? I'm afraid I won't be home in time."

Megan kissed him. "Of course."

"I could make an honest lassie out of ye someday, ye know."

"I'm not an honest woman now?"

Denver's eyes smiled. He kissed the top of her head, then breathed in her scent. "Aye, as honest as they come, I suspect. Except for preying on strange women named Sherry Lynn. You and your grandmother are two peas, ye are."

Knowing Bibi was busy reading Sarah's novels, searching for clues they'd missed, Megan nodded. "That we are."

Roger Becker lived in an older stone Colonial on the edge of Canal Street, not far from where the canal walking path began.

Like many of the homes along that stretch, the Beckers had a large stately house that sat atop a small yard. What the yard lacked in size, it more than made up for in landscaping. In the summer the white picket fence along the street was lined on either side with colorful perennial gardens, and Roger and Anita tended an elaborate *potager* alongside the house — a kitchen garden filled with flowers for cutting, culinary herbs, and vegetables. Even in the winter, their care showed. Wreathes had been placed at intervals along the fence and single electric candles burned in every window. Megan hated to disturb this cozy domestic scene with talk of murder, but she felt she had no choice. She rang the doorbell and waited.

Anita answered immediately. She was a short round woman with ebony black hair and enviably smooth mocha-colored skin. Megan saw her occasionally at the café, but usually Anita was there to buy groceries when she needed something in a hurry. Anita had been a special education teacher at a neighboring district for as long as Megan could remember, and she was as well known for her compassion as her amazing culinary skills.

"Megan, hello. Come in out of the cold."

Anita stepped back to let Megan inside. "Is everything okay?"

"We're fine, Anita. I'm here for sort of an odd reason. Did I come at a bad time?"

"No, no, not at all. I'm just making dinner. You're welcome to stay and eat with us." When Megan politely declined, Anita said, "Then if you don't mind, come into the kitchen. We can chat there."

Megan followed Anita and sat down at a stool by the island. Her kitchen felt small, but warm and inviting. A blocky wooden island with a cooktop center sat in the middle of the rectangular room. Two banks of counters lined the rear and north sides of the kitchen. The appliances were high-end but well-used, the counters stainless steel. It was a cook's kitchen, and Anita was busily chopping vegetables for what looked like a stir fry.

"I love what you're doing with the farm and the café, Megan. Alvaro is a gem of a chef." Anita chopped an onion with a stainless steel chef's knife, her strokes strong and sure. "But I doubt you came to talk about the café."

"No, unfortunately." After a few more minutes of chit chat, Megan explained that she was here about Blanche Fox. "Roger said the two of you were close friends up until she died."

"That's true. And even afterwards, I kept in contact with the family . . . for a while." She shook her head. "I heard Bobby arrested Becca for Paul's murder. So incredibly sad."

"Do you think Becca is capable of something like that?"

Anita seemed startled by the question. "No. Or at least I would have said no last week. I don't know what to think. After everything she's been through, now this."

"Then you know Becca claims her father killed Blanche."

"Yes, of course. She's been saying it for years."

"Do you think there's any truth to that, Anita?"

Anita's eyes looked sad when she said, "I just don't know. Becca is a troubled girl. She spent her childhood trying to please her father, and when her mother died, everything changed. And then the tables turned. The whole situation was heartbreaking."

"What do you mean 'everything changed'?"

Anita used a pastry scraper to transfer the onions into a glass bowl. "It was like she was suddenly seeing her father for who he was. His lies, his narcissism, his false bravado. She used to make excuses for him, and it all ended the second Blanche passed away." She tilted her head, thinking. "Becca didn't allow him to control her anymore."

"Control her in what way?"

Anita put down the scraper. She met Megan's gaze. "Paul was a master at manipulation, as you might have guessed. Especially with women. If he wanted to charm you, watch out. He could make even the most hardened libido feel desired. That's how he got his way. And if you didn't fall for it? Then he would try lies and bullying. But when it came to Blanche and Becca, his tactics were different."

"Different in what way?"

Anita took a moment before speaking. She looked around the room, searching, it seemed, for the right words. "It was as if he held their self-esteem hostage. He'd give just enough praise to make them believe him, but most of the time he degraded them — their looks, their intelligence, their ability to accomplish even little things." Anita regarded Megan, and Megan saw rage and remorse. "It took me years to realize what he was doing to them. By then, I urged Blanche to leave him, for the kids' sake as well as her own."

"I heard she was on the verge of divorce when she died."

"It's true." Anita sighed. She picked up the knife and began peeling the outer bark off a knuckle of ginger root. "She'd finally gotten the courage to end it."

"Do you think —"

"That he killed her so she couldn't leave him? I don't know, Megan. I'd hate to think that of anyone. But the truth is, she was no dummy. And she was quite knowledgeable when it came to the house. She'd even taken a class. It stumped me and Roger — how could she have left the gas on?"

But Megan was no longer listening. She was thinking about that home improvement class — and about someone else who admitted to being handy: Sherry Lynn Booker. She'd suspected Sherry Lynn of killing Paul, but now she wondered if Blanche had been a target too.

How much effort would it have taken Sherry Lynn to kill her competition? If Blanche sued for divorce, she would have received a good portion of Paul's estate and tied the couple up in a messy lawsuit. No Blanche meant Sherry Lynn could have Paul to herself. And a handy woman could figure out how to create a leaky stove — and might just know her way around paint thinner, or some other means of creating the gas that killed Paul Fox.

And conveniently inherit Paul's money.

So many things were clicking into place. Sherry Lynn's lack of mourning. The Sarah Estelle mystery novel in that bag. Megan's pulse picked up. Could that be right? Could Sherry Lynn be the missing link? The first time they'd met her, her worry over Paul had seemed genuine. But what if the emotion they were sensing was guilt? What if she had orchestrated this whole thing knowing she'd get everything in the end?

"What do you know about Sherry Lynn Booker?" Megan asked.

Anita's pleasant features twisted in disgust. "What about her?"

"I take it she's not your favorite person."

"I'm a churchgoing woman, Megan, and I believe in living the Lord's word, not just giving lip service, so I'm not going to express my full feelings for that woman. Suffice it to say I would not want to break bread with her, nor would I trust her with our hamster much less my husband."

"So you know about Sherry Lynn and Paul?"

"You'd have to be blind not to see the chemistry between the two of them. Well before they got together, I warned Blanche.

But she was too blind or trusting or naïve to see what was happening."

"Merry too?"

"Merry? Our Merry?" Anita looked confused.

"Was Merry too blind or trusting or naïve to see what was happening between Paul and Sherry Lynn?"

Anita took her time answering. She pulled two carrots out of the refrigerator and placed them on the counter. Then she crushed a clove of garlic with the back of her knife. "Merry knew. She must have."

Megan told her about the photo, about realizing that Merry had taken a photo of Sherry Lynn at Paul's shore house.

"That trip was an effort to mend the family," Anita said. "In her own way, Merry was as blind to Paul's shortcomings as Sherry Lynn. She truly believed she could bring him and Becca together again. And he pushed her to believe that. This trip — coming here at Christmas — was Paul's idea."

"He thought he could get Becca back?"

"He said he wanted a relationship with his daughter. I'm afraid he thought he could buy it."

Megan frowned. "What do you mean?"

Anita took a deep breath. She shifted uncomfortably, clearly feeling disloyal. "He gave Becca money for The Love Chemist. Funded her operation with a sizable investment."

Megan shook her head. "Merry gave her that money."

"Merry was the conduit. Paul was the financier."

Megan stared at her, open-mouthed. "Merry was acting on his behalf?"

Anita wacked another clove of garlic. "She thought she was doing the right thing, I guess. I told her it wasn't right, but you know how she can be." Anita shrugged. "She said Paul just wanted a relationship with his girl. Ask me? He wanted her to stop accusing him of Blanche's death. If Becca took his money, she'd owe him. That meant control."

Megan's head swam with the new information. Could that have been the investment he'd approached Sarah about? And could Sherry Lynn have killed him to stop more money from going to his daughter? But he was a wealthy man . . . why would he need Sarah's money?

Megan thanked Anita and said she would let herself out.

"Don't be silly, Megan." Anita led her back to the front door. "Here in Winsome, we still look after one another." She looked outside, squinting against the glow of the porch light. "It's starting to sleet or snow or something. You sure you don't want to stay?"

"I really can't. I have to feed Denver's dogs."

"Be careful."

Megan agreed, knowing Anita was thinking of the weather. It wasn't snow that scared Megan, though. It was things that went bump in the night.

Megan made her way outside and back to the truck. It was going to be a long evening.

THIRTY-FIVE

Megan drove slowly to Merry's house, conscious of slick roads and a rising feeling of dread. She was certain she'd be met with the same lukewarm reception she'd received the last several times she showed up, but she wanted to confirm what Anita had told her with Merry. She also wanted to ask Luke if he knew anything about his father's investments — or Paul's paramour.

This time when Megan arrived, the house was lit for the holidays. The outside lights were on, the window candles glowed, and even the Christmas tree twinkled and sparkled from its perch inside Merry's formal living space. Megan took a certain amount of comfort in that. Maybe Merry was back to her old self.

Luke answered the door on the second doorbell ring. He looked more rested and alert. His beard had been trimmed, and he wore a button-down blue gingham shirt with a gray vest, gray pants, and gray socks. He was carrying a newspaper.

"Hi, Megan. Looking for my aunt?"

"Is she up?"

"I can check. She was sleeping earlier."

"No change?"

Luke took a step back, inviting Megan into the center hall. "Better, I think. She's still not feeling one hundred percent. The doctor says she has a flu that might knock her out for a week or two. And then there's my sister." Luke's eyes clouded. "I'm sure you heard she's been formally charged."

"I did. I'm sorry. I imagine it's very upsetting to both of you."

Luke nodded. "I don't think they have the right person, but if this leads to Becca getting some help, then something positive will have come out of it. At least that's what I keep telling Aunt Merry."

Megan slid her coat off her shoulders. "May I come in?"

"Oh, sure. Please." Luke took her coat and hung it in the closet. "Let me check on Aunt Merry."

"Before you go, can I ask you a few questions?"

Impatience flashed across Luke's face. "I'm actually getting ready to head out."

"Oh? Something special?" Megan knew

370

she was bordering on intrusive, but she didn't care. "I don't want to hold you up, but it will only take a few minutes."

"I'm meeting with Becca's attorney." He glanced at his watch — a Cartier or a Cartier rip-off. "Fifteen minutes. Looks like it's starting to sleet. I want to get to the lawyer before she leaves."

Megan thanked him for his time. "I was wondering about your dad's investment business, Luke." She told him about Paul's request that Sarah make a sizable investment. "Do you know whether that was for Becca's business?"

Luke laughed. "The Love Chemist? Doubtful. If ever there was a business set to fail, that was it. Love potions? Pheromones?" He shook his head. "I don't think so."

"But your dad was trying to support Becca."

"Look, Becca hated Dad. I told you that, she told you that. My sister had this irrational belief that my father killed my mother. She wouldn't let it go. Why would he want to fund her business?"

They were still standing in the foyer. Megan shifted her weight so she could glance around the house. For what, she didn't know. "What if I told you your father had been married before? That his first wife died accidentally too."

Luke narrowed his eyes. "Bullshit."

"It's a matter of public record."

"I want to check that out for myself. Dad would have told us if he'd been married before."

"He was young, there were no kids, so not necessarily. And maybe your sister found out. Maybe that fueled her belief about your dad's guilt. Two deceased wives seems like quite a coincidence."

Luke looked skeptical. "Becca would have said something."

Megan hesitated before asking her next question. She knew she was walking on brittle glass, but she'd come too far to turn back. She'd push forward. "Is it possible Sherry Lynn found out?"

"Sherry Lynn?" His confusion appeared genuine. "Why would she care?"

"She had been your mother's best friend. I know things changed after her death, but if she caught wind that your father hadn't been completely honest —"

Luke waved his hand in a dismissive gesture. "I really have to go. It's getting late, and none of this is going to help my sister."

"Do you know Sherry Lynn well?"

"If you're asking me whether she could

have killed my father, the answer is no. Who should that joker King and his merry band of idiots be looking for? William Dorset . . . or some other disgruntled patient of my father's." Luke walked toward the stairs. "Now do you want to see Aunt Merry or not?"

"Yes, please." Megan started to follow him, but he motioned for her to stay put.

"Let me see if she's even awake. The doctor gave her a prescription that knocks her out."

Megan stood in the center hall while Luke disappeared outside. Megan was about to head into the living room for a quick peek around when Luke came barreling back down the stairs.

"She's really groggy, Megan. You may want to come back tomorrow."

"I'd like to see her now."

"I don't think —"

"I do." Megan pushed past him and up the steps. "I won't stay for more than five minutes."

"Then let yourself out," Luke called after her. "I'm not waiting around."

Megan expected to find Merry in bed, a repeat of the last visit. She was pleased to see her sitting in a chair by the window, a dark shawl around her frail-looking shoulders. The light in the room was dim, but Merry was awash in the soft glow from a table lamp. She turned her head to look at Megan when she entered. Her smile seemed wistful.

"Merry, we've been so worried about you. How are you feeling?"

"Better." Merry's voice was soft, raspy as though from disuse.

"I wanted to talk to you. First, to check on you, and second . . . well, I have some questions." But even as Megan spoke, she realized it was fruitless. Merry maintained the same wistful smile, the same glassy stare. Megan walked to the table and looked down at what Merry was doing. She had a pen and crossword in front of her, but only one word was filled in — and incorrectly.

Megan felt Merry's head. It was cool and clammy. She studied her friend. Her skin was pale, her hair unwashed. She wore a pink dressing gown under the shawl, and she smelled of Becca's rose perfume. "Do you want some ice water? Maybe a bite to eat?"

"No, thank you. I'm fine."

"Maybe a walk? Get out of this room for a spell?"

Merry looked up at her. Her eyes seemed

faraway. "I'm fine, Megan."

"Can we talk about Becca? About her relationship with Paul? I think it may be important, Merry. It might help your niece."

Merry closed her eyes slowly, then opened them again. It took her a moment to refocus. Her voice stronger but ignoring the question, she said, "Can you do me a favor?"

"Anything."

"I'm worried about the business. I've felt so ill."

"I understand. Whatever you need."

"My reputation is on the line. I can't afford to lose customers or suppliers."

Merry ripped a piece of paper out of the crossword book. "I need to cancel an order of trees and wreaths. I'm not feeling up to opening the store tomorrow. If I give you the name of the farm, will you cancel for me?"

"Sure, Merry."

Merry scribbled on the paper, folded it with shaking hands, and then handed it to Megan. "Thank you."

Megan nodded. She wasn't going to get more out of Merry today. She hugged Merry's rigid form and left, feeling a sense of hopelessness cascade over her. Downstairs was empty. The tree was unplugged, and there were no sounds except for the tick-tock of Merry's antique grandfather clock. Megan opened the closet door and tugged her coat off the hanger. It fell on the floor. Megan picked it up, her eyes latching onto something at the back of the closet.

It was a large leather laptop bag. Black, with a zippered top. Just like the one she'd seen in Sherry Lynn's car.

Megan left Merry's house with an impending feeling of doom. She wasn't sure what was going on in Winsome, but she was quite certain Becca's arrest was not the end of it. She had promised to let Denver's dogs out because he wouldn't be home until late. As she drove to his bungalow, she called Anita and Roger Becker. Roger answered.

"Megan!" He sounded pleased to hear from her. "I heard you spent some time with my wife today. She enjoyed seeing you despite the circumstances."

"Roger, I'm calling for a favor. It's Merry." Megan explained her visit to the older woman's house. "Luke said Merry's doctor prescribed meds for her flu. Can you call Dr. Schmidt and see if anything she prescribed would do this to Merry? I'm pretty sure Henrietta Schmidt is Merry's doctor. She won't tell you anything, but maybe she can at least confirm if the meds should make her so groggy."

"I'll do one better. Anita and I will go sit with Merry — and we'll call."

Megan thanked him. Denver's driveways had a fresh coat of snow and ice, so Megan pulled alongside the road near his house and killed the engine. "I locked the door on my way out," Megan said to Roger. "Luke went to meet with Becca's attorney."

"I have a key. No worries."

Next Megan dialed Bibi. "Have anything new for me?"

"Not really. I'm not seeing anything else in these books, Megan." Bibi's voice brightened. "I did call Vermont to get a copy of Paul's first wife's death certificate. I'm sure Bobby has one, but since it's a matter of public record, I figured we could take a look. See for ourselves if there's something wacky."

"Are they sending that?"

"Yes, but it will take weeks to get it. I have to send in a request by mail."

"Ah, well." Megan dug out the paper Merry had given her.

"I called the Department of Health to inquire. The nice lady in Vermont did tell me one thing. She said I'm not the only one who asked for this."

Megan stopped unfolding the paper. "Did

she say who else asked for it?"

"No, she just said it was a man."

"A man? Probably Bobby."

"Not unless he went in person."

Megan was thinking about this when she read the slip of torn crossword Merry had given her. "Alyssa Abrams" was written on the paper alongside the words "Killing Us All."

Was Alyssa the farmer? If so, it wasn't a name Megan recognized. But what about "Killing Us All"? Ramblings?

Then it hit her. Another book?

"Bibi, do me a favor." Megan gave her the information. "Do you know how to do some searches on the internet?" Bibi wasn't very tech savvy. She still couldn't quite master her phone, and she'd had it for months.

"I can get Porter to help me. He's still here."

"Yes, do that. Ask him to do some searches and see who this Alyssa is." She shared her concern that this was another author, another book. "Let's just be cautious and find out."

Bibi agreed. "Be careful, Megan."

"I will, Bibi. And could you have Porter stay with you until I get home? If we're right and there's more than Becca happening here, someone could get rather annoyed with us."

Bibi sounded like she was going to argue, but then she said, "Of course. It would be nice to feed that boy anyway. He looks like he hasn't seen the bottom of a plate in years."

Megan hung up, grateful for Brian Porter. With him and Gunther there, Bibi would be safe.

THIRTY-SIX

Megan pulled her metal flashlight from under the seat of the truck and climbed out. The street was slick from sleet and snow, and she tread carefully around to the back of the house. It would be easier to take the dogs out from there. The neighborhood was quiet, the nearest house, another small bungalow, dark and empty. Megan opened the gate and entered Denver's backyard. She climbed onto the deck and looked out over his wooded yard. The snow and sleet formed jagged icicles that hung from the trees and bushes. It would have been a pretty scene were it not for the oppressive sense of aloneness.

The dogs began barking, aware that their dinner was on its way. Megan was just fumbling with the back door key when she heard it: the sound of an engine followed by silence. She heard the sound of the gate — metal on metal. Someone was here.

Megan flicked off the flashlight and moved into the shadows at the side of the yard. Quickly, quietly, she followed the fence until she was entombed in the shadows of the trees. That's when she saw the figure come through the gate. Sheathed in black like the Canal Street stalker, it climbed the steps and jiggled the door handle. Met with a locked door, the figure left the porch and made its way into the yard. A flashlight flicked on. Whoever it was seemed to be headed toward Megan.

She looked around. Remembering the tipi tucked into the back area of the property, Megan followed a trail to the very back of the wooded yard. She circled around the back of the tipi and entered it quietly. She secured the flap that closed the structure, leaving enough space for a lookout. On her stomach, flashlight gripped in one hand like a weapon, Megan waited and watched.

She saw the glow of the figure's flashlight as it made its way to the back door, which was still locked, and through the lower portion of the yard. Her heart beat quickly — and so loudly she felt sure the intruder could hear it in the deafening silence of the woods. Still she watched, praying whoever it was would leave.

A few moments later, her prayer was

answered. The light weaved and bobbed through the yard, returning to the gate. Megan climbed out of the tipi and walked over toward the fence. The snow was coming down harder now, more flake than sleet. She heard an engine start and then fade as the car left Denver's neighborhood.

A figure in black. Someone who followed her here? Or someone who was after Denver?

Megan called the police and reported an intruder on Denver's property. She left the dogs inside for fear that their paw prints would ruin any scrap of evidence that might remain. Back in her car, she glanced at her phone. Three calls from Bibi.

Megan called her, still breathless from fear and adrenaline.

"Alyssa Abrams is your Aunt Sarah," Bibi said. "Here, talk to Porter."

Porter got on and explained the search they had done to find out the identity of Alyssa Abrams. "She's a short story writer," he said. "She writes crime fiction for magazines like *Alfred Hitchcock Mystery Magazine*, which is where this was published."

"Where what was published?"

" 'To Kill Us All.' It's a short story."

Megan started the car to warm it up. She

debated whether to wait for the local police to arrive but decided against it. The roads were getting slick and she didn't want to remain here, a sitting duck if the intruder returned.

"What's it about, Brian?"

Brian said, "We're still trying to find a copy. The tag line just says 'a chilling story of one deranged madman's act of revenge.' "

"Revenge again," Megan said. "Okay, can you continue to try and find it?"

"Yes. Want us to call your aunt?"

Megan glanced at the clock on the dashboard. 6:48. Plenty early for a visit. "No, I can do that. Just tell my grandmother I'll be home in an hour, okay?"

Porter agreed. "Bonnie wants to talk to you anyway."

"Why do you think Merry gave you that name?" Bibi asked when she was back on the phone.

"I don't know. I don't imagine we'll know until you and Porter can find the actual story — or I can reach Aunt Sarah."

"Call me, Megan. The second you know."

"I will. Can you do me one other favor?" She explained the intruder on Denver's property. "Can you or Brian call Denver and let him know?"

"You don't want to do it because he'll tell

you to go home and lock your door."

Megan didn't answer. Her grandmother knew her well.

"Megan? Please finish quickly and come home," Bibi said. "Denver would be right if you gave him the chance to tell you that. Whoever is wreaking havoc on the Fox family and our town isn't afraid to kill. And I have a very bad feeling we haven't seen the last of death's shadow tonight."

Megan hung up, spooked. Death's shadow. A very good way to describe the evil presence she was feeling.

THIRTY-SEVEN

Sarah didn't answer her phone. Megan left her a message and then pulled the truck out onto the road, debating what to do next. She could go home and help Bibi and Brian locate a copy of this Alyssa Abrams story. Or she could swing by Sarah's house.

The weather seemed to be letting up some, and the roads, while slippery, were mostly empty. The storm was keeping Winsome inside. Megan decided to take the risk and head to the outskirts of Winsome, to Sarah's cottage. Although it was only seven, it felt later. Houses dressed for merriment, with festive lights and lawn ornaments, only heightened Megan's tension. She wanted to go home and have this all be done with. A hot bath. A snuggle with the dogs. Some gift wrapping. That's what she should be doing days before Christmas — not driving around, seeking clues about murder.

Megan tried her aunt again. Still no

answer, but this time her cell phone went right to voicemail as though Aunt Sarah had turned her phone off. Frustrated, Megan increased her speed down the long curvy road that led to Sarah's home.

About an eighth of a mile from Aunt Sarah's, the unthinkable happened. Megan hit a patch of black ice and her truck swerved, then rolled into a frozen ditch on the side of the road. Megan slipped the truck into four-wheel drive and tried to back out. It was no use, the tires spun uselessly. She exited the truck and tried to push. Her feet slipped in the fresh mush and she landed on her knees and scraped her hand against the sharp edge of the bumper. Cursing her luck, Megan stood with some effort. Sleet was coming down again, and the pellets bit into her skin and stung her face.

Frustrated, Megan pulled the heavy metal flashlight, her keys, and her phone from the truck. If Mother Nature was going to place obstacles in her way, she'd climb over them. She texted Porter and asked him to call a tow truck. Then she set off to walk the rest of the way to Sarah's.

The cottage was lit up like a stadium during the Super Bowl. Megan crossed the driveway to the house, just happy her aunt was okay. Sarah's car sat in the driveway, and Megan could see one of her orange tabby cats lounging in an upstairs window-sill. Megan paused in the driveway to get the sleet out of her eyes. The air felt biting and cold, the sleet like a million tiny pin-pricks against her skin. Sarah would make her coffee. The world would be right again.

Megan was about to turn off her flashlight when the beam caught something in the wooded area behind Aunt Sarah's flower gardens. It looked like a car was parked between the trees. Curious, Megan made her way carefully across the icy pavement and into the edge of the forest. It was a car. A Honda with New Jersey license plates.

Sherry Lynn Booker's car.

From the look of it, it hadn't been here long. The tracks in the snow seemed fresh, and the car's windshield was still warm to the touch. Megan tried the door. Locked.

What was she doing here? Megan remem-bered the briefcase. And the book. And her hypothesis about Sherry Lynn's home repair prowess.

And the fact that Sherry Lynn would inherit the Fox estate with Paul dead. And with Becca out of the way? One less person to protest. But why Sarah? And why Sarah's books? And what did it mean that Sherry Lynn was likely inside Sarah's very well-lit cottage?

Megan stood in the cold, shivering, thinking about Sherry Lynn and the car parked in the woods. Her mind flashed to the laptop bag in Merry's closet. Could Sherry Lynn and Luke have been acting together all this time? Megan could envision it. An affair. A mutual desire to inherit Paul's money. The need to get rid of Paul — and have Becca out of the picture too.

A need for revenge.

But what about the books? And why would Sherry Lynn want revenge? She was the one set to inherit. Greed could have caused her to kill Paul, but Megan was hard-pressed to see why Sherry Lynn would carry on with the rest of the charade.

Maybe Paul had been cheating on Sherry Lynn too. It was his MO. But that wouldn't explain why she was here with Sarah.

Megan wanted to call the police, but she was suddenly aware of the quiet — and her vulnerable position. No car, no weapon. If someone heard her, she would be in danger. Megan turned the volume off on her phone. She was about to text Porter to ask him to call Bobby and 911 when she saw she'd received a text from Brian a few minutes earlier. It was about Alyssa Abrams and the short story. The text said, "Call us. Bibi said story is about a teen who holds a town hostage in his quest for revenge."

A chill snaked its way down Megan's spine. She knew the connections to Sarah's books weren't always literal, but this one struck her as different.

A town held hostage: by attacks and murders.

A teen boy seeking revenge: Luke Fox.

Revenge for what? Megan thought back to the photo on Sherry Lynn's Facebook page, the image of the father and son on one side, Blanche and Sherry Lynn on the other, and Becca in the middle. With a start, she saw the dynamic differently than she had before. Blanche and Paul looking at Becca. Sherry Lynn and Luke looking at Paul.

No one was looking at Luke. The responsible one. The less demanding child.

Merry had given Becca money — money from Paul. Money meant for Luke's newest venture? Merry being held hostage now, a prisoner in her own house. That was her message, slipped innocently to Megan under the guise of a business favor so her maniacal nephew wouldn't suspect her cry for help.

Hostage. Anita's words echoed in Megan's

ears: Paul had held his family hostage. He sadistically destroyed Becca and Blanche's self-image. He superficially propped up Luke's. Luke was turning the tables. Torturing those he blamed for torturing him.

She suddenly saw the man who was grinning in all those Facebook photos differently. A history of job hopping. Superficial friendships. Girlfriends who were unattractive in his father's eyes. An empty shell. A constant failure to the one man who Luke wanted desperately to please.

Megan imagined the entire period of the last few weeks as a play, with Luke as the playwright. First revenge against the man who jilted him one too many times — the man he couldn't please. His father's death would be staged over several days, while Paul was sleeping, and his final demise would take place in a taped-up room, with Paul fully aware of his impending death. Luke would have worn protective gear. He would have watched as his father, already weak from poison, coughed and sputtered and slowly suffocated, his mucous membranes scorched from the chemical, his lungs filling with fluid.

Then revenge against Dr. Kent, the woman who caused their family to leave Winsome, starting their string of bad luck.

Her revenge was swift and sudden — just like her actions against Luke's father. One blow to the head. Down and out.

Next, revenge against his sister — who in the end had the support and attention he felt he deserved. He could have forced her to set that fire, or set it himself and abandoned her there, threatening her life if she spoke up. Luke would have enjoyed torturing Becca most especially, doing to her the things her father had done. Filling her head with doubt, playing on her insecurities, and finally, simply threatening her if she didn't concede. Holding her hostage in her aunt's own home. No wonder Becca tried to run.

And Sarah . . . using her stories as clues. Drawing attention to the muse and the master, only in this instance he got to be the master, she the muse.

Sherry Lynn. The willing accomplice. Perhaps even Luke's lover. What had Becca said? There'd been competition between Luke and his father. And if Luke and Sherry Lynn were in this together, in Luke's mind he was the ultimate winner.

Sherry Lynn. Here now. With Sarah.

Megan glanced again at the car, her throat constricting in fear. She walked around the car, wondering whether she could jimmy open a door. She was feeling along the side by the handle when her fingers brushed something rough in the smooth surface of the Honda's paint job. Careful to hold the flashlight low, Megan pointed it at the side of the car. What she saw made her heart leap.

Scratches, all along the door. Scratches she was certain were not there earlier in the day.

Megan flipped off the flashlight. She knew with crushing certainty that Sherry Lynn was not a partner in crime.

Sherry Lynn was another victim.

THIRTY-EIGHT

Megan sent a group text asking Clay, Clover, Bobby, and Porter to alert the police and send someone to Sarah's house. Given the weather and the distance to Sarah from the town, she knew it would take some time for help to arrive. In the meantime, she needed to distract Luke from whatever it was he was doing in there — because she knew in her heart that Sarah was not fine.

Megan approached the house quietly. She walked from window to window to try and find where they were. Most windows were covered by window treatments or shades — the first defense of a savvy woman living alone. But Megan remembered the new kitchen and the treatment-less windows. She made her way around to the back of the house, her heart thumping steadily in her chest. Above, the skies had opened up and a steady sleety-rain was now pouring forth, drenching her clothes and dripping into Megan's eyes.

She steadied herself against the house and looked into the kitchen. Finally she spied him. Luke was wearing a black sweater and black pants. Like the intruder on Denver's property. Only he wasn't alone. He was sitting in a chair across from Sarah. She was smiling and speaking, her eyes and hands animated. Megan watched as Aunt Sarah lifted a glass of wine to her lips. Her small Christmas tree sparkled from its throne in the room behind her, brightly wrapped gifts circling its base. This looked like a scene from a holiday movie — not the horror show she was expecting.

Megan flipped around so her back was against the house. She forced herself to breathe. They seemed to be having a perfectly pleasant conversation. But then, Luke was as much an actor as his father. He'd seduce Sarah into thinking he was harmless. And then he'd pounce. Megan needed to get in there. She needed to warn Sarah.

Megan turned back toward the window. Her hand shot to her mouth to stifle a scream.

Aunt Sarah's eyes were wide, her mouth twisted in terror. The idyllic scene from a moment ago had given way to the macabre.

Luke was behind Sarah now, a rope in one hand, a sharp knife in the other. He watched with apparent pleasure as Aunt Sarah writhed in the chair, suffering, Megan believed, at the hands of whatever poison Luke had put into her glass. She seemed unable to defend herself while Luke placed the knife against her throat. Her mouth formed the "o" of an empty scream, her eyes struggled to stay open.

The knife pushed Megan into action. She ran to the back door and pounded, then stepped back into the shadows. She held the heavy metal flashlight with two hands, back behind her head. Luke opened the door. When no one was there, he ventured out onto the porch, his eyes searching the shadows. Before she could lose her nerve, Megan brought the flashlight down on the side of Luke's head with all of the energy she had left. The blow didn't knock him out, but it did knock him down.

Megan ran for the back door, hoping to get inside and lock it before Luke was back up. She was just about over the threshold when she felt his hand on her ankle. He tugged her down on top of him. His breath smelled of wine and cigars, his eyes looked demonic in the haze of the sleet and rain.

"Bitch," he muttered.

Megan's arm twisted and stretched, searching for the flashlight she knew was there somewhere. While her heart was racing, her mind was on Sarah. Was she still alive? Would she survive long enough to get help? Anger washed over Megan, a great wave of rage and bitterness. She finally felt a connection to her past, to her mother, to her grandfather — and this bastard, with his antisocial outlook on life and his disregard for anyone else, threatened to take it all away.

Luke used one hand to grab Megan's neck. The other was pinned under his body. Megan continued to search for the flashlight, her fingers crawling along the icy walkway.

Luke's fingers squeezed.

Megan's fingers grasped something hard. Only it wasn't a flashlight in her grasp. It was the knife Luke had been holding.

Megan raised the knife up over her head. Luke was squeezing harder now. Megan wrapped her free hand around his wrist and tried to pull his fingers off her throat but it was no use — he was too strong and the sleet had made him slippery. She could barely breathe, much less tell him to stop.

He grimaced with the effort of choking her. Nasty names spilled forth from his mouth, and his eyes searched hers as though waiting for the light to go out, anticipating the moment when she would succumb to his control.

One sociopath begot another, Megan thought.

Her vision was starting to dim. She was losing her grip on the knife.

Do it, she thought. Do it, Bibi said to her. Help me, Sarah whispered.

Megan plunged the knife down, aiming across Luke's torso and for his shoulder. She cringed as the knife point sliced into bone and muscle. As he released the grip on Megan's neck, it was she who screamed out in pain and anger. Blood gushed from Luke's chest. He looked at it, clearly enraged. His stare fell on Megan, locking onto her gaze. She scrambled backwards, off his body. Feeling for the door, Megan stood unsteadily. She backed up into the kitchen. The last thing she saw before she slammed and locked the door was the growing pool of blood under Luke's body.

Sarah sat draped over the table, unconscious. Megan felt for a pulse — it was there, but faint, just like her aunt's respiration. Megan dialed 911 and reported the crime in between crying gasps. "Police should be on the way," she said. "But we need an ambulance too." Thinking of Luke, she added, "Make that two."

Megan heard the faint wail of sirens, felt the chill in the room. She focused on tasks so she didn't need to think about whether Aunt Sarah would live or die, her own brush with death, or the fact that she may have killed another human being.

Megan grabbed an afghan she recognized as Bibi's off the couch in another room. Back in the kitchen, she wrapped it around her aunt and held her body close. "Stay with me," she whispered. "Please stay with me."

THIRTY-NINE

Megan sat in the safety of the patrol car for what felt like days. She watched as a cacophony of strobe lights swirled in blues and reds against the backdrop of Sarah's fairytale house. Pulling the blanket Bobby had given her tight around her shoulders, she stared at the ambulance that held her aunt. It pulled slowly out of the driveway, its wheels slipping on the sleet-covered surface. A few moments later, the sirens began to wail, a harbinger of evil in this holy season.

A second ambulance would follow in a few moments, Megan knew. This one would hold Luke, whose chest wound — a wound she had inflicted — ran deep. Not as deep as Luke's psychological wounds, perhaps. But deep enough to be fatal if the EMTs didn't act quickly. Megan could see them now, hunched over Luke's motionless body. Staunching blood flow. Administering medicines. All action and purpose. One of

Luke's gloves lay on the white snow in a pool of crimson. The color, so bright against its pale backdrop, would have looked festive had she not known what it was. Megan closed her eyes. A morbid thought, indeed.

But it was the Honda that pulled her attention in the final moments before she let her head hit the back of the seat. Before she acknowledged her own wounds, and the wounds of a town that would take years to recover.

Another body. Pulled from the trunk.

Sherry Lynn Booker. First a friend, then a mistress, then a victim.

Had she caught on to Luke's game, and he'd killed her?

Or had she been a willing accomplice whose life ended in another act of revenge?

Megan closed her eyes again, trying to push away the images that plagued her. Sarah, as the EMTs placed her on the gurney. Luke, his eyes blazing with misdirected hatred. A knife bloodied, buried in another human's body. The feel of the knife in her hand.

Soon Bobby would come to ask questions. For now, Megan closed her eyes against the barrage of pain and grief. Her body would heal. Of that she was certain.

She wasn't so sure about her spirit.

FORTY

This year's Christmas tree was the biggest and brightest they'd ever had. Denver received the honor of placing the angel atop the tree, and he needed a stool to reach. That finished, he stepped down and Bibi dimmed the lights. They all gathered around the tree — Bibi, Megan, Denver, Clay, Porter, Clover, Alvaro, his wife, Emily, Lily, and Bobby — and took in the sight. Handmade ornaments, strings of popcorn, candy canes, twinkling white lights, and that angel on the top, made so many years ago by a young Bonnie for her new husband. Megan felt tears sting her eyes. She wished Sarah could be here too. Maybe next year.

Alvaro was nursing a glass of vodka. He raised it in the air. "There is a saying in my birth country: *Arrieros somos y en el camino andamos.* We are all mule drivers in the fields." He took a drink. "Rich or poor, educated or uneducated, bad things happen. So I say let's sing, old woman."

"It's the first sensible thing you've said all night." Bibi looked at Alvaro with poorly veiled affection. " 'Silent Night.' I'll start."

Round after round they sang, one carol after another. Megan looked around the room, awash in gratitude. Her friends were here, her family. Even Lily, held closely by Clay as Emily stood near, was cooing along. The holiday may have brought them together, but the tree rooted them, its lights serving as beacons of hope and reminders that despite all that had happened, there was goodness in the world.

Bibi had made a turkey, garlic potatoes, green beans, glazed carrots, and salad. She insisted on eating in the dining room, and she placed the food on the long antique table alongside her good china dishes and crystal stemware.

"It's a special day," Bibi said. Megan knew she was celebrating more than the eve of Christmas.

Bobby cornered Megan as she was filling the wine glasses. "Thank you," he said. "I'm sorry for not listening. Without you . . . well, I hate to think how things would have turned out."

Megan had been hoping for a chance to

talk to the Chief alone. She had pieced most of it together but wanted confirmation. And an update. "How is Becca?"

"Back with Merry. They're both recovering. Merry has a therapist coming to her house, and Becca is seeing a psychologist." He looked at Megan pointedly. "A real psychologist."

"So Luke *was* holding them hostage."

"In a manner of speaking. At first it was just threats, but toward the end, he was using drugs to keep them docile, and he was threatening to hurt the other one if either refused to cooperate. That's how he got Becca to Emily's house. He told her he'd kill Merry if she didn't do what he told her." King shook his head in disgust. "Learned behavior. Based on what I've gathered, Paul really was a horrible person, and he passed that on to his son."

How awful, Megan thought. To live like that and have no one realize it. "So Merry was never under Dr. Schmidt's care?"

"No. As a matter of fact, when Roger called the doctor, she had no idea what he was talking about. Both of them called me. I was already on my way to Merry's when I was alerted to your call. You were the nail that sealed the coffin."

Bibi placed a platter of rolls and butter on

the table. Megan watched her grandmother work, thinking about a time when she would no longer be in her life. The pain she would feel, the heartbreak. How scary it must have been for Merry and Becca — living with the fear of losing one another.

"And Sherry Lynn?" Megan already knew the answer, which had been whispered from patron to patron at the café. The things she couldn't see from that patrol car. A body curled in fetal position in the trunk of Sherry Lynn's Accord. Bloodied fingernails the only testament to her struggle. A victim — not an accomplice.

"Part of his revenge story. Because she was set to inherit his father's money." King rubbed at his temples with thick fingers. "And there's the sick part. There was no money. Paul's new investment business? A sham. Just like everything else in his life. It took us a while to unravel things, but eventually we learned that he had built his own little pyramid scheme, borrowing from one investor to pay another." He shook his head. "Sherry Lynn died for nothing."

Perhaps that explained Sherry Lynn's altered behavior. And the reason Paul had hit Sarah up for money. Not blackmail — desperation. "The briefcase was Luke's. He had been in New Jersey when Bibi and I went to Sherry Lynn's house the second time."

King nodded. "Luke went down under the pretense of friendship, but then he kidnapped her, brought her to Winsome, killed her."

"And he knew we were there. He knew I was asking questions. That's why he followed me to Denver's."

"You would have been one of his victims, Megan." King shook his head. "A very sick man. He will never see daylight as a free man again."

"Dinner in five," Bibi called.

Megan watched King as his gaze followed Bibi make her way into the kitchen. There was a heaviness to her presence, a seriousness that underscored what they were all feeling.

"I understand why he went after Paul. He was angry that Paul had refused him investment money, giving it to Becca instead."

"And we think the will set him off initially. According to Luke, Paul told him he was writing Sherry Lynn into the will. Luke claims he didn't know there was no money. When Paul said no to the investment funds, that was the last straw. Luke killed Paul, and then set out to get revenge against everyone else who had done him wrong —

405

real or imagined." King held up a hand and counted on his fingers. "Paul, Becca, Sherry Lynn, Merry, Eloise —"

"Because she ended his contract?"

King nodded. "Eloise had a lot to say about Paul Fox and his so-called therapy sessions. Her patients didn't fare well in his care. And she blamed herself for not seeing through his façade. As for Sarah, well you know what happened there."

Ah, yes. Sarah. Megan sat down and picked up a glass of wine. She took a long sip, her eyes on the police chief. "I'm heading to the hospital in the morning. She seems to be holding on."

"Considering she was the crux of all of this, the catalyst, she's quite lucky she's still alive. In Luke's twisted mind, everything bad in his life started with Sarah. Had Sarah not told Eloise, they wouldn't have left Winsome and so on. So it was fitting to use her novels to mark his vengeful acts — and then to end this tirade with her death."

Megan thought about this. "It feels disproportional, Bobby. Reading all of her fiction? Pretty obsessive."

Bobby grabbed a glass off the table too. He held it to his lips and shook his head. "It was Paul who was obsessed with Sarah," he said after taking a drink. "They had a relationship while he was her therapist, and he never let it go. The more her fame grew, the angrier Paul became that she got away. It makes sense that Luke would have honed in on her."

Bibi was back in the dining room. She placed the turkey on the table and the savory scent wafted across the room, making Megan's stomach gurgle. Bibi wiped her hands on her "Winsome Rocks" apron and joined them in the back of the dining room.

"You said Becca is getting psychological help," Megan said. "She'll need it."

King nodded. "She's spending the holiday with Merry and the Beckers." He glanced at the long table, set out for a feast. "She'll be getting some help for some deep-rooted psychological issues. And continuing with her business."

Megan smiled. She'd had no time to buy gifts this year, so everyone was getting a box of Becca's special perfume or cologne. There'd be a lot of love in Winsome this spring.

"So her behavior — breaking into our home, the fire — was that drug induced or was that mental illness, Bobby?" Bibi asked.

"A mixture, I guess."

Megan turned to her grandmother. "Merry said Becca has post-traumatic stress disorder and suffers from some other issues. But much of what she was dealing with was quite real — and caused by her brother's threats. That day she broke in? He was stalking her outside. She was trying to tell us what was going on in the midst of what was likely a psychotic breakdown."

Bibi's mouth turned down in sadness. "We could have done more to help her. We might have believed her about her mother's death." Bibi searched King's eyes. "Do you think Paul killed Blanche?"

King shrugged. "We may never know for sure. What we do know is that Luke found out about the first wife. He used that information to fuel his frame-up of Becca."

"Because it fit with Sarah's book — *When Love Kills.*" Megan took another swallow of wine, enjoying the sting as it washed down her throat. The sting, the ability to taste, meant she was alive. "The attack outside the café, that was different. I know it couldn't have been Becca because she was locked up. William Dorset?"

King stood. "Yes. Becca paid him to follow you and leave the book. He attacked you because you caught him by surprise. He couldn't take a chance that you'd see him."

Bibi's eyes widened in surprise. "Why

would she do that? It doesn't sound like Becca at all."

"She wanted us to figure out what was happening," Megan said. "She knew the books were part of Luke's plan. By then she knew something was going on but couldn't tell anyone because Luke would have hurt Merry in retaliation." Megan glanced at Bobby, who nodded his agreement. "She wanted to give us a concrete clue about what Luke was up to. First the newspaper clippings, then the book. It was risky, but it worked."

King nodded. "She wanted you to figure it out. That was the first time we picked her up, and she couldn't get to you herself. Plus, Luke was threatening her. If she'd said something herself, Merry would have been in danger."

Denver entered the dining room. Spotting King, Bibi, and Megan, he joined them by the table. He leaned in and gave Megan a kiss, holding her gaze for a few seconds longer than necessary.

"Bonnie, that turkey is calling us. Shall I fetch the others?"

Bibi nodded. "Thank you, Denver."

"Ta, Bonnie. Thank *you*. For this," he waved at the table, "for this," he walked over to Megan, "and for having us all here together." He put his arms around Megan's shoulders protectively. "And I'm happy to say that Eloise is doing better. The doctors think any impairment is temporary."

Megan hugged him. Bibi grinned.

"All the more reason to celebrate," King said.

Bibi busied herself straightening the red cloth napkins and adjusting silverware that was already pin straight. Denver gave her a kiss and left the room, followed by King. When Megan moved to help Bibi with the remaining table settings that also didn't need adjustment, Bibi laid her hand on Megan's arm.

"They're fine," she said. "We're ready to eat."

Megan sighed. "I know."

"You were almost killed."

"But *I'm* fine."

"You did a brave thing, Megan."

"Stabbing Luke . . . feeling that knife in my hand. I don't think I will ever forget that, Bibi."

Her grandmother nodded. "It's the kind of thing that changes a person. But whether it changes you for the better or worse is up to you."

Megan looked away, wiping her eyes.

Bibi squeezed her arm. "Mick would be proud."

"You think so?" Megan's voice was husky.

"I know so." Bibi reached up and gave her granddaughter a kiss. "And I'm proud too."

FORTY-ONE

There was little more depressing than a hospital on Christmas Day. Walking quickly through the building, Megan noticed the holiday decorations — silver menorahs, Christmas trees, holly-studded garlands — that marked the nurses' stations and the waiting rooms. Like her drive to Sarah's cottage on that fateful day, the decorations didn't buoy her spirits. Rather, they reminded her that not everyone was feeling fortunate on such a celebrated occasion.

Megan reached Sarah's hall. She carried a large bouquet of mixed flowers and a box of chocolates from Bibi, and she hid behind the flowers, trying not to see the desperation in the faces of the other visitors walking the floor. The hospital smelled of disinfectant and sickness, and Megan's black boot heels clicked their way across the tiled floor. Megan searched for room 522, anxious to see Sarah and get home to Bibi and

Denver. To that hot bath and a hot lasagna and her two favorite dogs.

She found Sarah's room across from the nurses' station. A red-haired nurse with a pert nose and large bosom flashed her a warm, sympathetic smile. Megan managed to smile back.

"Sarah Birch?" Megan said.

"Right in there. I think she's sleeping finally."

Megan thanked her.

"Popular woman. You can go in too."

Too? Megan nodded and walked into room 522. She was expecting one of the Historical Society members, or maybe Merry. But the woman who sat by Sarah's bed was a stranger.

"Oh, I'm sorry," Megan said. She placed the flowers and candy on the bedside table. "I'll come back." When she looked back at the bed, she noticed the visitor studying her. The woman had black hair streaked with gray. It was pulled into a loose bun and wisps of hair framed a broad face and full lips. Her cheekbones were high, her skin creamy-pink.

"Megan?" the woman whispered.

Megan backed to the door. She looked from the bed to the woman and back again. Sarah was asleep. She would forgive

Megan's cowardice.

But Megan's feet rooted her in place.

The woman stood. Megan noticed wide hips, narrow shoulders. A black dress that was both modern and modest. A tight smile and eyes so sad they looked like pools of deepest regret.

"Megan."

Megan's heart raced, her breath slowed. She felt light-headed and euphoric at the same time. She'd waited her whole adult life for this moment. So many things ran through her head. Some kind, most not. Where were you when I needed you after my first breakup? When I got married? When Mick died?

Megan had an entire conversation with Charlotte Birch in the minute that she stood there, mute, staring at the woman who gave birth to her but who hadn't been part of her life since Megan was a child.

"Megan?" the woman said again. She took a step closer. Held out a hand, took it back. "I'm Charlotte."

"How is she?" Megan managed.

Charlotte turned back toward the bed. Her gaze was loving as she fixed a blanket, straightened a pillow. "Resting. The man who did this to her gave her a cocktail of Rohypnol and a few other drugs. Her body didn't react well." Charlotte smiled. "I heard what you did. Saving her life."

That man who was now in the same hospital, in a room guarded by police, Megan thought.

Charlotte smiled. "It was very brave."

Megan managed another nod.

Charlotte picked up a black wool coat from a nearby chair. "Sit, please. I was just leaving. I have a train to catch."

Don't go, Megan thought. But her voice had left her a dozen thoughts ago.

As though viewing a movie, Megan watched as her mother pulled on her coat, buttoned it with long, slim fingers, perfectly manicured nails. She was a polished version of Megan. Polished and demure. Sophisticated. Megan looked down at her jeans and vintage gray sweater, at the boots she wore over thick wool socks.

But Charlotte's eyes were on her face. And aside from the deep green pools of regret, she looked happy to see Megan.

"Merry Christmas, Megan," she said. She held a square black bag close to her side. "I'd hoped maybe I'd see you. I thought . . . if I see her, what would I say? How would I explain?" Her eyes beseeched Megan's. "But now that you're here, I know some things can't be explained. Or, perhaps, for-given."

Megan stood there, watching her. For someone whose prior career depended on words, they were failing her now.

Charlotte edged toward the door. "Well, maybe I'll see you again."

Megan pushed herself forward. She took a step, stopped. Someone in the corridor was crying and the sound echoed through insti-tutional green halls. "I'd like that," she man-aged.

Charlotte's eyes brightened. With a final nod, she left.

Megan wanted to run after her, tackle her, and ask her a million questions. She thought of Becca and the debilitating pain of losing a mother. Maybe it wasn't too late. Maybe Megan could still have hers.

She sat down next to Sarah. Her aunt's eyes fluttered but didn't open. Megan took her aunt's hand, squeezed gently, and whispered, "Merry Christmas."

Sarah squeezed back. The crying in the hall stopped. Megan saw the cards on the table next to the flower bouquet. One was addressed to Sarah. The other was ad-dressed to Megan in a script she didn't recognize. Her mother's handwriting. Her mother's card.

Sarah squeezed her hand again. Her aunt's eyes were opened. She smiled.

Megan smiled back. Perhaps everything would be all right. At least for today.

ABOUT THE AUTHOR

Wendy Tyson's background in law and psychology has provided inspiration for her mysteries and thrillers. Originally from the Philadelphia area, Wendy has returned to her roots and lives there again on a micro-farm with her husband, three sons and three dogs. Wendy's short fiction has appeared in literary journals, and she's a contributing editor and columnist for *The Big Thrill* and *The Thrill Begins,* International Thriller Writers' online magazines. Wendy is the author of the Allison Campbell Mystery Series and the Greenhouse Mystery Series.